M. B.

THE LIGHT AT WYNDCLIFF

THE LIGHT AT WYNDCLIFF

SARAH E. LADD

THORNDIKE PRESS
A part of Gale, a Cengage Company

LIBRARY OF CONGRESS CIP DATA ON FILE.
CATALOGUING IN PUBLICATION FOR THIS BOOK
IS AVAILABLE FROM THE LIBRARY OF CONGRESS.

ISBN-13: 979-8-8857-8095-7 (hardcover alk. paper)

Published in 2022 by arrangement with Thomas Nelson, Inc., a division of HarperCollins Christian Publishing, Inc.

Printed in Mexico
Print Number : 1   Print Year : 2022

To R.D. — with gratitude

PROLOGUE

Cornwall, 1808
Keverne Park

Evelyn Bray squinted in the bright Cornish sunlight and sidestepped to avoid a fat bumblebee circling the manicured roses at the drive's edge. Her mother, ignorant of the buzzing insect, tightened her hold on Evelyn's hand, her grip icy in the summer's warmth.

"This is a sad day for the Brays," Mother muttered, the swish of her emerald muslin skirt and the briskness of her steps swirling the road's dirt in the otherwise still morning air. "My only relief is that your father is not here to witness his own father's recklessness."

Evelyn trotted alongside her and wrinkled her nose in contemplation. She wasn't exactly sure why her mother was so angry with her grandfather, other than he'd lost a great deal of money.

7

She cast a glance back at Keverne Park, the ancient stone manor house with its sharply pitched slate roof and gabled windows that had been her home for all of her eight years. "Are we really not going to live here anymore?"

"No. We are not." Mother tugged on her hand, jerking Evelyn's attention forward once again.

As they walked, Evelyn adjusted the porcelain doll resting in the crook of her other arm. It was impossible not to admire the doll's elegantly curled hair that nearly matched the honey hue of her own, glass eyes the color of spring cornflowers, and lovely cherub face. She frowned. "But so many of my things are still inside. My books. My other dolls. I don't want to leave them behind."

"Those don't belong to you anymore," Mother snipped. "They belong to the house and the new master now. You can thank your grandfather for that."

The rigid clench of her mother's jaw wove a thread of uneasiness through Evelyn, and she eyed the trunk-laden cart still in Keverne's circular drive. They'd packed and repacked those trunks. Mother had been insistent. Evelyn could take only what fit into her two trunks. Not even a ribbon more.

As they made their way farther down the drive, Keverne's walled south garden came into view. The iron gates stood open, allowing passersby to glimpse inside. The flowers were in full bloom now, in vibrant crimson and gold.

"Do you think the new house will have a garden?"

Mother huffed, her annoyance becoming all too frequent of late. "Even if it does, it will not be the sort we're used to. Keverne Park employs both a gardener and a groundskeeper. There will be none of that at Wyndcliff Cottage. You must adjust your expectations."

Mother stopped abruptly, still gripping Evelyn's hand, and knelt to face her. Tears gleamed in her brown eyes, and her normally ruddy cheeks seemed wan. "Listen to me carefully, Evelyn. Nothing will be like it has been. You and I have no money of our own, so we must rely on your grandfather's generosity, such as it is, until another opportunity presents itself. But rest assured, my darling girl, something will come about."

Not entirely sure how to respond to her mother's statements, Evelyn only nodded and allowed herself to be led to the waiting

9

carriage.

Once settled inside the open vehicle, Evelyn looked around the foreign surroundings, from the worn wooden trim to the cracked leather padding of the short sidewall. She'd never been in this carriage before. It was not nearly as fine as the one they took to church on Sundays. It was more of a fancy cart, with a bench for the driver and smaller ones for the passengers.

A humid breeze, dense with the moisture from the previous night's rain and the nearby sea, lifted her loosely bound hair from her face and disrupted the yellow satin ribbons of her bonnet. Despite the heat, the rush of wind soothed her flushed cheeks and face, and if she beheld the blue sky and swooping swallows overhead, she could almost forget that her world was collapsing.

The carriage lurched into motion, and after they cleared Keverne's tall stone walls and spiked iron gates, small clusters of people from the village, clad in shades of brown and tan, lined the public road. Shabbily dressed women held infants in their arms. Children clothed in naught but rags stared, their small hands held above their eyes to shade them from the morning brightness.

Evelyn arched her head to see the children

10

as they turned the bend. "Why are they watching us?"

"Hold your head high." Mother didn't divert her gaze from the driver directly in front of her. "Don't look at them. People love nothing more than to witness the downfall of their betters. It's sickening."

"But why?" Evelyn could not tear her eyes from the children staring at her. "They don't even know us."

"Oh, they know us," Mother scoffed, swiping a bug from her sleeve with unnecessary force. "They know all about us. We just don't know them."

Unsure of her mother's meaning, Evelyn sat in silence as Keverne Park's pristine lawns dissolved into wild, open moorland. Smooth gray rock, waving grasses, and clumps of vibrant purple heather held a beauty and charm of their own, and Evelyn was quite content with the ride until several chimneys of blackened stone appeared at the moor's edge, rising above the heathland and reaching into the cloudless sky.

Excitement at the impressive structure surged through her. It appeared almost magical, like the ancient homes in the stories her father used to tell her before he died. "Is that where we're going to live?"

"No, that's Wyndcliff Hall, where Mr.

Treton lives. We're to live in a cottage. La, I never thought I would see the day." She shuddered, then nodded to her left. "There's your grandfather over by the gate."

The carriage slowed as it approached her grandfather and finally drew to a stop. Evelyn jumped down and sprinted toward the gray-haired man, who swept her up in his arms. His scent of tobacco encircled her, and the embrace felt familiar in a surrounding that was foreign and different. "There now, my little lamb." He gave her a little bounce in his arms. "Are you ready to see your new home?"

She nodded and wrapped her arms around his neck.

"Good. Now, close your eyes and don't open them until I say."

He lowered her to the ground, and she pressed her damp palms over her eyes, blocking out the light and any view of what might lay ahead.

He placed his hand on her shoulder to guide her, and they walked several paces before he stopped. "There now. Open them."

Excited and ready, she dropped her hands, but the sight that met her quickly squelched her building enthusiasm. Her shoulders slumped at the sight of trees before her.

12

Nothing was there. Then she peered closer. Beyond the tree line was a house so covered in vines and ivy that it blended into its surroundings, making it seem more like a forest.

Her zeal faded, and concern rushed in to take its place.

The windows looked black. The house seemed vacant, small and frightening in its darkness. Her stomach all fluttery, she scanned the grounds for sign of a garden — rhododendron, magnolia, even the sight of a simple primrose would set her heart and mind at ease.

She found none.

Every muscle in her body tensed. Suddenly her mother's frustration made sense. This simple cottage, although large compared to the houses in the village, paled horrifically in comparison to Keverne Park, with its magnificent columns and large windows.

"What do you think of it, lamb?"

She looked to her grandfather, shocked to find that he seemed almost happy. "I-I don't know."

"This is home now, and home is always a welcome sight. You must remember that. Now come. You'll sleep on the highest story, nearly touching the sky itself, and from your window you can see down to the sea."

The thought of waking up to the sight of the sea intrigued her, and yet she wanted to run back to Keverne Park, back to what was recognizable and comfortable.

But it did not belong to her anymore.

As Grandfather continued on toward the cottage, her mother approached and knelt at her side.

"I don't like it," Evelyn whispered as her mother's arm wrapped around her waist. "I don't want to go inside."

"I don't either." Mother's sigh was long and heavy. "I don't like it one bit. But as much as it pains me to say it, it doesn't matter where we live. Not really. Being together is what is important now. Besides, you must remember that you are a Bray, a descendant of one of the most magnificent families in all of Cornwall. This situation in this cottage is temporary, regardless of what your grandfather says. We are dependent upon him for the present, and we must be grateful. But I'll not rest until you and I are both restored to our rightful places in society. Do you trust me on that?"

Evelyn swallowed and nodded. She could not bring herself to say the words, but in her heart she knew life would never be the same.

CHAPTER 1

Cornwall, early autumn 1820
Wyndcliff Estate

Twenty-two years was a long time to wait for life to begin. Even now, as Liam Twethewey guided his bay horse down the narrow, deeply rutted path, he could barely prevent the grin from spreading on his face.

Only a mile or so more and he would be in his new home. Everything he'd been dreaming of — his plans for developing the moorland and making his own way in the world — was finally within his reach.

He filled his lungs with the damp earth-scented air. The rain had, for the moment, subsided. Night was falling and twilight's ominous light cast shadows on the barren land surrounding him, and he squinted to assess the ribbon of road winding before him through the moor's purple grasses and jagged crags.

He might be far from the home he'd

15

known for most of his life, but he already felt a connection to this bit of earth.

For he was now on Wyndcliff estate land.

And it all belonged to him.

Perhaps it would have been wiser to wait for his solicitor, Edwin Kinden, to join him as they'd originally planned. Liam had never set foot on Wyndcliff property, and the directions he'd received at the inn in town were vague at best. As the man tasked with overseeing the transfer of property, Kinden was the most appropriate person to handle all introductions to the place. But after nearly two hours of waiting for the older man to arrive, impatience won out. He'd anticipated this moment for far too long to spend another second sitting idly in a dark, smoky public house.

Liam had left word with the innkeeper for Mr. Kinden to meet him out at Wyndcliff Hall when he arrived. After all, how hard could it be to find a large manor house along the main road at the moor's edge?

Liam urged his horse to a quicker pace. This might be his property, but it wouldn't do to be caught in a storm on unfamiliar moorland, especially this close to nightfall.

A gentle rain began to drizzle from the heavens, and Liam was about to press his horse to an even faster pace when a sharp, panicked whinny met his ears. He slowed.

The sound echoed again, followed by a muffled voice.

Concern trumped his enthusiasm, and he halted his horse. But all was now silent. "Anyone there?"

"Yes!" a feminine voice snapped, high and sharp. "Here! Please help! My pony's caught."

Alarm pushed Liam from his saddle, and his boots landed with a splash in the mud. After securing his reins to a rugged piece of rock, he tracked the direction of the voice.

"Mind the bog!" The increasingly volatile wind distorted the woman's cries, tossing them amidst its gusts. "It's deep along the crag."

Heeding the warning, Liam stepped from stone to stone, testing each footfall before taking another step on the marshy ground. The wind tore at his greatcoat, threatening his balance. He cut through tall grasses and crested a rocky ridge, and then a flash of dark blue in the sea of brown and stone caught his attention.

A slight woman with windblown golden hair was yanking on the head collar of a gray pony knee-deep in mud.

Alarm at the potentially dangerous situation shook him from his surprise. One wrong step and the woman would be trapped in the bog, just like her pony. "Stay there. Don't move."

He retrieved the leather strap from his horse's head collar and returned back down to the little valley formed between the crags. He inched down the decline, testing the firmness of the ground before committing his full weight.

The mud-caked pony thrashed and awkwardly bucked to free itself. It reeled back, tossing its muzzle and squealing, but instead of helping the pony break loose, each movement tightened the murky substance around its legs.

"Whoa, whoa," Liam soothed, lowering and calming his voice. With careful, measured steps he approached the animal, ignoring the rain, now more like sharp bits of ice as it pounded his caped greatcoat and wide-brimmed hat.

He had to get closer.

In order to free his own movements he removed his coat, tossed it on higher land, and stepped farther into the bog. His foot instantly sank to his ankle. Like a noose, mud cinched around it. It would be unwise to go farther, so he reached as far as he could and made several attempts to secure the pony's head collar.

The pony tossed its head in distress, but Liam's fingers eventually caught on the head collar, and he pulled. He thrust all of his weight backward and pulled harder, careful not to lose control over his own stance.

The pony swung its head and, in a final display of momentum, freed a foreleg. The animal then broke free, and with all the wild gracelessness of a newborn foal it stumbled up onto dryer, firmer land.

Unsettled by the pony's momentum, Liam toppled back and fell against the damp earth.

With a cry the woman scrambled from her position on the bog's outer edge and staggered toward the pony. Sodden muck coated the bottom half of her blue gown, and dirt streaked across her cheek and coated the ends of her long hair. Without so much as a look at her rescuer, she knelt to assess the pony's legs. "Oh, is she all right, do you think?"

Liam paused to catch his breath, then stepped forward and brushed past the woman to run his hand down the pony's leg. He urged it to take a step and saw that a slight limp marred the pony's stride.

"She favors that leg." A frown wrinkled the woman's brow. "See?"

"Frightened 'tis all, I should think." He gently guided the pony to higher ground. "Even so, she's fortunate. I know horses who've had their legs snapped thrashing about in deep mud like that."

Thunder cracked above them, as if to agree with Liam's statement.

"I never should have brought her out." The woman shook her head. "I must get her home before the storm worsens."

Liam looked toward the clouds rolling in like a determined wave rushing for the shore, prepared to decimate all upon impact. They needed to get to some sort of shelter before the heavens opened up full force. He wanted nothing more than to be at his new home, to see the structure he'd tried to visualize a thousand times, but this woman needed help. He could not leave her here helpless, not with this injured pony.

He'd waited twenty-two years. He could wait a bit longer. "Allow me to assist you to your home. Is it far?"

"Oh no." She stepped back suddenly, the confidence she'd displayed earlier when caring for the pony fleeing. "I couldn't ask you to do that."

"You're not asking me. I'm offering." He smiled, attempting to appear as unthreatening as possible, and raised his voice to be heard above the rustling grasses. "But we must hurry — otherwise we'll all be caught out in the tempest."

She looked up at the turbulent sky, chewing her lower lip in a manner that suggested she did not like the thought, but as the rain pummeled them, practicality gave way. "I live at Wyndcliff Cottage at the moor's edge, about half a mile from here."

"Wyndcliff Cottage?" He started. "I'm on my way to Wyndcliff Hall. Are they close?"

Her gaze narrowed, her unusually colored green eyes vibrant against the stormy backdrop, and she tilted her head to the side. "What's your business at Wyndcliff Hall?"

The boldness — and perceived authority — in her voice caught him off guard. "My name is William Twethewey. I've recently inherited the property."

"Twethewey?" she repeated, as if searching her memory, and after a few seconds her fair brows rose and pink bloomed on her cheeks. "Of course. William Twethewey. We weren't expecting you. That is, we knew you were coming eventually, but . . ." Her voice faded before she straightened her shoulders and lifted her chin. "My name is Evelyn Bray. My grandfather is Rupert Bray, Wyndcliff's steward."

He shouldn't be surprised to find someone

associated with the place on the property, but at the moment it did not matter. The rain increased its intensity and thunder grumbled its ominous warning. The pony pranced nervously.

"Pleasure to meet you, Miss Bray, but I think further introductions can wait, don't you? You say we are not far? You are welcome to ride my horse if you like. I can lead the pony."

She eyed him, suspicion evident in the firm set of her jaw. She flicked her gaze to his horse, then stepped backward. "Thank you, but I will walk. Do you think Ada will be all right to walk the rest of the way?"

"She seems to be fine, and it will be easier to assess her out of this weather."

They fell into step with each other, each leading an animal. The wind now howled, making conversation nearly impossible. He cast a sideways glance at his unexpected traveling companion. In spite of the mud-streaked cheek and wind-tossed hair, her beauty was not lost on him.

An unconventional introduction, to be sure, but if Wyndcliff Hall came with such lovely neighbors, his new adventure could be off to a worse start.

CHAPTER 2

Mortified hardly described Evelyn's current state.

She drew her candle closer, leaned near the looking glass in the privacy of her small, darkened attic chamber, and scrubbed mud from her face with a cloth.

Being discovered helpless on the moors was humiliating enough, but to be discovered by Wyndcliff's new master, let alone a handsome stranger, was more than she could bear.

Burying her embarrassment, Evelyn exchanged her soaked shift for a dry one before attempting to brush the tangles and bits of mud from her damp hair. She should be grateful Ada had not been more seriously injured. The pony was not young, and Mr. Twethewey had been right. Many a pony — and horses and humans, for that matter — had endured harm in the moor's deceptive bogs.

Footsteps echoed on the stairs outside her chamber, and she turned as Bertie bustled in, the new servant girl Grandfather had recently engaged to look after them at Wyndcliff Cottage.

"Here's your gray gown." The maid shook out the folds of the garment as she approached. " 'Tis wrinkled, but at least it's dry."

Evelyn turned to allow the young woman to help her don the gown over her dry shift and stays.

"It will take quite a bit of work to get that mud out of your blue one," Bertie muttered as she smoothed the fabric. "How on earth did you manage to get it in such a state?"

Evelyn pivoted so Bertie could tie the fastenings at the back of her neck and between her shoulder blades. "Ada spooked and ran toward the marshland. You know how nervous she can be during storms. She got caught behind Aaron's Rock."

Bertie tsked and shook her dark-blonde head. "Your grandfather's warned you about riding out in the moors by yourself, especially in such weather. I've heard him say it a dozen times or more. He'll be powerful angry when he finds out you were out there alone."

Bertie was right, of course. Grandfather

was not shy about sharing his opinions, and he loathed disobedience. Bertie had only been at Wyndcliff a few weeks and already understood their unique relationship. Evelyn forced brightness to her tone. "Then let's hope he won't give it much of a thought now that Mr. Twethewey has arrived."

Once the fastenings were tied, Evelyn resumed the uncomfortable task of brushing mud from her hair. She needed to hurry. Marnie, Wyndcliff Hall's housekeeper, would need assistance — or at least moral support — with the new master's unexpected arrival.

"Now then, what's he like?" Bertie gathered the discarded shift and dirty linen cloths. "I saw only the back of 'im, and even then he was clear across the courtyard."

Evelyn's brushing slowed. She hardly knew how to respond. In truth she'd been startled by Mr. Twethewey. It was rare to run across strangers on that stretch of moorland. And yet she was impressed by him. He was young with striking black hair and brilliant blue eyes, and that alone was arresting. And he'd been kind to her. Many men might have passed her by to deal with the pony on her own. After being discovered in such a perilous position, she felt small. Silly. Incapable.

She tossed her damp hair. It would do no good to wallow in self-doubt. And as for Bertie's question, she was not willing to share her personal feelings with someone she'd known for such a short time. "I suppose we shall all find out soon enough. But for now I must go to Marnie. She is no doubt beside herself."

Bertie chuckled and looped the dirty garments over her arm. "She was already wary of his arrival when she thought it was a month hence. But for him to show up sudden-like, with no warning . . ." Bertie's words faded into the small chamber's deceptive stillness.

For it was not still at all.

The entire fabric of Wyndcliff Hall was rippling and evolving, even now as Mr. Twethewey roamed Wyndcliff grounds. She'd be lying to say she did not share Bertie's curiosity about the new master. As far as Evelyn was concerned, any change to Wyndcliff's sleepy patterns was welcome.

In that moment she could not help but wonder what Mother would think of Mr. Twethewey. Surely she'd think him a handsome man, as Evelyn did, and since he now possessed such expansive property, she'd surely consider him an ideal suitor — if it weren't for the fact that he was associated with Wyndcliff. Mother hated everything about Wyndcliff, and Evelyn doubted that any amount of money would change her mind.

After instructing Bertie to return to her normal evening duties, Evelyn adjusted the long sleeves of her clean gown, donned a fresh cloak of brown wool, and made her way from the cottage across the mist-laden cobbled courtyard to Wyndcliff Hall's kitchen entrance.

Light glowed from deep-set windows that on any other night would be dark at this hour. She pushed open the timber door. Warmth and spicy scents met her.

Marnie Taymer whirled from the fire, her wiry white hair hanging from beneath her dingy cap, her dark eyes wide. "He's here! An' without a proper warnin' neither."

"I know." Evelyn stepped farther into the room and closed the door behind her, barring the swirls of wind determined to make their way indoors. "But consider, Marnie. It's his home."

"Home or not, a bit of notice would've been sorely welcome. Probably just came early to catch us all unawares, I'd wager."

"Oh, I doubt that." Evelyn removed her cloak and hung it on the peg next to the door. "Besides, if you were Mr. Twethewey, wouldn't you be eager to lay claim to your estate?"

Ignoring Evelyn's reasoning, Marnie bustled across the kitchen to grip a copper pot. "And now we've got an entire house to get ready. La, my soul! Dusty an' dirty — we ain't even seen the inside of some of these chambers in years, what with naught but myself to see to it."

Evelyn shrugged in genuine empathy. For years Marnie and her late husband lived in the house and saw to its keeping, but since his death two years prior, everything shifted. Grandfather's main focus had always been the tenants, and as a result he neglected to add new staff to care for the house. That, compounded by Marnie's bad leg, hindered her ability to keep up with the duties.

"We'll send word for Kitty to come," Evelyn suggested. "She's a hard worker and fast. Lizzie Jones too. Don't fret. Mr. Tweth-ewey seems like a reasonable man, and everything will settle soon. Where is he now?"

"He and your grandfather are still in the stable, tendin' to his horse and that pony o' yours."

Evelyn bit her lip and looked out the window toward the stable. A simple lan-tern's glow hinted they were still inside. She wanted to check Ada for herself, but she'd seen the fire in her grandfather's eyes when she told him about what happened on the moors. Now was not the time to test him.

She snatched an apron from the hook, stepped farther into the kitchen, and refocused her attention on Marnie. "What are you doing now?"

Marnie nodded to a makeshift clothesline strung in front of the fire laden with men's attire: coats, a linen shirt, a striped waistcoat of gold and green, and two pair of breeches — much finer attire than they were used to seeing in the village. "Most of the clothes in his pack were soaked through. I've hung some of 'em to dry, but there are more. He asked to have a bath drawn, an' Tom took the tub up to the master's chamber, an' I'm heatin' the water."

Evelyn drew a deep breath, considering the state of the chambers upstairs after having been closed for so long. "Is the bedchamber ready?"

Marnie chortled. " 'Course not. Tom's to kindle a fire whilst he's up there with the tub, but la. The dust! No one's stepped foot up there in I don't know how long. If Mr. Twethewey had the courtesy to tell us he was comin', I'd have remedied that, but as things are . . . ."

Evelyn slid the apron straps over her shoulders. "I can have it tidied in no time."

"Oh, thank ye, child. Dear, these bones. The last thing I want to do is make the master angry an' be out on my side afore I can prove meself."

Evelyn placed a comforting hand on Marnie's shoulder. "Nothing is going to be very different, Marnie. Mark my words, he'll be far too occupied with the tenants and such to worry about the inner workings of Wyndcliff Hall. Grandfather will no doubt see to that."

Once the last of the clothing was hung to dry, Evelyn offered Marnie her arm and helped the older woman up the stairs, creaky and worn and uneven from centuries of use. The bedchambers were at the top of the stairs, but the master's chamber was at the far end of the house.

Evelyn had often roamed Wyndcliff's halls since her arrival more than a decade ago. With Grandfather gone most of the daytime hours and Mother away in Plymouth these past two years, she'd often found solace within Wyndcliff's thick stone walls by stealing into the library to read or daydream. And even though she enjoyed free rein of the house, she'd never really ventured into the upstairs rooms, especially the master's chambers — a cluster of three rooms that had been Mr. Treton's personal domain when he was alive.

With slight hesitation she followed the housekeeper into this space. As Marnie indicated, Tom had built a fire in the grate, and cheery flames danced and popped. The light flickered on paneled walls that were so dark, they appeared almost black, and ominous carvings of gargoyles on the bedposts met her with intimidating expressions.

Marnie clicked her tongue and propped her hands on her ample hips. "Master Treton died in this room, an' I'd ne'er step in it for the memory, if I can help it. A sad day for all of us."

Only half listening, Evelyn stepped to the bank of east-facing windows. Damp coolness seeped in from the cracks around the windows' leading, and light from the room directly below spilled to the courtyard. She'd only ever seen Mr. Treton in passing, and yet stories of him were shared so frequently, she felt as if she'd known him. He was as much a part of this home and land as the wild moors and windblown beaches, and people often spoke of him as if he alone were responsible for any positive aspects of the village.

She let the faded curtain fall and assessed

the oblong chamber as if she were seeing it for the first time. At the north end a large fireplace stood adjacent to a great carved oak bed, the heavy tapestry canopy having been a deep crimson at one time. A large trunk sat at the bed's end, and in the corner was a round table with two chairs. The plaster ceilings had at some point been painted white, the brightness of which stood in sharp contrast to the dark paneled walls. Beneath her feet a roughly woven rug covered the entirety of the planked floor, and chairs were scattered around the room. A thick layer of dust covered all, making everything appear ancient and almost other-worldly.

"Chilly in here, but there's naught that can be done for that but time." Marnie handed a cloth to Evelyn. "Here, see to that dust gathered on the table and chest. But first we need to freshen this air. Open that window there."

Evelyn obeyed and turned the archaic iron handle. With a creak the window swung outward, and the pungent moorland air swirled in, brimming with the scent of the sea, rain, and wet earth.

Evelyn took her rag and began to sweep away the dust on the wardrobe. Bertie's earlier question rang in her mind, and she absently repeated it. "I wonder what sort of man Mr. Twethewey is."

"Doesn't matter." Marnie huffed. "Kind or ill tempered, industrious or aloof, shouldn't affect us much. He's a young man. What is he, but two and twenty? He's just now findin' his way. As for me, I know my role here an' what's to be done."

Evelyn moved to the table and wiped it clean, her nose wrinkling in protest as the dust swirled upward. Marnie was right. The older woman's role as housekeeper was very defined — and about to get much busier. Evelyn, on the other hand, did not have an official role at Wyndcliff. Not really. She was the granddaughter of the steward and had no real responsibilities, and little of significance was expected of her by her family, other than to marry well.

But she was failing at that too, for at the moment her prospects were limited. Few suitable men resided in the village, and until her mother called her to Plymouth to introduce her to her acquaintances, there was little to do. In the meantime, Evelyn needed something to pass the time, and if that meant dusting the master's chamber, then so be it. But if she was honest, her curiosity about this new master, with the vibrant blue eyes and cleft chin and the

change he could bring to Wyndcliff, was
deepening with each passing moment.

CHAPTER 3

Liam blinked away the icy moisture and fixed his gaze on the soft glow emanating from the kitchen's square window before him. He had not been sure exactly what to expect when he arrived at Wyndcliff Hall, but he was certain this was not it.

Where are all the people?

Prior to his arrival, Kinden had informed him that a full staff was employed to see to the property's upkeep, but besides Miss Bray, a housekeeper, and the steward who now accompanied him, Liam had not encountered another soul. Even now as they crossed the courtyard after seeing to Miss Bray's pony and his own horse, all was still and eerily silent, save for the stormy gusts racing through bare branches and skittering dead leaves over the cobbled ground. He'd not seen enough of Wyndcliff yet for a true assessment, but judging by the size of the manor house alone, there should be evidence of stable hands or kitchen maids.

But Wyndcliff had not had a proper master since his great-uncle Treton died nearly a decade ago. He'd never met his father's uncle, but since Liam was the closest male heir, Treton left the property to him to inherit when he reached the age of two and twenty. During the interim the estate and tenants had been overseen by Rupert Bray, the steward, and Mr. Kinden oversaw the finances. It had seemed like a fairly simple arrangement, but as Liam looked from the muddy cobbles beneath his feet to the crack in the kitchen window at eye level to the black spire reaching toward the dark-purple sky, he wondered. He was far from the home he was so comfortable in and the people he loved.

They'd almost reached the kitchen door when Bray stopped abruptly. "Cellar door's open over there. I've a mind to go and close it. Go on in — don't wait on me." He crossed the courtyard.

The wind had caught the indicated door and it now swung on its hinges. Liam groaned. Clearly the latch either had given way or was in ill repair. Either way, the property seemed to have seen better days. With each passing moment the enthusiasm he brought with him was dissolving into concern.

Determined not to succumb to frustration, Liam entered the kitchen and was pleasantly surprised at the warmth it afforded. It possessed an unexpectedly high ceiling, with dried herbs and flowers hanging from the exposed wooden rafters. An open fireplace ran the width of the room at the far end, and in it raged a healthy fire that heated two large iron kettles. Inviting scents of stew and strong coffee reminded him that it had been hours since he last ate. The housekeeper, whom he'd met briefly upon his arrival, tended to one of the pots above the fire. Miss Bray stood near her.

He stepped farther into the kitchen, and the stone floor groaned beneath his wet boots. Both women snapped their gazes toward him.

"There now." Mrs. Taymer at last turned from the fire and swiped hair from her face. "Are the animals settled then?"

Liam nodded and removed his coat slowly so he didn't shake water all over the floor. He watched the younger woman from the corner of his eye, careful not to draw attention as he did so. How different she looked without the soiled cape over her shoulders. No trace of mud remained on the curve of her cheek. Her long, honey-blonde hair

37

draped damp and loose down her back.

How many times had he tried to imagine what his home and the people who worked and lived on Wyndcliff estate would be like? He'd received brief and random updates from Kinden's letters, including tidings of the old steward and the older housekeeper, but up until this point they had been figments of his imagination.

"Yes." Liam pulled himself from his silent musings and hung up his coat. "They're settled."

"And Ada?" Miss Bray advanced a pace, the fire's light accenting a slight dimple in her cheek. "How's her leg?"

Liam thought back to the frightened pony. "Her leg is perhaps bruised, or perhaps the muscle is strained, but she will recover."

Her shoulders relaxed in relief, but before anyone else had a chance to speak, Bray burst in behind him, accompanied by the damp scent of the outdoors and horses, and shed his coat and hat, revealing a shock of white hair and bushy white eyebrows. "Ah, Mrs. Taymer, I hope you've something warm to offer our young master. Traveling always takes it out of a man, 'specially when that travel is on horseback."

"I do, sir." The older woman twisted her hands before her. "Stew and coffee."

"You'll not find a more capable house-keeper than Mrs. Taymer in all of Cornwall." Bray advanced farther into the room. "She's been at Wyndcliff longer than any of us, myself included."

"My husband worked for Mr. Treton since he was a lad," Mrs. Taymer offered, a quiver in her thin voice. "An' I been here since I was but a bride meself. Nigh on thirty years, I reckon."

Bray's expression softened as he turned his attention to Miss Bray. "And then you've met my Evelyn here. Unexpectedly, I'll admit, but you've met her nonetheless."

Miss Bray smiled and offered a slight curtsy.

Liam returned the greeting with a slight bow. "And you are well after the ordeal?"

Before she could respond, Bray once again interjected himself and placed a hand on her shoulder. "We've spent the better part of the last half hour with that pony of yours. How many times have I told ye to stay off the moors, especially by the bogs? A dangerous bit of land. Best leave it to the wind and the fairies."

"Yes, you've told me." Her face flushed, and her former air of confidence faltered as she tucked her hands behind her back and diverted her gaze. "It won't happen again."

Bray straightened his shoulders, patted his granddaughter's cheek, and smoothed his hair neatly over his forehead. His control of this skeleton of a household was evident, proved by the knot of tension tightening in the air.

Attempting to lighten the atmosphere that Mr. Bray's reprimand had conjured, Liam turned to the housekeeper. "So I have met the three of you. Is there anyone else on the property I should know?"

Once again Bray answered in her stead. "Tom, our manservant, is about somewhere. You'll meet him soon enough. Kitty, the kitchen girl, comes during the day to help Mrs. Taymer as needed, and Joshua and Jeb, the boys I mentioned earlier, assist as needed with the grounds and the animals, not that there are many. And, of course, Evelyn and I have a housekeeper at the cottage called Bertie, but other than that we're a self-sufficient lot."

Liam shoved his disappointment down further as his suspicions were confirmed. There was a great deal to learn about Wyndcliff, and it would be best to avoid jumping to conclusions until he could see his property by day's light. He pushed his growing list of questions to the back of his mind and looked back to Mrs. Taymer. "I see."

She fussed with her apron. "I-I've set the stew on. If I'd have kn-known ye were comin', I would have prepared somethin' more fittin'. An' the water is hot for a bath in yer chamber."

Dinner and a bath would be most welcome. Liam's limbs ached with exhaustion, and his skin had been damp for quite some time from the rain and mud. He was eager to trade his damp clothes for dry ones. "Thank you. And I'll take dinner in my chamber tonight. I've no wish to disrupt things any more than I already have."

"Disrupt things?" Bray released a rough, almost abrasive laugh. "This is your home now, Mr. Twethewey. The house staff, such as it is, is at your service."

A fresh gust of wind rushed against the windowpane, rattling it and whistling through the cracks. Had Kinden arrived at the inn yet? Regardless, there was no way the man would venture out in this blustery weather. He turned to Bray. "I know you're acquainted with Mr. Kinden, my late uncle's solicitor."

"Yes, sir, I am."

"I was to meet him in the village earlier, but he did not arrive. I left a note at the inn for him to join me here. I doubt he'll come yet tonight, but he'll stay for a few days as

41

the transfer of property is finalized. I should like a room prepared for him."

"Of course." Bray bowed low. "Would you like to see the rest of Wyndcliff Hall before retiring?"

Liam glanced down a dark hall leading from the kitchen. He was curious to see the dining hall, but without the fires lit and the candles ablaze, he was not sure how much he would actually see. "It can wait until tomorrow's light."

"Very well. A thorough review of the house and grounds tomorrow then. It is Market Day tomorrow so the tenants may be away, but you'll see them soon enough."

"That is fine. But for now, if someone could show me to my chamber, I will leave you all to your evening." Liam took up a candle of his own. The warmth of the kitchen subsided as he followed the steward up the stairs. With each step the passageway grew narrower and the ambience grew darker, and the impending sense of dread of what would meet him eclipsed his excitement.

CHAPTER 4

Liam rolled his shoulders forward slightly to fit through the stairwell. The tight turn and the narrow passage made for an uncomfortable climb for a man of his height. If there had been any room for doubt, this walk confirmed it. Wyndcliff Hall was in quite a state of disrepair. Plaster curled off the walls. Dust and dirt covered each tread.

Despite the unsettling disappointment, he would hold out hope that the servants' staircase was not an indication of the rest of the house's condition. But for now his body ached from a long, arduous ride and a battle with a bog. At the moment he was hungry and in need of a hot bath and a warm bed. There would be time enough tomorrow for assessing the state of his property.

They reached the landing, and the air was even cooler. The light from his candle fell on thick cobwebs and reflected off shadowy dust motes balancing in the stale air. The corridor widened as they stepped past several closed doors, and eventually the plaster wall to his left opened to a banister.

"You can't see it now, but this walkway overlooks the great hall. The family sleeping chambers are on the other end, past the minstrel gallery. There's a portrait gallery as well. Some of the paintings there go back two centuries."

They continued down a labyrinth until at last Bray stopped before a wooden door. "We're here, the master's chamber. Of course, you can take any room you'd like. There are six sleeping chambers in this part of the house, but Mr. Treton was fond of this one on account of you can see the sea and the stable yard from the south windows."

"I'm sure it will suit me fine."

Bray's hand, trembling with age's effect, hovered over the tarnished iron handle for several seconds, and then it dropped. In a jerky motion, Bray spun back around to face Liam, the glint in his dark eyes hard and unwavering. His candle reflected light on the deep grooves in his cheeks that at one time might have been dimples but had been altered by decades of smiling. Or scowling. "Before I show you to this room, a word, if I may."

Liam eyed the man, his skepticism growing. He'd been in Bray's presence for well over an hour, and even in that short period an odd, unspoken challenge for dominance had hovered. Bray's harsh demeanor suggested he did not accept that Wyndcliff Hall was legally Liam's property now.

Liam hoped this transition would not be a problem.

He nodded and remained silent until Bray spoke again.

"You've indicated that you want to tour the estate tomorrow, which is right, but I feel a more appropriate introduction is in order before we proceed. After all, I've been at the helm here while you were coming of age and learning the ways of the world."

Liam stiffened at the whisper of condescension in the man's tone.

Bray did not wait for a response. "You'll come to hear my story sooner or later. Every soul in these parts is familiar with it, and every soul is keen on a bit of gossip. I was born not a mile from here at Keverne Park. I was married there. Raised a son there. Eventually welcomed a granddaughter and later buried my wife and son there. Yes, I had the same look of opportunity and optimism you have in your eyes, but foolish decisions on my part led to a reduction in circumstances, and I'm as you find me now — a steward. Nothing more, nothing less. I've seen this land from both sides — as a gentleman who enjoyed privileges and plenty and as one who worked the land, desperate for it to be kind and provide."

Liam watched the man, with his neatly combed white hair and his expertly tied crimson cravat. He did possess a certain air — the posture and self-assuredness of a member of the gentry.

"With age comes clarity and, dare I say, wisdom. I'm as loyal as they come, and I will serve you faithfully in the role bestowed upon me by Mr. Treton. But there is one thing you must understand."

Liam folded his arms over his chest. Now they were getting to it, the reason behind this man's monologue. "And that is?"

"My son is dead, and my daughter-in-law, fickle, vile woman that she is, chose to make a life for herself in Plymouth. Consequently, my granddaughter, Evelyn, is in my care." Bray's gaze narrowed. His voice lowered. "She's here as my family and is a lady in her own right. Let me be clear. Evelyn is not in the estate's employ."

Liam's shoulders tensed. He'd be lying if he said he hadn't been curious about the young woman. She seemed wildly out of place, but it was far too early to make assumptions.

"She's had free rein of the area, as well she should, but mind you, she's caught many an eye. She's all but spoken for, and . . ." He paused. "I'll not have any newcomer setting his sights on something that will not be."

Liam raised his brows. Had he heard correctly? Was Bray really suggesting that Liam would attempt to woo his granddaughter, mere hours after his arrival?

"I'd go to my grave to see her protected and happy." Bray's cheeks shook with intensity. "So as long as you and I are in agreement on that subject, I see no reason that we shouldn't look forward to a long and prosperous association."

Liam inhaled as anger seared through him. He should dismiss this man on the spot. The insinuation. The insolence. He may be young, but he would not be spoken to in such a manner on his own property.

Then reason stepped in.

Liam didn't know his tenants. Didn't know the inner workings of this estate. He was determined to make this estate profitable, and whether he liked it or not, he needed Bray.

Several seconds slid by, beckoning him to

47

remain calm. He met the man's sharp gaze, his unwavering determination standing testament to his past as a gentleman.

Liam forced confidence into his tone and refused to look away. "I understand your concerns, I do. I've three sisters whom I'd go to pistols to protect. I assure you, your granddaughter will be treated with nothing but the utmost respect."

The corner of Bray's mouth quirked in satisfaction.

Liam squared his shoulders. "You've served Wyndcliff faithfully and productively. That's not in question. I may have only assumed responsibility here just this day, but I'll not allow my integrity to be questioned, especially as it pertains to my behavior toward women."

Bray's brows shot up. The men locked eyes in a silent battle of wills — the older man intent upon clinging to his authority and Liam determined to take control.

Liam broke the tense silence. "And now it is my turn to ask. Do we understand each other?"

In a sudden turn of events, Bray emitted a condescending laugh, as an adult laughing to a child. "You've a great deal of your uncle's blood flowing through your veins, lad."

"I'm hardly a lad. And rest assured that the depth of my convictions has nothing to do with whom I'm related to or whose blood flows in my veins."

The steward stepped closer. His laughter faded to a throaty grunt. The hard glint returned to his gray eyes. "Yes, then. We understand each other, I think." Bray stepped back and pushed the door open. "Your chamber, sir. A bell pull is located inside the door to your left. Should you need anything, pull it and Tom or Mrs. Taymer will be summoned to assist you."

Liam nodded.

Bray retreated.

Once the steward's lumbering footsteps faded, Liam expelled his breath in a whoosh. Of all the unexpected events since his arrival, that was the oddest. Perhaps Bray was nothing more than an overprotective grandfather, but he suspected there was more to Bray's motives than Liam realized. Regardless, he was glad the man had finally left him in peace.

He entered his chamber and closed the door behind him. The fire in the grate provided most of the light, but candles and a lantern were scattered throughout the oblong room. As promised, a large copper tub had been brought, and steam rose from

49

the water within. Several items of clothing that had been packed in his satchel now hung near the fire, drying. He unbuttoned his damp coat and shrugged it from his shoulders. He looked around in the dark, low-ceilinged room, from the old canopied bed to the heavily carved wardrobe to the paneled walls to the uneven and worn floor.

This was what he'd waited for. Planned for. Now he was here in the master's chamber, where he assumed every master had laid his head since the building was constructed well over a century past.

As he loosened his neckcloth and began to unbutton his waistcoat, he moved to the window and looked down at the stable courtyard. An inky midnight mist obscured the cobbles and shrouded the grounds. With the exception of the occasional pop from the fire and the angry wind whistling through the window cracks, all was silent.

The silence and solitude were surprisingly unwelcome.

His thoughts turned to the others who resided on this land. Mrs. Taymer seemed a kind soul, if not a nervous one, and he'd yet to meet the elusive Tom.

Maybe Miss Bray was still in the kitchen below. Or perhaps she had gone back to her home. In the end he had to respect Bray's determination to protect his loved one. After all, Liam was not unreasonable. He understood why any guardian would be concerned with such a beautiful charge, for she was just that. It would have been impossible not to notice her blonde hair, the depth of her uniquely colored green eyes, and her complexion that rivaled porcelain.

He shook his head. No, his goal was clear. Before he could even think of a sweetheart, let alone a wife, he had to establish a living, one that would allow him to keep his home in better repair than he now found it.

He headed over to his bags and riffled through the letters he'd brought with him. He found the letter he sought — the one from Mr. Porter. Inside lay the plans for the china clay pits, the endeavor that would launch and ensure his future.

He opened the letter and read it again. It was not necessary to do so, for in truth he'd memorized every detail, from the timeline to the costs to the goals. No, he could not afford distractions. The sooner this night passed and the dawn broke so he could put his plans into action, the better.

CHAPTER 5

"Of all the self-important, impertinent . . . ."

Grandfather's grumbling echoed from the plaster walls, and his footsteps pounded the ancient stone stairs with unusual fervor, prompting Evelyn to peek up from the silver spoon she was polishing.

It had been nigh a quarter of an hour since Grandfather had accompanied Mr. Twethewey upstairs. She had wondered what was taking him so long to simply show the new master to his chamber, but as Grandfather entered the kitchen, the deep frown lines on his forehead suggested the interaction had not been pleasant.

As Grandfather crossed the threshold, Marnie ceased her sweeping and leaned on the broom handle. "There now, is he all settled?"

But Grandfather did not answer. Instead, his bushy brows furrowed and he snatched his hat from the table where he'd left it.

Evelyn tensed. She knew that look — that expression of simmering contemplation.

"The stew then? The bit we left in his chamber?" Marnie raised her voice, oblivious to Grandfather's irritation. "Did he like it?"

Grandfather huffed, stopped, and turned to face them both. His round, clean-shaven face flamed red, making his gray eyes more vibrant. He ignored Marnie's question and pulled his greatcoat from the hook before muttering, "We're in for a great deal of trouble with that one."

Evelyn and Marnie exchanged glances. It was not unusual for Grandfather to form opinions fast, but this one seemed decidedly negative.

Keeping her tone light, Evelyn returned to her task of polishing. "What makes you say that?"

"Fetch your things, Evie. Let's go home and put this day behind us."

This was not the time to challenge him. She lowered the silver, shrugged the work apron from her shoulders, hung it back on the hook, and offered Marnie an encouraging smile. "Try to get some rest. And I'm sure he enjoyed the stew."

"If I'd have known he was comin', I'd have used the salted pork. But who had time? Descended upon us with nary a warnin'." Marnie sniffed.

"Don't fret. Everything will be all right once everyone is settled in this new situation." Evelyn squeezed Marnie's hand as she walked past the older woman. "I'll be by in the morning."

Once at the door Evelyn retrieved her cloak, lifted a lantern, and followed her grandfather out into the damp, mist-laden night. He sighed, as if unburdening himself from the cares of the world, took her free hand in his, and looped it through his arm, protective and insistent, then patted it. His voice softened from the brash tone he'd used in the kitchen to one more suited to speaking with a child or a frightened kitten. "You know you're not to be polishing silver."

Evelyn swiped her hair away from her face. "I was only helping. Now that Mr. Twethewey has arrived, there's much to do. And you know how nervous Marnie gets."

"Let her see to it then, or ask Kitty or Lizzie by to help. You're not a hired hand, Evie. I've told you dozens of times, and I'll not have you acting like one."

Evelyn bit her lower lip. It would do no good to argue her point. Marnie was her friend — a relationship Grandfather tolerated — nay, permitted — most of the time.

Yet she'd not do anything to vex him further. "How did you leave Mr. Twethewey? Was he settled?"

"Bah." Grandfather snorted. "He's a high-and-mighty gent, or at least that is what he'd have us think. But he's naught more than a lad."

"He is two and twenty, is he not?" she asked, knowing full well the answer. Everyone knew of that particular term of the inheritance.

"Still a boy. It takes time and experience to be capable to run an estate like Wyndcliff. He's not had enough years on this earth for such an undertaking. He'd be wise to heed the expertise of his elders."

As they crossed the cobbled courtyard, Evelyn carefully adjusted her pace to match her grandfather's slower one. The damp weather was difficult on him, even though he'd never admit it. His lagging pace proved it. The rain had subsided, and a chill descended in its place. They continued in silence, and for that Evelyn was grateful. For all of his good qualities, the tendency toward anger was Grandfather's flaw, and when faced with something that vexed him, he was unlikely to dismiss it.

As they approached the canopied door of Wyndcliff Cottage, a broad-shouldered figure emerged from the shadows holding a lantern aloft.

Evelyn recognized Jim Bowen, keeper of the White Eagle Inn, instantly. Charlie Potts, a short, fair-haired miner from the village, walked next to him.

She didn't know Charlie well, but it was always good to see Jim. He and his father had been friends of her family for as long as she could remember.

Eager to put the day's events behind her, she drew a refreshing breath. A lighthearted conversation was just what she needed to end the day on a better note. "Jim, whatever are you doing poking around here in the dark?"

Despite her attempt at cheerfulness, lines of concern etched Jim's broad forehead. "Evening, Evelyn." He looked past her to Grandfather. "I heard that Mr. Twethewey has arrived. Heard he stopped by the inn earlier when I was out."

She raised her brows at the odd greeting. Normally Jim would have a playful word for her or, at the very least, flatter her in some manner. It had been their way with each other for years. But now a strange tension had invaded.

When Grandfather only nodded and grunted a reply to Jim, Evelyn forced a smile. "Yes, he has. I first encountered him on the moors. Ada got stuck in the bog and he helped me free her."

Jim smirked. "Did he now? Well, that's very friendly of him."

Evelyn sobered at the cynical tone of Jim's voice. It seemed no one was happy about Mr. Twethewey's arrival. But why?

Jim returned his attention to her grandfather. "The Kinden fellow's at the inn now and has been inquiring after him. He wanted a ride out tonight, but we talked him into waiting for the morrow."

Curious as to why Jim would feel the need to inform her grandfather of such a trifling detail, Evelyn pivoted to hear his response, but Grandfather gripped her hand looped through his arm. "Run along, lamb. Tell Bertie to fetch the port and prepare it for us in the parlor. We'll be in shortly."

She opened her mouth to protest, but Jim caught her eye. As if sensing her confusion over the odd conversation, he smiled. "Tomorrow's Market Day."

"It is," she answered slowly.

"Will you be there?"

"As long as the weather changes and I can be spared here." Evelyn tilted her head to the side. "Marnie's nearly beside herself."

"Oh, she'll be fine." The twinkle she'd

grown accustomed to returned to Jim's expression, and for a moment it felt like any other visit. "Maybe I can walk with ye a bit when you're in Pevlyn. What say you to that?"

Her shoulders relaxed slightly. "I suppose I can spare some time. That is, if you can free yourself. Your customers will be clamoring for your attention."

"I'll make time for you. You know I will. Besides, Charlie here will be wrestling. You wouldn't want to miss that, would you?"

Normally, a man talking so familiarly to her would embarrass her, but Jim . . . Jim was different. He was one of the few men her grandfather permitted her to speak with openly. He even encouraged it.

"Very well, Jim. Tomorrow then."

He bowed, and she left them and entered the cottage kitchen. Though it was much smaller and far less impressive than the massive space in Wyndcliff Hall, it held the familiar charm of home.

She placed her lantern on the table and called for Bertie.

No response.

Evelyn poked her head in the pantry and into the cellar.

Bertie was nowhere to be found.

Finding herself alone, Evelyn paused and

stood very still, attempting to overhear the men's conversation outside, but the blustery gusts of wind carried away the murmurings. With a sigh she untied her cloak, hung it on the hook, and turned to leave the kitchen when a missive on the table caught her eye.

The writing on the letter boasted large, strong strokes.

Her mother's handwriting.

She stared at it for several seconds as conflicted thoughts tumbled within her. How long had it been since she'd heard from her? A month? Perhaps more?

Mostly the child within Evelyn wanted to run to the letter, scoop it up, and devour every word her mother wanted to share with her.

The adult portion of her heart — more cautious and suspicious — argued to ignore it.

The contents might provide temporary happiness, a fleeting glimpse into the life of the mother who had left her two years prior, but the ensuing heartache that inevitably accompanied each missive would sneak in, winding its way into her emotions and tightening to the point of pain.

Despite the threat of sadness, the child within her won out.

Evelyn snatched the letter, lifted her

lantern once again, and made her way to the small parlor next to the kitchen. Once settled, she slid her finger under the fold to dislodge the wax seal. She unfolded the paper, drawing a deep breath to prepare herself for what lay inside.

It had been well over a year since she'd last seen her mother in person, and even then, it had been for but a day when Mother stopped in the village on her way to the coast. Now her mother's recent marriage and new family kept her busy. All the while Evelyn had expected to be included in her mother's new life. She would not get her hopes up that this would be the letter summoning her to Plymouth. It was easier that way.

Dear child,

So much has happened I hardly know where to begin! We have returned from a holiday in London to meet Mr. Drake's mother, and she could not have been more enchanting. My husband is from a long line of barristers, and they were a fascinating group, to be sure.

Evelyn's chest tightened as she skimmed the rest of the letter. It described in detail each of Mr. Drake's two daughters. Their

60

accomplishments, their beauty, their prospects. She swallowed the lump in her throat as the meaning behind the words sank in.

Her mother's efforts had paid off. She'd found happiness in a world outside of Wyndcliff. Happiness with another family, with new daughters, and with ample funds to live the life she expected.

But it was all without Evelyn.

Tears blurred the words as she continued to read.

One day, dear child, you will join me here and get to know your stepsisters. They ask about you frequently, and now that we are home from the season, we shall have you to Plymouth very soon for a proper introduction, once everything is settled.

Evelyn sniffed and tossed the letter onto the table.

"Once everything is settled." Mother had been writing those exact words ever since her first visit to Plymouth, when her intention had been merely to tend to her ill cousin. A trip that was supposed to last only a month stretched into a year, and then as her attachment to Mr. Drake intensified, she continued to remain away from Wyndcliff, all the while promising to call for

Evelyn to join her.

But she never did.

Now her mother was Mrs. Archibald Drake.

Now she was stepmother to two more daughters.

Anger and anguish twisted together within her so tightly, Evelyn could not accurately assess which emotion pulled strongest.

Was her mother embarrassed by her? Or did she simply want to start a new life and leave her old one, including her daughter from a disgraced family, behind?

A strange panic seized her. She'd never allowed herself to think that she wouldn't join her mother one day. But truths were truths. Evelyn was twenty and would quickly be past her prime. Perhaps her grandfather was right. He was always encouraging her to consider Jim as a suitor, and he made no effort to hide his esteem for the young innkeeper. After all, Jim was a leader in their little community. Influential. Liked and respected by all. And he was, at the very least, her friend. He was a far cry from the wealthy gentleman she and her mother had always dreamed of, but perhaps it was time to accept that that dream might never come true.

With a deep breath for fortitude, Evelyn

picked the letter back up and finished it. There was no invitation. No inquiry as to how she was faring.

A tear slipped. Then another.

But then a sharp tone, high and curt, from the courtyard caused her to jerk her head around. Were they arguing? Whatever it was, it was far from the friendly banter she usually overheard between Jim and her grandfather.

She made her way back to the kitchen and neared the door. The wind still whistled, but now the voices were louder, the edges sharper.

She recognized Jim's voice first. "What are you going to do about this?"

"What can I do about it?" Grandfather's retort was curt. "He owns the place. Every bit of sand on the shore, every bit of heather on the moorland."

"I thought he wasn't coming for two more months. How were you not aware he was to arrive? The timing couldn't be worse."

Evelyn held her breath. They were talking about Mr. Twethewey.

"He's naught but a boy with a shiny new toy, Jim. He's nothing to worry about."

"You know what's expected. Don't make me repeat it."

Silence ensued.

Frustration swelled within her. She did not like Jim's uncharacteristically harsh tone. Never had she heard anyone speak in such a threatening manner to Rupert Bray, except for perhaps her mother. Concerned, she tucked her letter in her pocket and opened the door once more. Surely they would not argue in front of her.

Both men turned to face her. Grandfather's eyes narrowed and he lifted his lantern. "I thought you were abed."

"It's far too early for bed." She stepped out into the night.

"Be on your way then, lass." Grandfather's voice was low. "We've business matters to discuss."

"Sounds more like you were arguing." She glanced pointedly at Jim. "I told myself surely that was not the case."

"Not all matters are pleasant to discuss," grunted Grandfather. "That's why it be men's talk, not suitable for a lady."

"Men's talk, is it? Well, if that's all it is, then . . ." She let her voice fade as she smirked and tilted her head to the side. "I'd hate to think there was an argument or such taking place right here in my courtyard."

"*Your* courtyard, is it?" Grandfather belted out a laugh, his countenance mellowing. "Well now, it might as well be."

She cut her eyes toward Jim. He'd not joined her grandfather's change in demeanor. His square, unshaved jaw clenched and then unclenched, and he gripped his hat with such force the rim folded.

Yes, she liked Jim, but her grandfather had been the only person to be constant in her life. The only person to truly show her love. She'd not tolerate any disrespect toward him if she could help it.

She waited for the customary smile that would crack Jim's scowl and reveal that this conversation was some sort of misunderstanding, but the expression in his dark eyes seemed unsettled. "It's late. I'd best get back to the inn. Evelyn, the rain is starting again. You'd best get back inside."

Why did everyone think they had the power to tell her when to go inside and when to go to bed and when to make herself scarce? Before she could respond, Jim, along with Charlie, had already turned, and the shrouded moonlight barely illuminated the dark cloak on his broad back.

"Why's he so upset?" Evelyn folded her arms over her chest and leaned back against the door frame. "Is it because Mr. Twethewey's arrived?"

Grandfather stared in the direction of Jim's departure, as if he could still see him.

"Jim's a good man but excitable. Don't give his behavior another thought."

"That doesn't sound like you to back down from someone who was speaking to you so brashly."

"Jim and his family have stood beside us when others wouldn't. One can forgive a great deal when you take such matters into account. Besides, he's got a great deal of responsibility on his shoulders. He's the sort of man who will make things happen, mark my words. He's the sort of man you need to align yourself with, child, and not the fancy sort your mother's got in mind for you."

Evelyn held her breath at the reference to her mother. Had he seen the letter on the table? As she shifted, the letter crinkled in her pocket.

Grandfather pushed past her and entered the cottage, leaving her alone in the court-yard. He would never see why it was so important for her to leave this village and be with her mother in Plymouth. Despite her seeming indifference, her mother always had spoken of plans for her — plans that had occupied her childhood daydreams and infiltrated her dreams at night. Here she might not be a lady, but her mother had expectations for her. And one day she would make her mother proud.

Yes, Grandfather would never understand. Perhaps it was time she stopped trying to convince him.

CHAPTER 6

Liam barely slept his first night at Wyndcliff Hall. He was never the sort of man who required a great deal of sleep, but after a long ride and an eventful day, he craved it.

And yet sleep would not come.

Instead, he spent the long midnight hours pacing his new chambers.

Thoughts of the home and family he'd left behind just the previous morning plagued him, and Bray's odd statements about his granddaughter, like a noisy gull, refused to leave him be.

After fleeting moments of rest, the first gray lights of dawn lured him to full consciousness, and he rose from the bed, eager to get on about the day. The fire still burned, offering its glowing contribution to the day's budding light, and he stepped toward it. His clothes, which had been hung near the hearth, were mostly dry now.

He donned buckskin breeches, appropriate for a day of exploring moorland and beach. As he buttoned his waistcoat, he peered through the bank of leaded windows. A faint fog hovered over the quiet courtyard and the slate-roofed stone stables, but past an expanse of purple-gray moorland, he glimpsed the sea.

At the sight, fresh enthusiasm flared through him, illuminating all of the opportunities that spread before him.

The master of the estate.

His lifelong ambition and dream.

Now it was here, and the possibilities were endless.

Once dressed, he found his way to the study on the home's main floor. Inside, books and leather-bound ledgers lined cluttered shelves, and a single stream of early-morning light slid through the tall windows and fell across a massive, messy oak desk in the room's center. He rubbed his hands together as he assessed the piles. At least here his restless energy could be put to use.

The study was a large, square room with a fireplace at the opposite end from the wall lined with bookshelves. Someone had been in here recently. Upon closer inspection he found ashes in the grate and papers and letters with recent dates on the desk. If the number of letters and agreements were painting an accurate picture, Bray had not been neglecting his duty as steward. In fact, the opposite appeared to be true. Even so, the numbers concerned him. It seemed that Wyndcliff estate was surviving, but barely.

Despite the unsettling realization, the day brightened with each passing minute, shedding fresh light on the study's stale contents. The increasing brightness forced his negative thoughts to the back of his mind and beckoned optimism to return. Gone were the steely clouds and threatening winds of the previous evening. Instead, a brilliant blue sky emerged. Seabirds swooped and dove in the open courtyard, and the rising sun glowed in faint pinks and oranges on the fluffy clouds.

He'd lost track of time when the sound of hoofbeats on the courtyard drew his attention. Liam stood from his desk and crossed the creaky floor to the window for a better view. Edwin Kinden rode in on a large gray horse. He'd only met the man in person once, but the exaggerated auburn side whiskers and portly build were unmistakable.

Eager to welcome his guest, Liam abandoned the study, crossed the great hall, and strode outside. A breeze swept down from the steeply pitched slate roof and met him as he stepped into the fresh air.

Kinden turned, his brows arched. "Ah there, Mr. Twethewey."

Liam crossed the courtyard and extended his hand. "So you found your way from the village after all."

"I did indeed." Kinden shook his hand.

"My apologies for not waiting to meet you at the inn, as we had discussed in our letters. It was getting late, and I was keen to arrive."

"Ah, the eagerness of youth." The man waved a thick hand and looped the reins over his horse's head. "It is I who should apologize. Abominably late. The true culprits are these moorland roads. The carriage broke a wheel and put me hours behind schedule. I didn't arrive at the inn until after dark, and I know better than to set foot on that stretch of moorland without light. But I'm here now, and we can get about these last pieces of business." He withdrew his handkerchief, wiped his florid face, and nodded to the house. "So what do you think of it? I've not been here in a year, but it appears as if everything's in order, at least from the outside."

Liam followed his gaze upward to the manor house's facade. "It's a little different than I imagined, but nothing a little hard

71

work won't remedy."

" 'Tis a pity, I'll agree. At one time I'm told this was the finest house in the area. But without a true master at the helm, it's what's to be expected. We all change over time, even buildings. You're quite a sight different from when I saw you last. Well, taller, at least. You were seventeen years of age when I called on you at Penwythe Hall?"

Liam stiffened at the reference to his age and only nodded his response. Yes, he was young, and it seemed no one would let him forget it. No doubt many thought him too young for such an undertaking. He kept his uncle Jac's advice in mind. *"Observe first. Then speak."*

A stable boy, one whom Liam had not yet met, trotted around from the side of Wyndcliff, interrupting their discussion, and sheepishly took control of Kinden's animal. After a quick introduction to the youth, Liam allowed the boy to be about his duties and ushered his guest through the main entrance, which really was impressive. Individual windows came together to form one large wall of glass that stretched up two stories. All around the second-floor perimeter, a thickly carved wooden banister allowed the upper level to be seen. It was a long, narrow space, but despite the dust and evident disuse, at one time it must have been quite grand. "I don't think anyone has truly set foot in this chamber in years. I have work ahead of me, to be sure, but we will see it restored to its former glory."

Kinden chuckled, his cheeks jiggling with the motion. "I wish you all the good fortune in the world, but you forget I've seen the finances of this place. Restoration takes capital."

The thought that the man might be finding humor in the situation did not sit well with Liam. But then again, what did it matter? He was in charge of this transformation, and he'd find a way to succeed, one way or another.

Liam ushered his guest toward the study.

Kinden removed his hat as he stepped through the doorway. "I assume you've spoken with Bray by now."

"I have." Liam glanced over to catch the amusement sparkling in Kinden's wide-set eyes. "He's an interesting man."

Inside the study Kinden clicked his tongue. "*Interesting* is one descriptor for him."

"I actually encountered his granddaughter first when I was on the moors last evening, and then I spoke with Bray in the stable shortly thereafter. Quite an opinionated fellow."

Kinden pulled one of the chairs to the side and sat before he crossed one thick leg over the other. "He was great friends with your great-uncle before he died, you know. In fact, Bray's son was your uncle's godson."

Liam raised an eyebrow.

"Bray wasn't always a steward, as I'm sure you will hear, if you haven't already." Kinden brushed dirt from his hat before he deposited it on a nearby table. "He used to own the estate to the north of here. Your uncle gave him the steward position here and saved his family from the poorhouse. But it wasn't all charity. Bray knows the area and the people as well as anyone, and they respect him. You'll want him on your side."

Liam took his chair behind the desk. "On my side? Why?"

" 'Course I only know what I've been told, but I've heard the Pevlyn villagers can be difficult."

Liam's stomach tightened. He didn't relish the idea of relying on a man he did not know, but neither did he like the prospect of disagreeable locals. "And the granddaughter?"

Kinden shrugged. "Don't know much about her, but she's been here every time I came to visit, not that I've visited often. What's her name? Elizabeth? Eve? Bah. Doesn't matter. He keeps her pretty much hidden as far as I can tell."

Recalling Bray's harsh words of warning regarding his granddaughter, he changed the subject. "Are you familiar with a man by the name of George Porter?"

Kinden looked toward the ceiling, as if the answer might be written on the plaster there, then shook his head. "Seems I've heard it before. Can't place it, though."

"His business is mining china clay. He's out of Staffordshire and oversees some other pits here in Cornwall. He said he was in works with my uncle before he died to dig a china clay pit on Wyndcliff moorland."

"Ah yes! China clay. Dusty stuff. But isn't that the same as copper and tin? Leave it to the Cornishmen to find the gold buried beneath the earth."

"He contacted me several years ago to inform me of the plans he had with my great-uncle, and we have stayed in contact."

"Yes, yes, I do recall Treton's enthusiasm for the project, now that you mention it. He died before the paperwork could be signed, if I recall correctly."

"Well, the plans were put into place, and now that I am owner I fully intend to pursue them." Liam folded his arms across his chest. "Porter is to come out within the week."

"Within the week? Ah, you are an eager one, aren't you?" Kinden chortled, and the chair beneath him groaned as he shifted. "And why not? You're young. You have assets. Well, some, anyway."

Movement in the courtyard caught Liam's eye. Bray was crossing from the cottage. Liam leaned forward and tapped on the front window to capture the steward's attention. Bray looked up, and Liam motioned for him to come in.

Bray did as bid, and as he entered the study he swept his wide-brimmed hat from his head and smoothed his white hair into place before shaking hands with Kinden.

The man did not appear much different by daylight. He was not a tall man, not by any measure. The top of his head came only to Kinden's shoulder, and Bray's person was quite small by comparison. He appeared to be wearing the same crimson neckcloth he'd worn the previous night, and if possible the firm angles of his face and deep-set eyes looked even more intense.

"Kinden will be joining us as we go out to call on the tenants," Liam explained.

"Very well, but there's something you

need to know before we depart." Bray shifted his gaze from one man to the other. "Soldiers are patrolling the cliffs above the cove as we speak."

"Soldiers?" Liam frowned. "Why?"

Bray tugged at the cravat about his neck and smoothed the front of his striped waistcoat. "We've been having a bit of trouble with the Customs officers from over in Plymouth. The cove is a dangerous strip of coastline, and it's seen more than its fair share of wrecks, especially recently. As a result, they're accusing the locals of plundering and smuggling and the sort. Seems there's been an increase in free trading, or at least the officials believe that to be the case, and they are keeping a close eye on the cove."

Liam jerked. "Shipwrecks and free trading?"

" 'Tis not to be taken lightly," Bray snapped, his brows drawing together in intense focus. "Shipwrecks must be dealt with, and as keepers of the land we must address the issue, whether you're aware of the happenings or not. The villagers — who have lived their lives here and made their livelihood from the land — think they've a God-given right to whatever washes ashore, or at least a right to be compensated for retrieving what washes ashore. Alternatively, the king believes he's owed a bit as well and sends his Customs men to collect. It's a tedious lot, and one that must be handled with utmost care."

Kinden cleared his throat and leaned forward in his chair. "It's true. My experience here has been limited, but Bray has kept me abreast. He's been acting as your wrecking agent and handling all the details."

"They're called wrecking rights," Bray blurted. "If a ship and its cargo wash ashore and no one on board is alive to claim it, or if it hasn't been claimed in a year and a day, you — as landowner — pay duties on it and then it's yours to do with as you see fit. But the law is worried that whatever comes ashore might be smuggled goods. Therein lies the obvious issue."

It wasn't so obvious to Liam, but he'd not given his coastline a thought. He'd been focused on the tenants. The farmable land. The moorland that could be used for china clay pits. But the coastline? Never.

Bray nodded. "I've got the situation in hand and will apprise you of the details and inner workings in good time. Prepare yourself. The officers will probably call once they learn of your arrival. No doubt they'll paint you a grim picture."

Liam stiffened at the gravity of Bray's words. "I'd no idea that shipwrecks were so prevalent."

"Aye. It's dangerous on account of the ridge not far off the coast. On a clear day you can see the rocks offshore from atop the cliffs when the tide's out and the sun hits the sea just right. But the ships coming in along the coast have no idea what's below 'em."

"Is there naught that can be done for it?" Liam asked.

"Not really. We keep an eye out, especially during storms. Often our men risk life and limb to get out and rescue sailors or help the ships. Other times they rescue the goods. They get paid for the salvage, of course."

The conversation shifted back to the tenants, but even as the men went to their horses, a nagging sense of dread hovered over Liam. He didn't know exactly why, but he suspected there was much more to the shipwrecks than he'd been told, and he was determined to get to the bottom of it.

CHAPTER 7

"Isn't he wonderful?" Jenna Shaw looped her arm through Evelyn's and squeezed. Admiration glimmered in her light-brown eyes as the wrestling match unfolded before her, and she bit her lower lip, almost as if to keep her giddiness from spilling forward.

Evelyn followed her friend's gaze back to Charlie Potts and tilted her head as she studied his short, stocky frame and his wild shock of white-blond hair. His round face flushed crimson with exertion, and his dark eyes were a startling contrast to his otherwise fair features. At present the man in question was sweaty, bare chested, and already developing red and purple welts from his beating. And yet those around him cheered him on.

"Evie?"

Evelyn snapped her attention back to her friend — and her question. "Yes, he is."

Content with the affirmation, Jenna returned her gaze to the display of strength unfolding before them. "He promised me that once he makes enough money we'll marry. Likely before the end of the year. Well, at least the banns can be read then. Isn't that a grand thought?"

Evelyn forced a smile, despite the knot settling in her stomach. She knew well her friend's desire to be married and settled. But to Charlie Potts?

Apparently she hadn't feigned enough excitement, for Jenna's sharp sniff and toss of her chestnut hair added to the frustration in her voice. "I suppose it's easy to lack interest in such things when one's future is so certain."

Evelyn tilted her head to the side at the odd statement. "I'm sorry, Jenna. My thoughts were elsewhere. Yes, it is very exciting."

Jenna dropped her arm from Evelyn's but did not respond, leaving Jenna's last words hanging as thick as the dust in the air.

The match ended. The men shook hands. Charlie, victorious and breathless, winked at Jenna.

The smile returned to her face.

Even though Evelyn did not understand the appeal of the short, red-faced man, she did feel a thread of envy tighten through her.

Charlie had his faults, but Jenna accepted him. What would it be like to care for someone in such a way and have someone care for you in return?

She'd never even come close to a romance. With the exception of Jim, Charlie, Jenna, and a few other select individuals, Grandfather did not approve of her interacting with the village folks.

Not that they would have her.

She still cringed when she thought of the way her mother had treated the less fortunate while she still lived at Wyndcliff Cottage, and apparently the villagers remembered it as well. Even so, Evelyn longed for the sort of connection that Jenna seemed to have — the feeling that she truly belonged somewhere, and to someone.

"Is that him?" Jenna gripped Evelyn's arm again.

The brightness in Jenna's tone suggested that Evelyn's preoccupation had been forgiven — or at least momentarily dismissed — and Evelyn followed her friend's gaze. There, in the distance beyond the makeshift wrestling ring, stood two men who were not from the village: one in a black coat, one in an emerald green, and both in tall beaver hats.

His name had been the topic of every whispered conversation: Mr. William Twethewey.

"Look how dapper he is." Jenna laughed, shielding her eyes with her free hand, making no effort to hide her assessment or her amusement. "He looks fit for a visit to the palace instead of a call to the pub."

Mr. Twethewey did cut a striking, albeit out of place, figure in a fitted black tailcoat, as did Mr. Kinden, whose green coat was a strange sight in the midst of a mass of grays and tans.

"Who's that with 'im?" Jenna asked.

"Mr. Kinden." Evelyn leaned closer to be heard over the voices and movement around them. "The solicitor who's overseen the estate until Mr. Twethewey came of age."

"And Mr. Twethewey, is he handsome then? You've seen him up close? One can't tell from this distance."

Evelyn tensed. Yes, William Twethewey was handsome, with his dark hair and striking blue eyes. And yet it felt like a question she shouldn't answer. He was, after all, her grandfather's employer. They lived on his property. "That doesn't matter really, does it?"

Jenna laughed again and threw back her head. "Oh, Evie. It always matters, and your refusal to answer confirms he must be very handsome indeed."

Evelyn returned her gaze to the festivities. "What matters is if he is kind. If he is —"

"You should know that men like him are never kind. Resourceful, efficient even. But kind?" She huffed. "My father says Mr. Twethewey's priority now is squeezing every farthing from Wyndcliff that he can, with no thought to the cost to those who work it."

"Oh, I don't think that is necessarily the case." Evelyn bristled, attempting to keep her tone level. "Remember, my grandfather once owned an estate. He was kind and well respected."

"Yes, but you were a child then. You don't know how he was, not for certain. We remember things the way we want to remember them. Just like we judge the present in the manner we wish to see it."

Evelyn's chest burned with the perceived injustice in Jenna's words, slowly at first and then hotter and stronger. Yes, Grandfather had a temper, but what man was completely without some flaw? She owed her very life to her grandfather. Why did it seem that everyone refused to see his kinder side?

She looked back to the men. Grandfather

was with them now, and they were speaking with Jim just outside the inn's main door.

"Well, handsome or not, it's good that you're not falling prey to the new master's charms," Jenna teased. "Your Jim might be jealous."

The memory of his odd behavior toward her grandfather the previous night still did not sit right with her. "I'd hardly call him *my* Jim."

"Wouldn't you?" Jenna grinned smugly and folded her arms across her chest. "He referred to you as *his* Evelyn. Told Charlie so himself."

"Well, it isn't true, and you mustn't believe it."

"And what would be so bad 'bout Jim? He's handsome, in his own way. He's certainly well respected. Seems to me a maid could do a great deal worse."

Evelyn gazed back to Jim across High Street. His sand-colored hair was wild and tousled about his tanned face. He looked very different from the other two men, with no coat on, his plain tan waistcoat, and his white sleeves rolled up to his elbows. She shrugged. "There's nothing wrong with Jim. I like him. I do. It is just that I have other plans."

"Yes, I know. I know." Jenna sighed and

rolled her eyes. "Your mother's to send for you, and you will go to Plymouth and live with her happily, as if she never left in the first place. And then you'll find the man of your dreams and leave this little village once and for all and live out your days in luxury and comfort."

The unmasked sarcasm in the words stung. Evelyn bit her lower lip.

Jenna, as if realizing she'd taken her assessment too far, softened her tone. "I'm sorry. 'Tis only I don't want you to let an opportunity pass you by when you're chasing something that perhaps is not meant to be."

Evelyn nodded but could not speak on the topic. The rejection in the letter from the previous night still ached. With each new letter the bandage was unbound afresh, leaving the wound raw and tender. Now, to hear her friend almost mock the situation was salt to the injury.

Yes, she could encourage Jim as Jenna suggested. It would certainly please her grandfather. Then her future would at last be secure and steady. After all, it was happening all around her. Many women her age were already married with babes in their arms and more on the way.

How long would she have to endure this

battle warring within her? The thought of a husband appealed to her. A home of her own. She wanted to please her grandfather, who had cared for her all these years. But another part of her longed to grab hold of the future she and her mother had dreamt of. To make a suitable match that would secure her future. To make her mother proud. To truly *belong.*

Jenna placed her work-worn hand on Evelyn's arm. "You know, it isn't wrong to want a husband and a family, even if you think your mother expects something different."

Evelyn bristled. "It's not just my mother."

"Then what is it?" After waiting for a response, Jenna sighed. "Evie. Dearest. I know you love your mother, and she loves you, but she has been saying this for years. You have been living in perpetual anticipation. In the meantime, your youth is passing you by. At some point you must make decisions for yourself and do what is best for you."

The advice was sound. But Evelyn could not bring herself to believe that perhaps her friend might be right.

CHAPTER 8

Liam ducked to step inside the inn's low-beamed door and squinted as his eyes adjusted from the brightness of the late-afternoon sun to the dimly lit space before him. Kinden and Bray followed, both covered with dust from their ride across the moors.

Immediately the thick atmosphere of the taproom pressed in on him. No breeze or drafts moved the damp air. It stood stagnant and pungent, like a heavy blanket draped over all. Scents of tobacco smoke, spirits, dirty men, and burnt bread battled for dominance, and yet according to Bray, this was the place to go in the village to encounter the tenants: the White Eagle Inn.

Liam, along with Kinden and Bray, had spent the morning and early afternoon riding over the Wyndcliff estate. He'd been pleasantly surprised by the number of cottages and farms he encountered. He'd even glimpsed the coastline and cove that Bray had told him about just that morning. As satisfying as it was to finally be able to assess his property, what he saw distressed him. Poverty was everywhere — from the underfed cows in a tenant's pasture to the tattered clothing hanging on makeshift laundry lines.

Wyndcliff Hall would never be truly successful unless he could help those who lived and worked on his property — his uncle Jac had taught him that. And even though he'd met few of his tenants, the evident need fueled his desire even more to begin work on the china clay pits and start providing an additional source of income. For everyone.

"So this is it . . . the White Eagle Inn." Bray stepped in front of Liam, sweeping his arm out toward the inn's patrons. "You wanted to meet your tenants. Well, they're all here."

Slowly the voices in the chamber softened to whispers before the sound disappeared completely. All eyes turned to him. No one moved. Men of every age — from gangly youths to the elderly — were huddled around roughly fashioned tables or standing in corners. Their shabby clothing and unkempt appearance unified them and at the same time made Liam feel wholly out of place.

At the sight before him, a sense of obligation rushed him. He thought of the relationship Uncle Jac had with his tenants. One of respect. Pride. Trust.

Was it possible Liam could have such a relationship with these people?

"Take note, men," Bray called, pushing his way past them and moving to the center of the front room. "This is William Twethewey, Wyndcliff Hall's new master. Those of you who have business with Wyndcliff will continue to work with me. You'll all meet him in due time, as needed."

Liam was not expecting the introduction, especially such a blunt one.

The room fell silent again. All eyes remained on him, watching and waiting to see what he would do.

He nodded curtly in the direction of the men before he joined Bray and Kinden at a table along the outer wall.

After several awkward, silent moments, conversation gradually resumed, and Liam leaned on the table, very conscious of the stares in his direction, and fixed his own stare on Bray. "Was that necessary?"

Bray shrugged his narrow shoulders and smoothed the lapels on his coat. "Sure it was. Don't forget, you're the most impor-

90

tant and influential man in Pevlyn now. The sooner they recognize it, the smoother things will go for everyone."

"Yes, but I've no wish to —"

"These men need to know you. Every single one of them." Bray's expression hardened, his gray eyes unblinking, and he leaned with his elbow on the rough table. "They need to respect you and your position. Best set the expectation early. I'm only trying to help you."

Liam did not like being interrupted. Nor did he want that sort of help. But everything was new here. He'd be wise to observe before responding.

Liam exchanged glances with Kinden, whose brows were raised in what could only be annoyance. It had become painfully evident throughout the course of the day that a band of tension pulled between Kinden and Bray. Liam hadn't noticed it at first, but as the hours dragged on, their disdain for each other intensified. Now they would barely speak to each other.

Time passed in the crowded public house. Liam had taken it upon himself to introduce himself to the men around him. Bray departed not long after they arrived, claiming he had business that needed tending, leaving Liam and Kinden to take their evening meal at the inn. The sun started to set, casting beams of dusty light through the dirty windows and across the packed taproom. The crowd grew rowdier and louder. Needing to stretch his muscles after hours of riding, Liam stood and moved to the window. Outside, women, men, and children milled about, merchants lined the streets with their wares, and farmers organized baskets of autumn harvest.

But this activity was not what captured his attention.

Miss Bray stood at the road's edge, talking with another woman. In a gown of cerulean blue and with her long golden hair loose in the bright sunlight, she was impossible not to notice.

He remained at the window for several moments, allowing himself to enjoy the sight. So far, the most pleasant interactions he'd had at Wyndcliff had been with her, fleeting though they were. And while it would be highly improper for him to speak with her, the tension he'd been carrying in his shoulders seemed to ease at the sight of her.

"She's a pretty one, isn't she?"

Liam turned to find Jim Bowen at his side. Clearly Liam was not the only man in the village to appreciate Miss Bray's beauty.

When Liam did not respond, Bowen leaned with his thick shoulder on the stone wall and faced him. "The lovely Evelyn Bray. I spoke with her just last night. She told me she'd met you already."

Liam stiffened. It had already been dark when he bid her farewell the previous evening. She spoke with Bowen after that? Of course it was no business of his, but what would a woman be doing speaking to the innkeeper after nightfall?

Bowen extended the mug of ale in his hand toward Liam. " 'Tis for you." He nodded toward his patrons. "This is an ornery lot. But no doubt you're finding that out on your own. As for me, I'm glad to see you here. Welcome to Pevlyn."

Liam accepted the outstretched mug without a word, then Bowen clamped a hand on Liam's shoulder and walked back to the bar.

It was an odd welcome, but then again, pretty much everything about his arrival here had not fit a mold. He turned back to the table to find Kinden teasing the raven-haired barmaid, whose every movement and bat of her eyes encouraged his attentions. The volume of Kinden's laughter increased. The ale was loosening the man's professional side, and Liam didn't like it.

93

Liam returned to the table, interrupting the flirtation. Kinden patted the barmaid's hand, perhaps a bit too freely, before she refilled his mug and moved on to the next customer. Only then did Kinden regain his composure. He cleared his throat before he nodded toward Bowen. "I'm not in this village often, but best keep an eye on that one."

"Why?" Liam dropped back into his chair.

"Bray told you about the Customs officers this morning, remember? Now, I don't know much, but the last time I was in Pevlyn, the Customs officers had just conducted a raid on this very inn. They were certain that the spirits Bowen sells are contraband, be it from a wreck or smuggling."

Liam shrugged as he watched Bowen lean over a table and talk to a patron. "What's that to do with me?"

"Think on it a minute. Who owns the coastline along this stretch of the world? You, that's who."

The meaning behind Kinden's words sank in. Liam sobered.

"Like I said, I'd just watch that one." He sloppily lifted the mug to his lips.

Liam did not like the glassy look in Kinden's eyes or his boisterous laughter. This was not the man he'd spent the day with but an altered version of him — one brought on by drink. The hour was growing late. The sun had long since set, and now naught but candlelight and firelight lit the space. Women had joined the men, and the leer in Kinden's eyes could be nothing but trouble.

The barmaid passed by again, and Kinden swung his arm out, wrapped it around the barmaid's ample waist, and pulled her onto his lap. She giggled and spilled the mug she'd been holding.

Determined to stop this before it got out of hand, Liam stepped toward Kinden. "Let's go."

"What? Why?" he demanded as the busty woman put her bare arm around his shoulders. "You aren't ready for me to leave, are you, luv?"

She giggled again and smoothed Kinden's unruly, wiry auburn hair.

Anger tightened in Liam's chest at the ridiculous display. Liam reached for his hat. "You can stay, then. I'm going."

The young barmaid stood and moved to another customer, and Kinden slunk in his seat. "Bah, you scared her away with your sour mood."

Liam turned to leave, and Kinden sputtered in protest, "No, man. No! You can't go back at this hour. You're young. You've your whole life to spend in that dusty abode.

This is Market Day! Make merry and meet your neighbors, like this lovely." Kinden stood and reached out for the barmaid again, who was serving the next table, and tugged her hand.

The large, broad-shouldered man she'd been speaking with positioned himself between Kinden and the woman, his eyes radiating rage.

The man, whoever he was, bested Kinden in both size and brawn, and his black brows drew into a harsh line. He cast an intimidating glance toward Liam before speaking. "I don't care who you are or who you are a guest of. You can get up, take yer fancy hat, and get out. Or I can show you out meself."

Kinden cackled, the laugh of a man used to behavior without consequence. "Is that so? Foolish man. I'd think twice before —"

The man jerked Kinden up in the air by his coat and dropped him to the dusty inn floor.

Cheers circled the group of rowdy miners and laborers.

Any respect for their position had dwindled with time and drink. Now Liam and Kinden were invaders on their turf. Liam stooped to grab Kinden's coat and yanked him to his feet.

Once steady, Kinden, red-faced, pushed

past Liam and lunged toward the burly man. It was a ridiculous match. Kinden, older by possibly decades and smaller by at least a head, stood no chance.

The man whirled and drew back his fist and slammed it against Kinden's cheek. Kinden hurtled back against a wall.

Liam groaned. This was not how he'd wanted to arrive in his new town, his new home.

Master, indeed.

The men in the crowd heckled Kinden.

Kinden spewed profanities.

In an effort to end the debacle as soon as possible, Liam dragged Kinden out the door and all the way to where they had tied their horses. Sweating with exertion in the cool night, Liam lifted the man to his horse and dropped him over the saddle.

As Kinden continued to protest, Liam hissed, "What were you thinking?"

"My last visit to ol' Pevlyn. I'll not be returning here." He smirked. "Might as well make it a good one."

CHAPTER 9

Evelyn pulled an errant stitch from her sewing and adjusted the position of her chair so the fire's light could illuminate her work more fully. She clicked her tongue in frustration as the knot she'd created refused to give way.

Sewing had never been her strong suit. She hadn't the patience for it. The sewing she'd learned as a child had been more ornamental than practical, and now as she attempted to help Marnie mend an apron, feelings of inadequacy flooded her. She was almost certain she was making it worse, but she would sit here by the fire and keep her friend company for as long as needed.

"My, but the hour be late." Marnie looked up from the hem she was mending to cast a glance toward the mantel clock. "Ye'd think they'd have sent word if they weren't goin' to eat their evenin' meal here."

Evelyn followed Marnie's gaze to the

clock. It was past ten. "I told you I saw Mr. Twethewey and Grandfather at the inn, didn't I? I wonder if they took their meal there."

"La. Ye did tell me that. Bless my soul, it's goin' to take me quite some time gettin' used to someone else's hours. I'm set in me ways."

"We all are." Evelyn reached for the sewing scissors on the table between them. "I fear Grandfather will have a difficult time relinquishing the responsibility for Wyndcliff to Mr. Twethewey. He's been so used to being in control of every detail."

"Yer grandfather's a reasonable man. He'll adjust."

Evelyn did not respond. Instead, she pierced her needle into the fabric. She'd seen the twitch in her grandfather's eye the previous night. He was not used to being questioned, and he was accustomed to having the final word. No one in the whole of Pevlyn dared question him, be it tenant, villager, staff, or even herself.

She'd returned to Wyndcliff shortly after the wrestling match, knowing the merrymaking would continue late into the night. Jenna would enjoy time with her family and her beau, but Grandfather would expect Evelyn to return home, so she passed the evening by telling Marnie of the gossip she'd gleaned and the wrestling match she'd watched.

In the evening's quiet time, when both women worked in silence, she tried not to think about Jenna's words regarding both her future and her mother, but they hung heavy in her heart. The judgmental sentiment intermingled with the thinly veiled rejection in her mother's latest letter, making Evelyn question every desire she'd held for her future.

Her thoughts turned to Jim. It seemed everyone thought him a suitable match for her, but their relationship had always been playful. Flirtatious at most. But surely his interest stopped there, or he would have met her for a walk during Market Day as he'd promised the previous night.

Something banged into the kitchen door with a loud crash.

Evelyn jumped and nearly dropped her sewing.

The door flung inward.

Marnie cried out, and her hand flew to her chest.

Mr. Kinden, face flushed, hair disheveled, burst through the threshold, bouncing his shoulder against the door frame as he did.

Evelyn laughed at first, dismissing her

surprise. "Mr. Kinden! You gave me a fright."

He chuckled and shrugged his coat from his shoulders.

Evelyn had only glimpsed the solicitor earlier that morning, and she'd not spoken with him. But as the moments passed, the wild sloppiness in his expression made her increasingly uncomfortable. His cravat hung crooked and threatened to become untied. He wore no hat, and his copper hair hung free of his queue and untidy about his round cheeks. His face flushed an unbecoming pinkish gray. He took a step forward and stumbled.

"Merciful heavens." Marnie's eyes widened. "He's drunk."

Evelyn assessed him with fresh eyes. Marnie was right — there was no mistaking it.

Marnie slammed her sewing into the basket. "The nerve he has to come in here like this an' —"

Mr. Kinden ignored Marnie's disapproval and fixed his pale-brown eyes on Evelyn. "Ah, the pretty lass of Wyndcliff Hall."

Alarm pricked Evelyn's spine. She dropped her sewing to her chair, stood, and inched back against the wall, adding distance between her and Mr. Kinden. "I'll fetch my grandfather. He'll want to know you've returned." She eyed the door, marking it as her target. She skirted around the edge of the nearby table, but in a sudden sidestep, Mr. Kinden blocked her path.

"Must ye be off in such a hurry there, luv?" He stepped even closer.

She lifted her chin and forced her voice to remain level. "Let me pass."

He reached for her waist.

At the touch fear ratcheted into anger. She didn't think. She smacked him across his face. Hard.

So hard that it stung her palm's soft flesh.

She gasped in surprise at her own action.

Mr. Kinden stumbled back, nearly falling to the ground. "Why, you —"

"Enough!" a voice boomed.

Evelyn jerked her head upward.

William Twethewey stood in the doorway, his face red, his blue eyes wide. He said nothing else but closed the space and grabbed Mr. Kinden's arm.

Mr. Kinden's face shook with mounting rage. "What's wrong with you?"

"I'll not tolerate such reprehensible behavior under my roof, do you hear?"

"Bah." Mr. Kinden jerked his arm free, swinging it wide. "She's just the granddaughter of your steward."

"Doesn't matter who she is. I said I won't

tolerate it."

"Ha! But you're a boy, playing grown-up master of the castle."

Evelyn did not remain to hear the rest of the conversation. Palm stinging, pulse racing, she flung open the door and ran through. Tears burned in her eyes as she ran blindly into the dark night.

"Just the granddaughter of your steward."

The words pounded in her head as surely as her feet pounded the cobblestones as she raced back to her cottage.

Her snug little world, safe and secure, was starting to crumble, cracking under the stress of change.

The dream was always the same eerie vision.

It regularly snuck in like a ghostly caller and invaded Evelyn's midnight thoughts. And now it haunted her as she woke to morning's early light.

The premise was a dismal one — she was a young child again, clad in a white linen nightdress with her hair loose about her shoulders, crying and looking for her parents. Eventually she'd locate her father, but when she reached him she'd find naught but a faceless apparition who would not speak.

But it was only a dream. A product of her innermost thoughts.

Evelyn stood from her bed and stretched the tightness from her muscles. The worn wooden planks were cold beneath her bare feet, and a shiver traversed her spine as a gust buffeted her. She looked toward the window. The rag she'd used to plug the hole in the glass had fallen again, and chilly morning air curled in. With a huff of frustration she crossed to the window, retrieved the rag, and stuffed it back into the cracked glass. She'd mentioned it to Grandfather several times, and yet he failed to have the glazier out to repair it.

As she finished her task, movement in Wyndcliff's front courtyard caught her eye.

Mr. Twethewey and Mr. Kinden stood facing each other. Mr. Kinden had his gloved hand on a gray horse, and Mr. Twethewey's arms were folded across his chest.

The memory of the previous evening swept in, calling forth anger, then embarrassment. She'd smacked a man. She'd never smacked anyone before.

Her own actions shocked her. But he'd frightened her, and an almost primal need to defend herself from the man with the dark, beady eyes and grabby hands had taken control.

She swallowed the uncertainty rising within her. No doubt Mr. Twethewey would think her wild. Or unmannered. It would reflect poorly on her grandfather.

Even so, why should she care?

Because he was her superior in station, and in many respects, he had authority over her.

She watched the ensuing interaction with interest. The wind, which threatened a storm, swept down from the gables, disrupting Mr. Twethewey's black hair and fluttering the cape of Mr. Kinden's greatcoat. She was too far away to make out their expressions, much less hear their words, but after a brief discussion, Mr. Kinden mounted his horse and urged it through the iron gate out toward the open moorland.

Mr. Twethewey watched Mr. Kinden depart, then he looked toward the cottage.

Fearing discovery, she whirled away from the window and stood very still, as if any movement might attract attention. After several seconds, she mustered her courage to peer back down to the courtyard.

But he was gone.

Relieved, Evelyn checked to make sure the rag was secure in the window, dressed quickly in a gown of thick brown wool, and made her way down to the kitchen where

Bertie was already about her morning duties. The scents of coffee and freshly baked bread tantalized her. Bertie's dark-blonde hair was bound in a cloth on her head, and a stained apron covered her faded gown. She lifted her head as Evelyn entered, then she wrapped a rag around her hand to remove a pot from above the fire. "I heard about what happened last night. I just got back from Wyndcliff's kitchen after fetching some more bread. Marnie told me."

Evelyn, not knowing how to respond, simply nodded and took an apple from the basket near the pantry.

The situation had been humiliating, and it should be no surprise that people would talk about it. Marnie was not known for her discretion, and with so few people on Wyndcliff grounds, keeping a secret was nigh impossible. But if Bertie knew of the events, then Grandfather would know, and there was no telling how he'd react to such news.

Bertie returned the pot to the fire and swiped her hair from her forehead. "Marnie said Mr. Twethewey made him leave first thing. Woke him up before dawn, yanked him right out of his bed, and told the scoundrel to leave, just like that. Seems Mr. Kinden caused quite a stir at the White Eagle last night too. La, I hope these newcomers do not bring us too much trouble. Things are nice and quiet around here. Would be a shame for that to change for all of their carousing and tomfoolery."

Evelyn took a bite of the apple. "Where is Grandfather now, do you know?"

"I ain't seen him this morning." Bertie shrugged her narrow shoulders. "But you know how he is. Up and out before the light of day."

Ready to be alone with her thoughts, Evelyn eyed the maid with suspicion. Bertie seemed to know more about her grandfather than she did lately. Dismissing the sentiment, she lifted an empty basket from the shelf next to the door. "I'm out to the garden. Please let me know if Grandfather returns." And with the final words, Evelyn grabbed her shawl and stepped out into the cool morning and low-hanging mists.

CHAPTER 10

Liam sat in Wyndcliff's dining hall, alone with naught but the ticking mantel clock for company.

His untouched breakfast of bread, pork, and eggs sat before him. His coffee, also untouched, had grown cold.

Brilliant sunlight streamed through the dirty paned windows, signaling the morning's late hour, and yet here he sat. His appetite had left with Kinden, and now anger blazed through him, increasing with each passing moment.

It was an emotion he did not experience often. Normally he considered himself practical. Even-tempered. Reasonable. But Kinden had played him for a fool. He'd taken advantage of a situation, and it made Liam sick.

Yes, Kinden's facilitation of the transfer of the estate from the trust to Liam had been valuable, and he'd played an important role over the years in helping to prepare Liam to manage what would one day be his property. He'd anticipated Kinden's ongoing assistance with various financial and legal matters, but that association was now dead.

When Liam considered the damage that had been done, his jaw tightened. No doubt the solicitor's ridiculous actions were on the tongue of every villager who'd been at the White Eagle Inn, and the look of fear in Miss Bray's eyes haunted him even now. But it was more than the embarrassment and injustice of his actions.

At the end of the day, failure was not an option. He had to make Wyndcliff successful, and that task would be even more difficult without Kinden's expertise. He owed it to the memory of his parents, not to mention Uncle Jac, his father's younger brother who had stepped in as his guardian after his father's death. He also owed it to his siblings, especially his sisters, who would one day require dowries.

Uncle Jac's advice rang afresh in his mind. *"Trust is to be earned, not something freely given."*

Liam had been lulled into a false sense of security with Kinden. Just because his great-uncle Treton had trusted him wholly, he should not have trusted so blindly. Liam would not make that mistake again — not with Bray, not with anyone.

He took a drink of the cold coffee and stood from his chair to pace the chamber.

He'd half expected to see Rupert Bray when he escorted Kinden from the house earlier that morning. Surely someone had told him about the incident between Miss Bray and the solicitor. The man always seemed to have his finger on the pulse of every event, but he did not appear.

Beyond the courtyard's outer stone wall, over the stretch of dew-covered lawn, he saw the steward's cottage. It was a tidy dwelling with a steeply sloped slate roof, very like that of Wyndcliff Hall.

Miss Bray was likely inside.

He thought of her, with her porcelain skin and sharp eyes — and the expression of abhorrence as she ran from the kitchen.

He'd need to speak with her at some point to offer an apology and an assurance that she'd never again be treated so unscrupulously on his property. And what made matters worse, he felt personally responsible. Great-Uncle Treton may have made Kinden the solicitor, but Liam had invited him to stay at Wyndcliff. Perhaps she now associated him with Kinden's behavior. The thought of her keeping her distance from him saddened Liam.

He saw her then. As she stepped away from the cottage door, the breeze caught her golden hair, which always seemed to be wild and down about her shoulders. She was clad in a gray gown, and she stopped to pet a white cat crossing the yard. Then, without a glance toward the main house, she straightened and continued around to the back of the cottage.

Bray had made it clear that she was not a member of the household staff. Yet she seemed to be a part of the very fabric of Wyndcliff. She roamed the house, the cottage, the gardens, the grounds, as if she belonged here.

Perhaps she did.

Liam should take advantage of this moment and make sure she was well. It would be an awkward conversation, but an apology was required. He dropped his things to the desk and made his way through the great room. But by the time he made his way to the main entrance, she was gone.

His opportunity, for the moment, was lost.

He drew a deep breath and went back inside. This would not be the last difficult situation he'd come up against as master of Wyndcliff, and yet Liam had not expected trouble to find him so quickly. And even though the support he thought he had in his corner in Kinden had faded away, he was not without resources.

He cleared his throat and began clearing the clutter on his desk. He might have encountered an initial setback, but he would not give up without a fight.

A breeze whipped over the purple and brown moorland, waving the tall grasses and tugging at Liam's coat. Gray clouds had obscured the earlier morning's blue skies, and the scent of rain hovered all around them, intermingling with the land's earthy aroma.

Before him spread Aulder Hill, the highest point in this stretch of moorland. *His* moorland. Wide. Open. And tinged with autumn's tawny hues.

Today he was seeing it through fresh eyes.

Next to him stood George Porter, the man whose plan for china clay pits would provide a sound future for the estate. The gentleman had arrived not even an hour prior, and now they stood shoulder to shoulder in the moorland winds, assessing the land before them.

It looked like so many other bits of moorland, except for one significant difference: long perpendicular grooves crossed the landscape. Time had done its best to camouflage the man-made pits, but they were still evident in neat, straight rows.

"I remember the day we dug these sample pits very well." Porter knelt and ran his fingers over the loose dirt. "Most people might see this type of land as a wasteland, but not me. It's what's beneath the surface that beckons, and it will save your estate from ruin, mark my words."

It was odd to hear another man speak so openly about Liam's fortune, but in truth, this man was hardly a stranger. Even though today was their first meeting face-to-face, many letters had been exchanged over the past two years regarding the future of this moorland once Liam fully inherited.

Making the china clay pits profitable was more important than he had first imagined. According to Wyndcliff's ledgers, many tenants were behind in their rent. With relatively little other income coming in, something had to be done. If he wanted to build something worth handing down to his own children someday, and if he wanted to provide any support to his sisters and family at Penwythe Hall, he needed to act soon.

"It's been nearly a decade since we dug these pits to assess them for china clay," Porter said. "Your uncle saw the value in it.

Whereas most Cornishmen would see their fortune in copper or tin, this is true sustainability. Its mining is not nearly as dramatic as the metals, but it's steady, and our job is to extract it as quickly as possible. We were all set to start digging when Mr. Treton died. Then the legal issues arose, and the contract he signed with me was declared null and void. But now that you're at the helm, hopefully we can resume activity. Here, let me show you."

Porter strode to his horse and pulled a rolled-up map from his saddlebag, and returned to Liam. He knelt on the rocky ground, motioned for Liam to do the same, and smoothed the paper, using rocks to anchor the four corners.

Porter pointed to the center of the drawing. "Here's where the primary pit will go, and it will spread out to the north. The countinghouse obviously needs to be constructed still, but it will be a modest building. We'll put it on that flat bit of land over there. The pits will be shallow, so as not to require a water pump, at least initially, and we'll cut the road through here to meet up with the main road."

Liam drew a deep breath of satisfaction. For the first time since his arrival, fresh optimism — real and invigorating, as vitalizing and crisp as the biting wind — surged within him. The odd events with Kinden and Bray shrank into the background. This was his purpose. This was how he would make his mark on this estate. This was how he would provide for those he loved and contribute to the Twethewey legacy.

Porter returned the map to his satchel and retrieved a small bundle. He unwrapped it, revealing a sizeable lump of white clay. "This is what we are after. This will become the finest piece of porcelain you have ever seen."

Liam took the clay and ran his finger over it.

"Of course we'll want to recheck samples, but with what I saw with your uncle, you are sitting on china clay ripe for the picking. Before now, it was impossible for potters and the like to replicate the fine porcelain coming out of the Far East, but this china clay, which is actually a decomposed form of granite, allows us to produce such porcelain, and now we can compete, and the buyers in Staffordshire are clamoring for it. At the end of the day, my business is mining this china clay from the earth and preparing it for market. The arrangement will be very much like one a miner would come to with a landowner in copper or tin mining. We'll sign the agreement for my company to work this site, and if it goes well, we might look beyond these initial boundaries.

"As the landowner you have the option to take either a silent or participatory role. You will, of course, be paid a percentage of the profits, and the land will remain completely under your ownership. My company takes on every bit of the risk. We are essentially renting land from you for this purpose, and with a seat on the board, you'll have input on how things are run. If we're successful, it provides you with a nice income. If things should not go exactly as planned, you are out nothing, just a few grooves in your land, and in the process several men will have employ for as long as we are here."

"I was hoping to hire local men," Liam said. "I know that was important to my great-uncle, and it is important to me as well."

Porter stared out to the grooved ground, his brows drawn. "We will do what we can. Unfortunately, many men left their positions at the mines based on our original plans all those years ago, and when your uncle died, the positions they had been promised were no longer there, and many went without work. Hopefully enough time has passed that the anger will be forgotten. Besides, money always speaks."

Liam nodded, the sight of the shoddy tenant farms fresh in his mind. "Assuming they are willing, how many locals will you hire?"

"I'll need some of my men from Staffordshire to open the pits and instruct the men in what needs to be done. Beyond that we'll require at least a few dozen local men, working different shifts throughout the day. It may seem like a large number, but the men will be compensated based on their production, not time. We can adjust as needs change, of course. It's different from metal mining, which I assume most of the men around here have experience with, but it is work — honest, true, and most importantly, steady."

Liam surveyed the moorland once more. In his mind's eye he could already see the countinghouse with smoke curling from a stone chimney and a newly cut road winding through the waving grasses. The future seemed as wide as the open moorland and as bright as the sky. "I see no reason to delay. Based on the estate ledgers I've seen, the sooner we can generate income, the better."

"I agree completely. I've written up the terms for officially opening these Aulder

Hill pits, based on the conversations I had with your uncle. I will leave the contract with you. All it needs is your signature and my men will start working and hiring local laborers. Do you prefer me to work with your man, or shall I contact you directly?"

"My man?" Liam tilted his head to the side, his brow furrowed.

"Rupert Bray. He's still employed at Wyndcliff, is he not? He was involved in the process initially, and I was to work with him to hire locals before Mr. Treton died."

Liam shook his head. He'd purposely left Bray out of the visit to the moors. Yes, the man had vast experience and knowledge of the area, but something about him made Liam uncomfortable. He would keep his cards close to his chest — at least for now.

"No, you can address everything to me for now." Liam accepted the contract from Porter. "I'll review it and be in touch with you soon."

CHAPTER 11

As Evelyn made her way back to the cottage, gusts fluttered the satin ribbons on her cape and tugged at her long, unfettered locks. She lifted her skirts to step over a fallen log along the tree line that ran perpendicular to the courtyard's outer stone wall.

Dusk was falling, and the weather had taken a turn. Everyone who lived on the moors was accustomed to the weather changing quickly, but the fluffy white clouds that had gathered earlier in the day now donned ominous shades of slate and gray, and the wind swept up from the sea, angry and foreboding.

Despite the tempestuous bent of the weather, Evelyn had avoided both Wyndcliff Cottage and the main house all day in favor of her garden's solace. The drystone walls provided protection from the weather — and from any visitors who might happen by.

Mr. Kinden had departed, and for that

she was grateful. She'd watched him do so with her own eyes, and yet uneasiness prevailed. Mr. Twethewey was still here, and she vividly recalled the anger brewing in his expression after the incident with Mr. Kinden. Even though she knew the response was directed toward Mr. Kinden and not her, she was not ready to encounter him. Not yet.

After she deposited her garden tools in the cottage, she found herself drawn to the kitchen in the main house, as she usually was, to pass time with Marnie.

"An' where have ye been all afternoon?" Marnie looked up from stirring her stew. Her white hair hung in long, frazzled locks about her face, which was blotchy from the fire's heat. "I've been on watch for ye all this day."

"I've been drying flowers from the back garden." Evelyn tied the apron strings around her waist and smoothed her hand down the front of it. "Took me hours to clear out the last of the lavender before the frost comes."

"I've been worried about ye." Marnie lifted her brow. "Ye didn't even come in to see me this mornin'. 'Tis unlike ye."

Evelyn fiddled with her apron's tie. "There's no need to worry after me, Marnie. You know that."

"That Mr. Kinden got what he deserved." Marnie sniffed. "An' good riddance, I say."

The creak of a door followed by voices sounded from the great hall. Evelyn recognized Mr. Twethewey's baritone but couldn't place the other voice. "Who's here?"

"Mr. Porter, a china clay man from Staffordshire." Marnie clicked her tongue. "Been here most the day. 'Course, you wouldn't remember, but he used to come 'round when Mr. Treton was alive. We've not seen 'im since, though. He knows all about china clay an' the sort. Apparently there's a great deal of it on the Wyndcliff moors. Mr. Twethewey's plannin' to follow in his uncle's footsteps an' take up the matter."

Evelyn stepped to the corridor leading to the great hall and angled her head to see around the corner. Mr. Twethewey's back was to her, and he stood a full head taller than his guest. She'd heard of china clay before, but to her knowledge there were no pits in the immediate area. Copper and tin were king as far as mining was concerned. "I suppose it will be just the first of many changes around here, if it happens."

"If?" Marnie's eyebrows rose. "Based on

what I've heard 'em say, they're to start as soon as Mr. Twethewey signs the agreement. They're makin' no effort to be quiet, talkin' about money an' figures out in the open in the great hall. Sounds to me like somethin' that should be discussed in private. Mr. Twethewey be a determined young man, make no mistake 'bout that. I've the feelin' he might have a good many ideas in that head of his."

Evelyn stepped a little farther out to get a better view of the great hall, then returned to her task in the kitchen. "Is Grandfather not with them?"

"I've not seen 'im all day."

Evelyn frowned. Normally Grandfather would be at the heart of such conversations.

Marnie lifted her head. "Speakin' of lavender, have ye any more of that lavender dried at the cottage? I need some for the salve. My leg's been botherin' me again, an' if I want it ready for tomorrow, best to get it simmerin' sooner than later."

Evelyn nodded. Marnie rarely complained of her leg, so any request for assistance could not be ignored. She donned her cape and stepped back out into the evening. She hurried to a small storeroom off of the kitchen, where her garden herbs were hung to dry. After selecting some she had previously dried, she wrapped them in a cloth and headed back toward Wyndcliff's kitchen.

As she strode down the stone path from the cottage to the main road, a visitor caught her eye. She slowed her steps, swiped a strand of hair away from her face, and stopped at the courtyard gate. It was the first time she'd seen him since their odd interaction — and since he'd failed to meet her for their planned walk.

"Jim, what are you doing here?"

He lifted his head and smiled. "I've come to speak with your grandfather. Have you seen him?"

"No, I haven't." She paused, noting the tightness in Jim's normally nonchalant expression. It seemed no one knew of Grandfather's whereabouts as of late. "Where's Charlie? He usually joins you on these calls to my grandfather."

When Jim only shrugged and did not return with any playful banter, Evelyn drew her brows together. "Is everything all right?"

Jim removed his hat and swept his fingers through his tousled, sand-colored hair. He shook his head, as if searching for words, and then took a step toward her. "Last night Mr. Twethewey's guest, that Kinden fellow, caused quite a disturbance at the inn. I've

123

come to make sure it doesn't happen again."

The memory of Kinden's hand on her waist sent a shiver through her. Even so, she straightened her shoulders and lifted her chin. "Well then, I'll put your mind at ease. Mr. Kinden left early this morning. I saw him ride out myself."

"Glad to hear it. We don't need that sort in Pevlyn. I don't care who he's in town to visit." Jim nodded at the carriage in the courtyard. "Twethewey's a regular host, isn't he?"

She followed his gaze to the vehicle. It was true. Normally months would pass without a single guest to Wyndcliff grounds, other than a tenant or a local businessman. In the manner of a few days, they'd had more outside guests than they'd had in well over a year. "That carriage belongs to a Mr. Porter from Staffordshire."

"You seem to know all of the comings and goings," he teased.

"Oh, you know how it is. Everything's been so sleepy here for so long. Nothing ever happens, and now it seems like everything about Wyndcliff Hall has changed overnight."

"And you are not happy about it?"

She shrugged and adjusted the bundle of lavender in her arms. "Oh, it's not that at all. Change is to be expected."

They stood in silence for a few moments, and then he said in a low voice, "I've a confession."

She met his gaze, tilting her head to the side in question.

"I didn't come just to talk to your grandfather. Actually, I've come to see you."

"Me?" The thought of anyone visiting her specifically was almost amusing. With the exception of Marnie and very rarely Jenna, she never had visitors.

"Yes. I owe you an apology. I wasn't able to get away last night to meet you on Market Day."

She shrugged and waved a hand dismissively. "Don't give it another thought. It sounds like you were quite occupied, and with Mr. Kinden's misbehavior I completely understand."

"But I don't want you to think that I forgot," he added hurriedly. "Or that it wasn't important to me."

"Jim, it was just a walk." She raised an eyebrow. "It was nothing."

"It wasn't nothing to me. You know, I got to thinking. Plymouth is far away." He took a step closer. "Your grandfather and I were discussing it just the other day. I don't like the thought of you being so far removed from Pevlyn."

She tried to hide the nervous quake within her. "Well, 'tis nothing worth thinking on now. Mother's not sent for me, and I don't know when she will."

"Do you never think you should make plans for yourself? Outside of what your mother wants?"

The ensuing silence pressed heavily. No one had ever asked her about her own plans. Not her mother. Not her grandfather. Never.

The strange turn of questions caught her off guard, and in that sliver of time, she noticed that Jim looked different. His hair had been parted and combed. He wore a coat instead of his customary waistcoat and shirt with his sleeves rolled to his elbows. She narrowed her eyes. "What are you getting at, Jim?"

"I, for one, would be sad if you were to leave Pevlyn."

She studied her fingers as she gripped the edge of the gate. Her stomach tightened and her head felt light.

She'd told herself repeatedly that Jim was not the right sort of suitor for her, but then again, he'd never spoken to her like this.

No man had.

Mother would no doubt find her an appropriate beau soon who would get her out of this village. But her mother did not seem keen on summoning her, and Evelyn grew older by the day.

And this man's eyes were fixed on her in a way no other man's had ever been.

"Next Sunday, then," he blurted in his usual booming voice, recapturing her attention. "We could walk down by the pond on the moor's edge, if the weather's fine, of course."

She opened her mouth to respond, but the main door to Wyndcliff Hall swung open, and Mr. Twethewey stepped outside. The wind caught his coat and whipped his hair. He held the door for Mr. Porter, who followed him.

He straightened and Evelyn took a step back, surprised at the unexpected interruption.

How different the men were. Mr. Twethewey, with hair so dark it appeared almost black and his clothes pristine and sharp. And Jim, with his sandy hair in need of a cut, his tan coat dusty from the moorland, and his neckcloth, even though she knew it was his best, faded.

And yet similarities also struck her. Both men were tall and broad shouldered. Both men exuded a confidence that commanded attention and even respect.

Mr. Twethewey saw his guest into the carriage, and after it rumbled away, he took notice of them, nodded a greeting, and walked in their direction.

Evelyn curtsied as he drew near. Jim stood firm.

Mr. Twethewey spoke first. "About last night at your inn. I must apologize to both of you for Mr. Kinden's behavior. It was reprehensible."

"We don't welcome that sort here in Pevlyn," Jim snapped.

"And I don't expect you to. You've my word that he'll not return, at least as a guest of Wyndcliff Hall. I do hope this incident will be behind us."

Jim grunted, folding his thick arms over his barrel chest. Evelyn offered a smile and a slight nod.

Mr. Twethewey extended his hand toward Jim, and after a moment of hesitation, Jim shook it. Mr. Twethewey drew a deep breath. "Perhaps, Mr. Bowen, I can beg your assistance on a matter."

Jim's glare hardened. "Depends."

"We intend to revive my great-uncle's plan of mining for china clay on Wyndcliff Moor, near Aulder Hill. Before the end of the month we'll be hiring men — local men —

to see to the mining of it. Perhaps you could spread the word."

Evelyn expected Jim's reaction to be one of appreciation or, at the very least, interest. Employment was scarce, and many a local man had been forced to mines in neighboring villages to provide for their families, and the effect was heartbreaking.

But Jim made no reaction. He stood there in the wind for several moments, as if considering the request, then leaned against the gate door. "Maybe you don't know, but when your uncle died and the plans for the clay pits fell through, it left many a man without a source of income. Dozens of men left good employ to help chase his dream, only to come out with nothing. They were angry about it, and memories last long around here. I bet your china clay man didn't tell you that, now did he?"

Mr. Twethewey's gaze did not waver. "I'm certain my great-uncle could hardly have anticipated his own demise, let alone prepare for it. Times have changed, and I'll venture that fair wage for fair work can hardly be frowned upon, by anyone."

A muscle in Jim's clean-shaven jaw twitched.

There'd been enough arguments, enough strife for one week. Evelyn leaned forward, hoping to defuse the tense conversation. "I am sure the men would be very glad to hear of this, Mr. Twethewey. Grandfather and Jim will spread the word as well, I'm certain. And surely Charlie will help as well to share the news with those miners out of work to the north of here."

Mr. Twethewey glanced back at her, almost as if he'd forgotten she was there, and then he stepped back. His eyes narrowed, and his expression was cautious. "I thank you for your help, Mr. Bowen, and for your warm welcome."

He bowed in parting, and Evelyn curtsied once more, but Jim remained rigid.

Once Mr. Twethewey was out of earshot, Jim huffed a sarcastic laugh.

Evelyn pursed her lips. "That was uncalled for."

"What are you talking about?"

"Do you mean to make an enemy of the man?"

Jim smirked and straightened his coat. "I've no need to make a friend of Mr. Twethewey."

"Still, I think it best to at least attempt to get along with him. He is, or will be, very influential."

Jim's amusement faded. "You think I care what a man like Twethewey can do to me?

I've made my own success in life, and it's not on account of playing nice to men of self-important privilege." His smile resumed. "Sunday then. Tell your grandfather I stopped by."

She watched him as he disappeared down the road to where his horse was tied and rode away. An uncomfortable sense of disquiet wound through her. Jim was a good man but a strong one, influential in his own right.

She hated confrontation of any kind, and the strife brewing between her grandfather, Jim, and Mr. Twethewey was unsettling.

CHAPTER 12

Outside the study window, a gentle rain tapped on the panes. Night had fallen, snuffing out all but a bit of gray light and obscuring the landscape — and his view of Wyndcliff Cottage. Liam pulled the candle closer to review, yet again, the contract Porter had left.

But he couldn't concentrate.

What was Miss Bray doing talking alone with that innkeeper? Liam did not consider himself the jealous sort, but the sight of Bowen talking so closely to Miss Bray at the gate incited the strangest jolt through him. He could no longer consider Kinden a reliable source, but he had warned him of Bowen while they were at the inn.

And yet Miss Bray seemed friendly enough with him. Rupert Bray did too.

A knock sounded at the study door, interrupting his thoughts. Bray stood in the threshold holding a lantern in one hand and a bag in the other. "I heard Porter was here about the china clay pits over by Aulder Hill." His voice was low. Hard.

"He was." Liam leaned back from the desk and slid the contract into the top drawer of his desk. "He departed an hour ago."

"I missed him then. A true shame."

Liam stiffened and nodded to the canvas bag in Bray's hand. "What's that?"

"Apples from the Smith orchard. They asked me to deliver them on their behalf." He dropped the bag on the desktop. "They intend it as a welcome."

Bray's anger at not being included in the walk on the moor radiated from his movements. Liam knew Bray was used to being involved in every aspect of the property, and no doubt his exclusion was seen as a slight, but if Liam was going to take charge of this estate, he needed to stand on his own early on.

"Were you satisfied with what Porter had to say?" Bray directed the conversation back to the clay pits.

"Quite." Liam straightened a stack of papers on the desk and returned his quill to the holder.

Even though he could see the objections and questions lingering in the older man's eyes, opening the china clay pits was Liam's plan. He would not be deterred.

Bray placed the lantern on the desk with a thud. "And you intend to sign the contract? I assume that is the document you just hid in your desk."

Annoyance growing at the man's impertinence, Liam cleared his throat. "I do."

Bray sat across from Liam without invitation. "And the workers? Have you given a thought to that?"

"Once the papers are signed, Porter will release a notice to the local men."

"Have you considered you'll pull miners from the tin mines? That won't sit well with the owners."

Bray's words were nearly identical to Bowen's, as if the topic had been discussed. His defenses began to rise. "All men are free to work where they will. There are plenty of folks around here without work who will be grateful for it, and to be frank, the mine owners are not my concern. Providing income for the estate and the tenants is." Liam lifted the thick ledger from its position on the corner of the desk. "As far as I can tell, with little other income than my tenant rent, or lack thereof, the estate is in dire straits."

Bray stared at him for several moments, his steely gray eyes fixed on him, steady and unblinking. He leaned forward with his thick hand on the desk. "You do have income, beyond the tenants, beyond the rent that is recorded in that ledger."

Liam lifted a brow at Bray's cryptic words.

Bray stood and went to a mahogany cabinet Liam had not paid any attention to until now. He reached for a key on top of the cabinet and stooped to unlock the lower door. "It isn't popular to talk of, especially in the current landscape with excise men and the law breathing down our necks, and the lawmen themselves looking for a hand-out."

At the mention of the law, understanding crept in. "You're talking about the ship-wrecks."

Bray nodded in the direction of the sea. "The entire edge of your property lies against the coast — and wrecks happen all the time, just like we were speaking of earlier. In the cellar below the kitchen and stables is where the collected cargo is being stored. It's all been logged and tracked. With all the shipwrecks and materials that wash up on your shore, the estate has profited and will continue to profit."

Liam narrowed his gaze. Was this man serious? He didn't like the thought of making money off another's misfortune, and the sickening suspicion that more was going on than he realized tugged at his gut.

Bray reached in and grabbed a leather-bound book, then closed the cabinet door. "Everything that lands on that property, from every shipwreck, belongs to you. There were two shipwrecks last month alone. Almost every day something washes ashore. Of course, the beachcombers usually find the smaller things, and there's naught much you can do on that account. But the true shipwrecks, that's where we come in. It isn't pretty to think on, and not too gentlemanly, but it is a fact and a part of living here, as sure as pulling tin or copper — or *china clay* — from the ground.

"If a ship washes ashore and there is no living crew member, the items tossed over-board or retrieved from the water or the shore belong to you. The law says you must hold them for a year and a day, lest someone comes with a credible claim to them. In that case you return them to the proven owner. If not, you pay your duties and you are free to do with the items what you will."

Liam shook his head. " 'Tis not the business I wish to be in."

"Like it or not, you *are* in it, by the sheer fact that you own that stretch of beach." Bray dropped the ledger on the desk in front

136

of him. "You've a legal responsibility to do so; otherwise, the excise men will be down your throat so fast you won't know what happened. Before you turn your nose up at it, you must realize the villagers depend on it too. They salvage what they can and return it, and they get a finder's fee either from the Wyndcliff estate or from the owner, if they've a mind to claim it."

Liam fixed his gaze on Bray. "I've heard they sell it as contraband."

"Some do. You can't control the people, and you always have folks looking to get something for nothing. But most would rather come by it honest and salvage than deal with the possibility of getting caught up in the grip of free trading. As steward I've assumed the role of wrecking agent and have seen to these tasks. It has provided a small profit, which I am sure the solicitor outlined in the paperwork provided."

Liam shifted uncomfortably. Every hour that passed, every conversation he had, uncovered yet another part of this life he was not expecting.

Liam opened the book. Page after page was filled with an accounting of items — spirits, cloth, silver — and quantities and amounts. "What's all this?"

"That's the record of what we've either

stored in the cellars, paid out in finder's fees, or paid duties on. It's all there — records for the last decade or so." He turned a few pages and pointed to a number. "There. That's your income for this year. After these autumn storms, I expect that number to be larger next year. And that's what'll help you get this place up and running."

Liam's mouth felt dry. "I suppose there is nothing that can be done about the weather."

"No, and like I said, there's a rocky ridge out from the coast, and it'll rip the bottom clean out from under a boat afore the crew knows what's happened. They occur most often in the winter when the storms are worse, but they happen anytime. Moody Cornish weather." Bray stepped to the window and looked out to the courtyard. "Laws are laws. I can handle the excise men. But my advice, from an old landowner to a new one, is not to turn up your nose at what's sitting right underneath you. Best make it work for the good of everyone involved instead of having it squandered by the free traders. Think on that."

Liam hated this feeling of being told what to do by someone who knew his land better than he did.

But what could be done?

He closed the ledger. Its thud echoed in the room. "I'll review this, and we can talk further at another time."

"I'll show you the cellar whenever you've a mind for it. I keep the key on my person at all times." Bray patted his chest. "We wouldn't want anything happening to it."

Once Bray departed, Liam blew out a breath and sank back down into his chair. A fresh gust of wind rattled the windows. He could not help but wonder what effect these gusts were having on the sea. He stood and walked to the window, staring into the black soggy night. Perhaps Bray was right and Liam should pay more attention to what happened on his coast. Tomorrow morning he would ride down to the beach and study the coast more closely for himself.

CHAPTER 13

Clang-clang. Clang-clang.

The echoing toll invaded Liam's dream.

Each peal of the distant bell pulled him further from sleep.

Clang-clang. Clang-clang.

Liam jerked upright, his eyes wide and alert. He blinked.

It was a bell. There was no doubt. But where was it coming from?

Then the clanging stopped.

He held his breath. Had he dreamt it?

He snatched his pocket watch from his bedside table, but before he even opened it, the tolling sounded again.

Clang-clang. Clang-clang.

Footsteps pounded in the stable yard below his window.

Liam jumped from the bed. His bare feet smacked the wooden floor. Fully alert, he hurried to the window and looked to the ground, where shadowy figures raced in the direction of the sea.

He grabbed his breeches and boots from where he'd left them, yanked the breeches on over his nightshirt, and hurried from his chamber down the corridor, pulling on his boots with each step.

As he approached the kitchen, the shouts and voices intensified. Shuffling and movement echoed from the plaster walls. The bell tolls seemed faster.

He burst into the kitchen. Nearly a dozen lanterns flickered and glowed on the table. The light shone on people he did not recognize, all busy about a task. No one noticed him. He quickly located Mrs. Taymer, who was distributing the lanterns out the door, one by one, to the kitchen yard, and then Miss Bray, who was at a smaller cellar door, struggling and pulling at something inside.

He rushed toward her. "What is it? What's going on?"

"Shipwreck." Without pausing in her task, Miss Bray shoved a canvas bundle toward him. "We must hurry."

She reached for another bundle and then piled it in his arms. "Hear the bells? Four tolls in quick succession mean there are survivors. We need to get these supplies to the west end of the cove, where the rescuers gather to organize."

Liam grabbed the bundle to prevent it from falling and struggled to make sense of Miss Bray's words. The very word *survivors* suggested that some did not survive. He was not prepared to face the thought that there would be loss of life on his land.

His breath caught in his throat. "What can I do?"

"Carry this. It needs to go to the beach." She struggled to lift a length of rope from the closet. "The men will bring others from the shed. Follow me."

She hurried from the kitchen, a bundle in her arms, out the very door ushering in the gusts. He followed her outside. The wind swooped around the stone corner, folding them into the murky night's chaos. Figures, black and ant-like, cascaded down the road that separated the courtyard from the cottage grounds. Bells rang and voices, grotesquely distorted by the whistling wind, shouted from every direction.

Miss Bray, oblivious to the disorder, ran fearless and determined into the dark. Clearly her footsteps knew where to land.

His did not.

The threat of a storm hung thick, and yet dawn peeked from the east, seeping through the breaks in the gossamer clouds and shedding just enough pewter light to help him catch his bearings. He had to stay close, lest he lose her in the fog and mist. She sprinted in the direction of the beach, her skirt billowing behind her, and disappeared through a copse of trees.

He adjusted the rope over his shoulder and continued to run after her, following the white flutter of her gown. She wove her way through the trees, fleeting, like a bird in flight. At length she paused as the tree line gave way to the grassland that bordered the sea cliffs and waited for him.

"What now?" he shouted above the wind and tolling bells as he took the large bundle of canvas from her arms.

She looped her skirt over her arm so she could move more quickly amidst the brush. "This way."

They didn't speak further, but with every step the hair on his arms prickled. Men calling to one another sharpened into focus. The damp wind cried over the sea grass, and as they approached the moor's edge, he saw it, spreading out far and wide. All along the curve of the cove's coast dark figures darted and dashed. Fires blazed in intermittent places on the shore, sputtering in the drizzling rain. Smaller lanterns dotted the beach, and dozens — nay, hundreds — of people were crammed in the space, crawling, waiting.

He lifted his eyes to the shivering sea and saw it — the source of all the commotion — the very thing that roused these people from their nighttime slumber. Barely visible in the predawn light, a vessel tossed in the sea, its white sails ragged and torn and fluttering in the gales. She was on her side, the masts pointed to the east instead of to the sky.

Lightning rippled through the heavens, sharply highlighting the sea's white waves crashing against her, determined to pull her beneath with its violent arms. In the lightning's brilliant flashes he saw a chain of men already stretching out in the sea. Two smaller boats were attempting to reach it, but with each wave they were pushed toward the shore.

Miss Bray started to climb down, and he touched her arm to get her attention. "Where are we going?" he shouted.

"Over there. To that stone. Brayden's Crag."

He reached out to assist her down the cliff to the beach.

She gripped his hand and lifted her skirt to start her descent to the sand. "Rocks are lowest there. The men'll try to row out, but most often it's too dangerous. See? They're making a chain out from that point. The water's not deep there, but they still must be careful because the seabed is naught but sharp rock. Come on."

He lumbered behind her as she picked a strong foothold in the jagged cliffs that surrounded the beach. Once they hit the beach, people raced past them.

She led him to Bray, who was shouting, pointing, and yelling orders.

Liam dropped the supplies on a pile of other supplies and stepped in front of him. "Tell me what to do."

"Grab a line along the rope there," Bray barked. "See them there? Whatever you do, don't let go of it, lest the undertow pull you right out."

Liam licked his lips. They were salty. It was impossible to tell if it was from the sea spray splashing against his face or the perspiration dripping from his temples. He moved into the water, icy and strong, and grabbed hold of the rope between two men he did not know.

The sand shifted and sank beneath his weight, and his boot caught on a rock. He anchored his foot against it and held the rope firm, ignoring how its rough fibers gnawed and ripped at his bare wet hands.

Shadows covered all the faces around him. Perhaps he'd seen them in the village on Market Day, perhaps he had not. There was no distinction here — no way to decipher miners from farmers. Everyone was equal and, for the moment, dedicated to the task of finding and saving who they could. The waves pushed and tugged, pulling him from his feet.

Methodically, carefully, they stepped farther out. Not a single man was in more than waist-deep water, but more than once the sharp withdraw of water from the beach to the sea took Liam's feet out from under him. Behind him, the other end of the rope was tightly secured in an attempt to keep as little slack to it as possible. In front of him men manned the rope all the way to a small boat attempting to reach the distressed vessel.

The saltwater burned his eyes, and yet through his blurred vision, he could see someone waving a lantern, its yellow light eerie and frantic in the intermittent mist as the rescuers mounted the distressed vessel. Eventually tension pulled the rope.

"They've reached it!" the muted voices in front of him shouted, running the message back down the line.

Liam, in turn, shouted his message to

146

those onshore. He blew the spraying seawater out of his mouth and braced himself once more.

Another message was coming down the line, over the crashing waves and whistling wind.

"A child!"

And then he could see it — a white parcel, barely visible in the dark, held above the water, passing down the line from one stronghold along the rope to another.

"You!" the man next to him shouted above the crashing waves. "Pass 'er to shore. Another one's coming."

Terror pinched Liam as the bundle approached him. The tiny body was not limp but tensed and alert. A wet, tangled mess of hair obscured her face. He lifted the small body over his shoulder to keep it above the gripping waves. As he took hold, the tiny, trembling fingernails clutched his arm. He shouted the same message he'd just received to the man behind him and passed the child.

Shouts roared again, and then he heard a crack, like the splintering of wood. A loud crash sent a tremor through him.

He whirled back in the direction of the boat. One of the masts, with its white ghostlike sail, sank into the sea.

And the light aboard the vessel disappeared.

CHAPTER 14

Evelyn braced her feet in the sand, standing still and straight on the shoreline, refusing to sway with the gusts as the wind tore at her gown and her unbound hair. Determined to ignore the shiver of cold that began in her chest and flowed to her limbs, she watched in breathless anticipation and fear as the mayhem unfolded before her.

How familiar it was. How terribly, eerily, chillingly familiar. The sight was much *too* familiar, especially as of late, and each instance hit close to her heart.

Perhaps the men would rescue someone. Perhaps not.

She could not help but wonder if the situation had been the same all those years ago when her father had lost his life assisting in a rescue. She'd been too young to understand then, and no one ever spoke of it, especially her grandfather, but with every shipwreck she saw, it seemed a little bit more of him was taken from her.

A man ran past, nearly knocking her down. She stumbled backward into Bertie and some of the other women gathered.

The excise men could not be aware of the shipwreck yet. Otherwise uniformed men would make their presence known and there would be more order, or at least more discretion, among the villagers racing to grab whatever they could.

Aye, several men were attempting to rescue survivors presumably still aboard, but as she looked farther down shore, dawn's faint glow cast light on men and women who were equally intent upon reaching the crates and debris being pushed onto the shore and into the arms of those waiting to receive them.

She turned her attention back to the men forming the lifeline. It was not raining now, and a figure clad in white appeared in the distance.

Her pulse jumped, and she stepped toward the water so the waves lapped at her skirts. She shielded her eyes against bits of sand caught in the gale and watched as the bundle was passed slowly down the rope until the very last man carried the small body over one shoulder to the shoreline. He dropped to his knees and lowered the body to the ground.

Evelyn rushed forward and stooped next to the tiny body, fearing what she might see. It was a child. A girl. And her breath came in great, airy gulps. Black eyes stared up at her, wide and wild, from a ghostly white face. Long streaks of black hair clung to her forehead, her cheeks, her neck. Her blue lips shivered, but raspy breaths, gasping coughs, and darting glances confirmed she was alive. The child struggled to sit up, but Evelyn put a gentle hand on her shoulder.

Dr. Smith, the mining surgeon, pushed past Evelyn and knelt by the girl. "Are you hurt, child? What is your name?"

The child did not respond but shivered violently. The bottom of her white gown was torn, and it clung to her tiny body. She wore no boots, no stockings.

One of the women lifted a light behind the surgeon so he could assess the child's condition. After several moments he sat back. "I think she's all right, just stunned most likely, but we must get her dry and warm. Take her back to Wyndcliff. I'll stay here. I think there are more coming. Can you carry her, Miss Bray, or shall I call one of the men?"

Evelyn looked back to the men, lit only by lantern light and torchlight and a faint sliver of moonlight through the rolling clouds. They were engaged along the rope for another rescue and were needed here. She nodded. "We'll manage."

She took the child's shivering shoulders in her hands and looked at her. "You must hold on to me tightly, just for a while, then you will be able to rest, I promise."

The child did not respond. Her teeth chattered, but she did as bid. She wrapped her arms about Evelyn's neck and her legs around her waist as much as her trembling limbs would allow. Evelyn's own wet skirts hindered her walking, and already at the edge of the beach her muscles burned with the effort.

Slowly but surely they made their way back up the crag where the beach gave way to a copse of trees and then to moorland. Fortunately the child clutched her as if her very life depended on it, as it very well may have, easing some of the burden of the weight.

Evelyn climbed the rocks, her skirts catching on the crags and the brush. Before her, the lights of Wyndcliff blazed, and she fixed her sights on it, placing one foot in front of the other.

The kitchen light shone like a beacon, calling to her, urging her to hurry. After what seemed an eternity, they burst through the door, breathless and windblown, and Marnie whirled to face them. "Merciful heavens! What be this?" She reached out and accepted the girl.

Evelyn's arms and legs burned from the physical exertion. Her own limbs trembled with the cold, and she knelt on the flagstone floor before the fire. "We must get her warm."

Marnie knelt next to her, dry linens in her hands. "Are there more coming?"

"I think there will be. We must get her dry."

The child's black eyes were wide, and she allowed the women to wipe water from her face.

"Ye must too. Yer soaked to the skin. Ye'll catch yer death, and then where will we be?" Marnie looked over at Evelyn. "Go now. Change that gown. I'll need yer help if more are comin'. I can take care of this wee one."

"Very well. I'll get her some dry clothes from the cottage." Evelyn looked the child in the eye. "I will be back shortly, all right? This is Marnie. She will take care of you."

The child flicked her gaze up at Marnie, then back to Evelyn, but said nothing.

"I'll be right back."

Once in the cottage she tore to her chamber, pausing only to light a candle from the fire glowing in the parlor grate. She'd seen Bertie at the beach with everyone else, so with trembling fingers Evelyn shed her wet gown and underthings by herself and traded them for dry articles from her wardrobe. Her skin now ached from shivering and the rub of wet fabric against it. She dressed quickly in a warm, winter flannel gown, but the soft, dry fabric did little to alleviate her chill. She snatched a warm flannel night-dress for the child and two thick shawls from the chest at the foot of her bed.

When she returned to the kitchen at the manor moments later, Evelyn found the girl wrapped in a blanket and sitting next to the fire. It was the first good look Evelyn got of her. Her discarded gown was hanging in front of the fire. Her tiny, white-knuckled fist clutched the blanket to her. Evelyn didn't know much about children, but surely the girl was no more than four or five. Her skin was ghostly pale, and her large eyes took in every bit of her surroundings.

Evelyn and Marnie helped the child into the warm flannel nightdress, which was ridiculously large on her, and wrapped her in the two wool shawls. Evelyn smoothed her black hair down her back and untangled it as best she could with her fingers. Even now she smelled of salt water and cold.

Kitty, the kitchen girl, ran past her, and Evelyn instructed her to light the fires in all of the guest chambers. They might be needed.

Outside, shouts rang and footsteps pounded. Indoors, the fires were stoked, preparing for others who would need warmth very soon.

And in her arms, a child shivered and curled against her.

CHAPTER 15

Liam sputtered on the salt water splashing in his mouth and nose as the waves crashed against him, threatening his balance and fighting his efforts. His arms, chest, and leg muscles burned from the exertion necessary to hold his footing in the shifting sand.

The rain had started again, and the morning sky, streaked with pale gray, cast somber shadows on the chaos below.

He was not sure how long he'd been standing here, holding the rope. Half an hour? Longer? The men who'd reached the vessel were no longer attempting to right the ship. She was too far gone. Now the focus was retrieving any survivors.

He prayed there would be more.

He tightened his numb fingers, regripped the rope, and strained to see. The ship was tilting farther now. Her white sails draped over the surging sea like an unearthly specter, swaying and dancing at the whim of the waves. Stretching out before him, he could make out the rescue line. Many men, unable to compete with the strong currents, had abandoned their posts out of fear for their own safety, but a skeleton crew stood firm.

Another group of men, much larger and rowdier, were coming at the ship from a different angle. They also had smaller vessels, but instead of participating in any rescue efforts, they were breaking it apart, scavenging wood and metal.

This was what Bray had been referring to. Men clawing and scratching their way to whatever part of the ship held any value. The entire situation was sickening.

Cries from the ship recaptured his attention.

His heart leapt as welcome news rushed down the rescue line. "A woman!"

Then the second bundle started — a larger white figure was lowered from the ship. Men shouted and struggled in waist-deep water to keep the woman above water. But as she came closer, it was clear something was wrong. Whereas the child had been alert and tense, this woman was limp.

Liam was now the closest man to shore. He took the woman's body from the man in front of him, hoisted her over his shoulder, and still gripping the rope with one hand, waded through the rushing water and insistent undertow to reach shore. Once free of the water, he dropped to his knees.

People rushed to them and surrounded the woman immediately. She was taken from him and placed on the beach. Chest heaving, he leaned forward with his fists on the sand, attempting to catch his breath as the waves pounded relentlessly against him. He glanced at her and noticed the blood on her white face. Her eyes were closed. Her head rolled to the side.

A man pushed him to the side and leaned over her. He checked her pulse and then pressed his ear to her chest. "She's alive, but barely," he called. "Get her to Wyndcliff."

Another man shouted from the rescue line, "She's the last one!"

Liam's relief was quickly quelled. His stomach clenched.

One woman.

One child.

Only.

Several people gathered around, drawn by the spectacle, but many of the men rushed off toward the other group on the beach.

Was no one going to help the woman?

If they were going to his home, he'd lead

the way. With a fresh burst of determination, he pushed his way back to his feet and lifted her in his arms again. She was cold. Unresponsive.

And he thought he might be sick.

He said nothing but trudged his way back to the beach's edge, the same way Miss Bray had brought him down.

His muscles screamed in protest and his chest ached under the weight of this unconscious woman. He cast a glance back at the beach. The man in black, who must be a surgeon, followed. Liam did not stop walking, but from here he could see a much broader scope. The gray light of daybreak intensified with each passing minute, illuminating the men crawling around like insects. Piles of rubble were everywhere. White waves crashed onto the shore. Thunder rumbled low, and rain was misting. Giant fires burned. This was organized chaos.

He turned his attention back to the woman and made his way across the moorland — his moorland. It was a short walk before he saw the blazing light of Wyndcliff Hall.

Evelyn sat in silence in the wooden settee next to the kitchen fire. Next to her, the tiny child slumbered, still and finally warm,

159

her head on Evelyn's lap.

At least the girl was dry. Peaceful. Safe. Her breath came in steady, even measures.

She'd fallen asleep quickly once she was out of her wet clothing, yet Evelyn could not relax. She did not even know this child's name yet. She wanted to run back to the beach, to offer assistance where she could. Undoubtedly there were others who needed help.

But this was where she was needed. This poor child was alone.

At Wyndcliff's every creak and moan she expected the stable yard door to fly open with news. Or another survivor. But the minutes stretched on. None came. Kitty had prepared the fires in the upstairs chambers in anticipation of more survivors, and across the broad kitchen, Marnie heated food over the fire for the hungry guests who inevitably would pass Wyndcliff's door this day. Otherwise, for the moment, all was quiet in Wyndcliff Hall.

Suddenly the door flung open and damp air swirled in.

Mr. Twethewey, soaked and heaving for air, filled the doorway with a woman — clad in white, soaked, and limp — in his arms. Blood covered her gown. Her head hung back, and her arm flailed involuntarily with each movement. Dr. Smith followed closely behind him.

Spurred to action, Evelyn moved the sleeping child, who did not wake at the door's opening, from her lap and stood.

"Where can I put her?" Mr. Twethewey breathed, his eyes wide.

"Stay with the child, Kitty," Evelyn instructed. She hurried to Mr. Twethewey, paused to place the woman's limp, icy arm over his shoulder to make it easier for him to carry her up the stairs, then led him to the first chamber off the landing.

Heat from the fire in the hearth rushed at them as they entered. He placed her on the bed.

Evelyn gasped as she got her first real sight of the woman. A deep gash cut her forehead, and blood streaked down her corpselike white cheek. Her eyes were closed, and her hair, sandy and dark with the sea's moisture, clung to her face and neck in knotted clumps. Her pale lips were parted, and her head rolled to the side.

She appeared lifeless.

The surgeon pushed past them both and began assessing her.

Evelyn looked around, nervous. Needing to do something, she opened the drapes to allow any bit of morning light to assist the surgeon in his task, then she moved next to Mr. Twethewey.

She cast a sideways glance at the master of Wyndcliff estate as they stood there in silence, watching. His face, which had been alarmingly pale upon arrival, was now red and ruddy. His wet hair clung to his temples and draped over his forehead. He looked cold and the scent of the sea clung to him, and even now seawater dripped to the planked floor. Sand and dirt encrusted his sodden boots.

"Are there others?" she asked. "We need to prepare the —"

"No," he blurted. "No more survivors."

Horror shot through her. She jerked her head forward. She'd seen enough wrecks to know that there should have been a fairly sizable crew on a ship like the one in the cove.

Evelyn looked back at him. His jaw clenched tightly, and blood marred his shirt.

"And you? Are you all right? That isn't your blood, is it?"

"No. I'm fine."

But he wasn't fine. His arms were crossed over his chest, but his hand, as it gripped his opposite arm, was shivering. His breath was coming in noisy gasps. The toe of his dripping boot tapped erratically.

162

At length the surgeon straightened.

Mr. Twethewey dropped his hands to his sides. "Well?"

Dr. Smith removed his spectacles and drew a deep breath before he looked back to his patient once more. "She's alive. She's breathing, at least. But her pulse is weak. That is a nasty gash to the head, and I suspect she's lost a great deal of blood. Whatever hit her did so very hard, and without knowing how long she has been in this condition . . ."

"Do you think she'll survive?" Evelyn asked, hopeful.

"I've seen men at the mine come back from worse than this, but she's a slight thing. We'll have to wait and see."

Marnie appeared with a basin of water and a basket of linens, and the surgeon set about tending and bandaging the wound.

Mr. Twethewey turned toward Evelyn. "I'm going back to the beach."

She looked to the wet fabric clinging to him. "You'd be wise to change clothes first. It's cold. Even colder with the sea winds. You'll do no one any good if you fall ill."

He jerked, as if he planned to dismiss her words entirely, then he paused and nodded.

Evelyn next saw Mr. Twethewey in the kitchen a quarter of an hour later. He'd changed into dry clothing — buckskin breeches and a thick wool coat — but his hair was still wet, his cheeks still ruddy. "I passed by the room with the woman. Mrs. Taymer asked for you to join her. They're done bandaging her head, but she needs your help getting her into dry clothing."

Evelyn nodded and handed him a cup of tea. "Drink this before you go back out. It will be a long day."

He drank it and gazed at the child still asleep on the settee. "She looks so peaceful. The irony is almost painful, isn't it?"

Evelyn followed his gaze to the sleeping child. Her lashes were fanned on her cheeks, and her breath came in steady puffs. "She's exhausted. There's no telling how long she's been awake if their ship was in a storm."

"Is there somewhere she would be more comfortable?" he asked, glancing around.

"We've another room prepared upstairs."

"I'll carry her up before I go. Show me where." He leaned forward and picked up the sleeping child. She rolled against him and did not wake.

Evelyn lifted a candle and led the way up the back corridor and the uncomfortably narrow winding steps to the second level. She showed him to a small room with a canopied bed positioned by the window.

The fire cast a soft glow on the modest contents.

Evelyn pulled back the coverlet, and he placed the child on the bed. Evelyn reached in front of him to tuck her in.

"I now see," he muttered as she stepped back from the bed.

"See what?"

"A shipwreck," he whispered, as if it took too much effort to say the word aloud. "Are they always like this?"

The air seemed too thin with the question. She could barely remember a time when shipwrecks were not a part of the fabric of their life. She repeated what she'd been told so many times. "It's a dangerous coast, and there is a wind that blows the ships north. Winter is always the worst, and with the weather being what it is . . ."

He sniffed, interrupting her, as if her very words were poison and he needed to be away from them quickly. "I'd best get back to the beach." He departed, and with him went the scent of cold and sea.

Evelyn hurried to the Blue Room to help Marnie put dry clothing on the injured woman. When they finished, the two women returned to the kitchen, and Marnie poured them each a cup of tea. Even now that all was quiet and calm, Evelyn found sitting still difficult. She hated to be useless. She grabbed her cloak and stepped out into the courtyard. A wild wind howled down from the stable's slate roof, whipping her hair and distorting the morning's sounds. A strange energy charged the gray air, and the fires that had been lit in the courtyard sputtered in the drizzling rain. Men carrying crates and oddly shaped lengths of timber headed toward the storage cellars when a voice rose above the wind.

"Who rang the warning bell?"

Evelyn winced at the sharp tone of the rough, masculine voice, and she stood very still to hear over the wind.

"Don't know," responded a lower, raspier voice. "But whoever did is a dead man."

She drew a sharp breath. Why would they not ring the warning bell?

"All I know is I wouldn't be disobeying orders like that," responded the first voice. "I like livin' too much."

Footsteps pounded, and not wishing to be caught eavesdropping, Evelyn hurried back inside. Heart racing, she stood in the kitchen's unnerving silence for several moments, but when she stepped back out to the courtyard, all was still once again and not a soul could be seen.

Orders? Who would be giving orders?

Anger at ringing the warning bell?

None of it made sense.

The shipwreck might be over, but Evelyn sensed that the true storm was just now brewing.

CHAPTER 16

Liam fell into step next to Bray as they walked along the cliff overlooking the cove. The entire afternoon had been spent ensuring that the cargo washed ashore was safely stored in Wyndcliff's cellars.

"Have any other crew members been located?" Liam asked as they watched two men lift a crate.

"No, just the four dead that washed ashore. All men."

Liam swallowed the taste of bile at the thought. "Surely the crew was larger than four men."

"I agree."

Liam let out his breath in a whoosh, as if by doing so he could expel the doubt and concern welling within him. "Perhaps we will find someone alive still."

The sun never fully emerged from behind the clouds, and rain continued to drizzle from the heavens, covering all in a damp shroud. The gruesome day seemed to grow darker, and each hour ushered in yet another grim task to attend to.

A group of villagers on the beach lifted a large wooden crate and balanced it on their shoulders, each man taking a corner and then attempting to carry it up the cliff. Others tried to pull crates up with rope pullies, and some carried broken timber from the ship. Children were crawling among the rocks that appeared after the tide receded. Another group wrestled with a large piece of sail.

Never had Liam had to deal with death so bluntly. He'd been at his father's side when he died several years prior, but never had he encountered death on this scale. He had to look away as the vicar, clad in his black robe, stood over the bodies of the four men spread out on the beach, a visual confirmation of the day's lurid events.

"I wouldn't be surprised if more washed ashore in the coming days," Bray said, seemingly immune to the somber events around him. "I'm sure some tried to swim for it, but even the best swimmers are little match for the undertow. We'll keep a watch out."

"Is there any way to find out the name of the ship?"

"As far as I know, no one has discovered

any documentation, but with half the ship already under water when we arrived, it isn't that unusual. Usually members of the crew survive and are able to tell us everything we need to know, but in this instance . . ."

Bray's voice trailed away, but the meaning behind his words echoed in the wind's mournful cry.

"What's to be done then?" Liam attempted to focus on the practical.

"Excise men will be here at any time. I'm surprised they aren't already here. They will likely contact their counterparts in Plymouth and other nearby harbor towns to see if any ships are unaccounted for, but most likely we'll have to wait for whoever owned that ship — or anyone who had interest in her — to begin searching for her. Ideally the woman will wake and be able to tell us what we need to know, but according to the surgeon that seems improbable. The child may be able to tell us something, but I doubt she would know many specifics, being as young as she is. But even knowing its destination would be helpful.

"Come on." Bray motioned for Liam to follow him. "Let's go get something to eat. These men have it under control, and it will be a long night, for 'tis under the cover of darkness that the free traders will try to take what they can. We'll want our wits about us then."

They walked back toward Wyndcliff Hall in silence, back up the cliffs, across the moor, and through the copse of woods he had first followed Miss Bray through during the early-morning hours. His clothes were damp and wet again. Hours spent organizing and lugging the items washed ashore had taken a toll. "How long do you think the recovery will take?"

"Usually a couple of days. The excise men will want to know what is happening with the salvage. Every item that is recovered, from the largest crate to the smallest piece of timber, will be recorded."

"And these people who are doing this work?"

"Villagers. Miners. Everyone around here knows that salvagers will be paid, and everyone around here needs money. Badly. We'll want to see to that as soon as possible."

"We?" Liam raised an eyebrow.

"Yes. Well, *you.* The cargo washed up on your shores. You own the land, and you have wrecker's rights. Like I said, if the cargo isn't claimed in one year and a day, you pay duties on it and it is yours to do with as you will."

Liam shook his head. "But paying the salvagers?"

"Since you will likely profit from the wreck, it's expected that you'll pay a finder's fee. 'Tis law, actually. They are the ones doing the work and recovering it. As your acting wrecking agent, I've been overseeing the payments. If someone claims the cargo within the appropriate time frame, they will reimburse you for the finder's fees you paid the salvagers. Of course, there are always those who will keep what they find on the beach for themselves, and in the chaos of a wreck, that is hard to control, but I think we've done a pretty good job of reprimanding and punishing those who go against the set rules."

Liam's mind reeled with what he'd heard. The entire shipwreck process, chaotic and wild as it seemed, was, according to Bray, a rather coordinated effort.

"The men on the line who rescued the lady and the child will expect to be paid as well, but being as they are still alive, whoever their people are will likely pay the fee. But for those who are dead, it falls to the estate — again, you — to pay for their recovery and burial.

"There's much to consider, and that's why I'm here. Been around forever, I've seen more than my fair share of these wrecks, and I'll not lead you astray. But yet another word of caution. Prepare yourself for the excise men. They'll have very specific demands. Just don't commit to anything or claim anything other than the facts you saw with your own eyes. They're a deceptive lot, and they have more to gain than anyone by tending a shipwreck. I'm surprised the bloodthirsty mongrels weren't here at the first sound of the bell. Must have been a wreck elsewhere to take their attention."

Liam stiffened at the anger in the man's voice, but really, after what they'd just experienced, anger seemed a viable response. Now that he had witnessed the aftermath of a shipwreck firsthand, he was beginning to fully grip the seriousness of these events.

Liam, tired, worn, and damp from the day's events, swept his hat from his head and stepped into the room where the child was sleeping.

He'd seen a great many things this day — things he never expected to see and things he would prefer to forget — but the sight of this child, frightened and wide-eyed, freezing in the fury of the tempestuous sea, haunted him above all.

Now the bedchamber was silent. Miss Bray was present, as he expected. She sat by the window sewing. It was a simple bedchamber with a canopied bed, two chairs, and a wardrobe. No whistling wind or shouting men could be heard, just the rhythmic crackle of the fire in the grate and steady, even breathing. If it weren't for the tragedy that presently consumed his every thought, this chamber — and this moment — might even be considered peaceful.

He walked farther in. The boards creaked beneath his boots, and Miss Bray turned at the sound. He lifted his hand in greeting but said nothing.

Miss Bray stood, set her sewing on the chair, and after adjusting the shawl around her shoulders, moved closer to him.

Her scent of lavender met him first, the softness and sweetness of it catching him off guard after the scents of salt and rain had been seared into his senses.

He whispered as she approached, "How is she?"

Her fair brows drawn, Miss Bray glanced at the bed. "I'm pleased she's been sleeping so well, and she's starting to stir a bit. I expect she'll wake soon."

They stood in silence for several moments, both locked in the discomfort of uncertainty. She leaned her head closer. "What news from the cove?"

Liam hesitated, not exactly sure what she wanted to know or how much it was proper to reveal. "I don't think they know a great deal yet."

"Have the excise men arrived?"

"No. Any updates on the woman?"

She shook her head.

He cast a downward glance at the steward's granddaughter. The top of her blonde head barely reached his shoulder. Her hair was down, her cheeks were pale, and her shawl was drawn tight. In all practicality she was, essentially, a stranger to him, but the day's events seemed to have drawn them together in an unexpected way. It was strange, but at the moment he felt more at ease in her presence than with anyone else in Pevlyn.

Perhaps it was because she was closer to his age than the others he had encountered. Or maybe it was the calmness and kindness she exuded. Or perhaps it was the soft curve of her cheek and the sweet expression in her eyes. Regardless, he liked her. And he cared about how these events were affecting her.

He wanted to ask her how she was faring after such a day, but instead he looked back to the child, deciding it best to keep to the topic at hand. Something about the child's wild dark locks and delicate features reminded him of his sister Sophy when she was around that age. "How old do you think she is? Four? Five?"

"I'm not sure." Miss Bray shrugged. "I'm not around children a great deal. It's hard for me to tell."

It was odd to hear a woman say such a thing. The women he knew always seemed to be surrounded by children, whether their own family members or village children. But then he considered her life. By nearly everyone's account her grandfather kept her close to the cottage and guarded who she interacted with. He'd not seen a single child in the area, except for those he saw playing on Market Day.

"Life is so fragile, is it not?" she continued absently, her arms wrapped around her waist as she stared at the child.

Her statement was a short one, and yet it felt almost like an invitation for a more in-depth interaction — instead of a polite exchange between master of the estate and steward's daughter. And why shouldn't it? They had both endured a significant event this day.

He kept his voice low. "It is. And how

quickly life can change."

"This child's life will never be the same. And yet she'll survive. She's a fighting spirit in her. I could tell by the way she clung to me."

"I hope you're right. And I hope the woman in the next room has a fighting spirit too."

Suddenly the child's eyes opened, as if she'd been startled awake. She pushed herself up and pressed herself back against her pillow. She whirled her head to the left, then to the right. Panic widened her eyes. "Mama! Mama! Where's my mama?"

The child attempted to climb down from the bed, her movements frantic. Miss Bray hurried to the bedside, sat next to her, and took her hand in her own. "Shh, dearest. Shh." She brushed the child's hair from her face and spoke in soft tones until the child started to calm. "Do you remember me?" Miss Bray leaned close. "I'm Evelyn. Do you remember?"

The child's movements slowed. She sniffed and nodded, then cast a dubious glance in Liam's direction.

Miss Bray followed the shift in the child's attention. "That's Mr. Twethewey. Do you remember him?"

The child's dark eyes met his. She made

no response.

Miss Bray's voice was gentle. "This is his house. It's called Wyndcliff Hall. Isn't that a pretty name?"

The child snapped her attention back to Miss Bray. "Where's my mama?"

Miss Bray swallowed and looked up to Liam, as if for support.

But what could be said?

She turned back to the child. "Let's start with introductions. I don't even know your name. Can you tell me what it is?"

The girl swallowed and pulled the blanket up to her. "Mary."

"Ah. Mary." Miss Bray smiled. "Such a pretty name. And what is your surname? Mine's Bray."

Mary eyed Liam again. "Williams."

"Well, Miss Mary Williams, it is so nice to make your acquaintance." Miss Bray stood and gave a formal curtsy in such a dramatic fashion that it incited a cautious giggle from Mary.

Miss Bray sat down and took Mary's hands once more. "Do you remember the ship you were sailing on?"

Mary nodded.

"There's someone else who's here from it. She's in the room next to you. I'm not sure if she's your mama or not, but she's sleeping. I will take you to see her, but it is very important that we remain quiet so as not to wake her. Do you think we can do that?"

Mary swiped her hand across her nose and nodded.

Miss Bray removed her shawl, wrapped it around Mary's shoulders, and lifted her in her arms. Together they made their way past Liam to the room next door.

Liam trailed them, feeling more like an observer than a participant.

"That's my mama!" Mary cried the moment they crossed the threshold. She wiggled to get down from Miss Bray's arms. "What's that on her head? Why is she sleeping? Let me down. I want to go to her!"

But Miss Bray held her firm. "Remember? We must let her sleep. And that is a bandage on her head."

Mary stopped squirming. A frown curved her small lips. "But when will she wake up?"

"I'm not sure, but she needs rest. Just like you needed rest." Miss Bray lightened her tone and brushed hair from Mary's face. "You must be hungry. You haven't eaten all day! You've been very brave, and you need your strength. Let's go find something to eat."

"But I want to stay with her." The child squirmed to get down again.

179

Miss Bray did not loosen her hold on her. "I know you do. But she's sleeping, see? And we shouldn't disturb her. Did you know there's a kitten who lives in the kitchen?"

At this the child stopped wiggling.

Brilliant. All children liked animals.

Miss Bray adjusted her grip. "She's gray, and ever so tiny. She hurt her paw somehow, so now she rarely goes outside. The house-keeper feeds her by hand. Maybe we can help. Shall we go find her?"

Mary nodded cautiously.

Miss Bray swept by him with Mary in her arms, whispering about kittens. She'd done it. She'd managed to calm the child and identify the woman as the child's mother.

Amazed and impressed at Miss Bray's ability to handle the situation, he retreated from the room, drew the door closed once again, and followed them down to the kitchen in time to find them looking in the basket and near the settee for the kitten.

Once the kitten had been located and tarts had been served, Liam sat next to Mary at the table. The child eyed him skeptically. She drew the kitten close in one arm, her tart close in the other hand, and scooted nearer to Miss Bray.

He shouldn't have been surprised she was

frightened of him. After all, he was a stranger and he lacked Miss Bray's soothing nature. But he had younger siblings, had he not? He knew how to talk with children.

Determined to develop a good rapport with Mary, he smiled. "How's the tart?"

Her expression did not change. "Good."

"You can have all you'd like." He pushed the plate with the tarts toward her.

At this the corner of her mouth twitched, and she reached for another.

The conversation started to flow, and for a few moments Liam felt a slight weight lift from his shoulders. For a few moments he allowed himself to laugh. After the tarts had been eaten and the kitten had a new bed made from an old kitchen apron, Miss Bray gathered the child on her lap. She, too, had seemed to enjoy their interaction, but now her expression sobered once again. "May I ask you a question, Mary? Can you tell me your mama's name? She's been asleep so I haven't been able to ask her myself."

Mary's countenance darkened, as if she had just remembered that her mother was upstairs.

"It would be so helpful if you could tell me. That way, when she wakes, she won't be frightened either."

Mary leaned her head against Miss Bray's

shoulder. "Elizabeth Williams."

"Ah. I knew it would be a pretty name."

Pleased with the praise, the child smiled.

"And do you know where you were sailing to before the ship had trouble?" Miss Bray's tone was remarkably light and conversational, as if nothing unpleasant had transpired.

Mary simply shook her head and returned her attention to the kitten in her lap.

Two names — Elizabeth and Mary Williams. It was not a great deal to go on, but it was a start. If they were to find the answers they needed, they had to start somewhere, and at the moment he would take anything he could get.

CHAPTER 17

Minutes slipped to hours, and after a day that seemed endless, night fell.

When Evelyn finally quit Wyndcliff Hall and stepped foot in Wyndcliff Cottage, all was quiet. The kitchen was dark. Not a single lantern burned; no fire was in the grate. No doubt, shipwreck activity was keeping the cottage's other occupants occupied.

In truth she did not mind solitude. The sleepy silence on this bitter autumn night was a welcome relief from the day's harrowing events. Her mind was alive with all she'd seen and heard, but her body longed for rest, and her mind craved seclusion to review all she'd endured.

She lit a candle and made her way through the house. The cottage had but two sleeping chambers, and for the first year or so of their residence Evelyn shared one of them with her mother. Eventually the arrangement felt cramped, and the attic was arranged as her own private space. Even after her mother's relocation to Plymouth two years prior, Evelyn never moved back to the room.

She climbed the narrow staircase that led from the kitchen, and once she came to the first landing, she paused. The door on her left was her mother's old room. On a whim she opened the door. The chamber was dark, and she filled her lungs with the stale air. For several months after her mother left, the scent of her mother's rosewater seemed to linger in this space, allowing Evelyn to cling to the past, but after time passed the scent completely vanished.

Now a sliver of moonlight slanted in through the windows, falling on the simple furnishings. She lifted her gaze to the ceiling to a square trapdoor that was another access point to her attic apartment. When she was younger she'd often descend through this small door to be at her mother's side when she became frightened of a storm or a nightmare, but she'd not opened it in at least two years.

How her mother had despised everything about life at Wyndcliff Cottage. Evelyn never really understood it. Perhaps it was because Mother associated the nearby sea with her father's death. Perhaps it was because she despised Grandfather for losing their fortune. Regardless of the reason, her mother never was shy to share her opinions.

Evelyn drew the door closed and continued to climb the main staircase to her attic room. A window at the chamber's north end framed the moorlands, and another at the south end showed the distant sea during daylight. Two east-facing dormer windows, deeply set in the cottage's granite stone, overlooked Wyndcliff Hall and the front courtyard.

The attic itself was sparsely furnished. A wardrobe stood in the room's tallest point, and her bed was positioned under a window and would catch the morning's light. A small writing desk and chair she had wrestled up from the parlor were beneath another window.

It was this writing desk she went to upon entering the chamber. She opened the drawer and saw the letter her mother had written her. Her stomach soured at the sight. Shipwrecks were an aspect of Pevlyn life that her mother had abhorred. Even before her husband's demise, she regarded the scavenging traditions of the villagers as barbaric.

Even so, Evelyn would write to her mother

and inform her of the events, just as she did whenever anything of significance occurred in the otherwise quiet village. She pulled a piece of paper from her desk and unstopped her inkwell. She drew her candle closer, and her quill hovered over the blank page.

But as she considered which words to write, sadness prevailed. She thought of Elizabeth Williams fighting for her life in Wyndcliff Hall. And of Mary, so innocent and so unaware of the true danger her mother was in.

Evelyn could not help but compare the situation to her own. Her mother had left her. Not by an accident or a force of nature, like the one that threatened to separate Elizabeth Williams from her daughter. No, her mother chose to live away, chose to keep Evelyn at a distance.

The ache was as real as if she, too, had received a blow.

Abandoning the letter, Evelyn stood from the desk and stepped to the chest in the corner. She'd not opened it in quite some time. It contained remnants of her former life and bits that seemed otherworldly now.

But she was drawn to it.

She knelt before the wooden chest, unlatched the creaky iron holds, and pushed up the lid. After tucking her hair behind her ear and drawing her candle closer, she rummaged through the items, pushing aside old gowns and shifts, stockings, and ribbons. Not that there were many. New gowns were expensive, and normally once she outgrew a gown it would be made over into a new one. But these early articles from her childhood — beautifully fashioned and elegantly decorated, from a time when the Brays cared naught for finances — had been too precious to deconstruct.

She lifted the yellow muslin and satin gown she'd worn the day she first arrived at the cottage. The fabric shimmered buttery and lovely in the meager candlelight. It really was beautiful, with lace trimming and tiny pearl embellishments on the bodice.

How vividly she remembered that day. The scent of the flowers. The intensity of her mother's fingers clutching her own. The stares of the villagers as she passed them on the road.

The gown conjured so many memories, yet preserving the gown would profit no one, especially when a frightened child facing an uncertain future was in need of attire. Keeping it hidden away in this trunk would not bring their fortune — or Evelyn's mother — back.

Perhaps Jenna was right. Evelyn was clinging to a hope that might not be.

Sounds of hoofbeats drew her from her thoughts, and she returned to the window. Three soldiers rode into the courtyard, their red coats vibrant even in the dusk. They tied their horses, then pounded on the manor house's door. Shadows moved in the dimly lit study. Her grandfather, as if expecting them, came around from the stable yard.

She bit her lower lip and let the curtain fall. She'd seen enough wrecks and watched her grandfather enough to know that even though the contents of the ship had been cleared from the beach, events were far from over.

Liam paced the great hall and rubbed his hands together, generating warmth. He'd been indoors about half an hour, and still the damp chilliness from the cove clung to him, like a fine mist that refused to dry up.

He stepped closer to the fire and stared into the leaping flames. What he said to Miss Bray earlier in the day had been true. He'd never seen anything like it. The ship-wreck. The cove. The villagers crawling about, everyone eager for something to gain.

Other than quick visits back to Wyndcliff for a change of clothes or to inquire after the Williams duo, he'd spent the entire day on the sandy beach, where despite the incessant drizzle and battering winds, a concerted effort to bring the cargo ashore had been under way. Horses and wagons had been brought down to heave and transport timber and cargo. Men organized the bundles and formed a chain to get it off the beach and to the cellars for storage.

But his mind was occupied by another weighty matter — that of a young child and her unconscious mother. They were under his care for the time being, and the importance of the responsibility was not lost on him.

Horses' hooves crunched on the courtyard, and he looked out the window. Three men in uniform rode together across the space.

The excise men, no doubt.

Not surprisingly, Bray also approached. As boots stomped down the great hall to the study, Liam straightened his damp coat and combed his fingers through his tangled hair. Bray ushered them in, and each one ducked through the low door frame and straightened once inside.

"Gentlemen," Liam greeted.

The tallest man with dark hair and bushy side whiskers spoke first. "You're Mr. Twethewey, I trust. I'm Captain Hollingswood with His Majesty's excise office. This is Captain Andrews."

Liam nodded and extended his hand toward the chairs in front of the desk. "Yes, I've been expecting you. Please, be seated."

Captain Hollingswood nodded. "We heard you'd arrived and hoped to pay you a visit before."

"Before?" Liam raised his eyebrows.

"A wreck. Dastardly weather as of late." He shook his head sharply. "Third wreck this month in your cove alone."

Third?

Liam's stomach clenched at the number. He turned to the side table. "Can I offer you a beverage?"

Captain Hollingswood's stark expression did not change. "No, I thank you. I'm told there are survivors."

Liam stepped back to his desk, grateful to avoid small talk and eager to discuss the matter at hand. "Yes. A young girl, maybe four or five years of age, and her mother."

"And what is their status?"

"The child is well. She's sleeping now. But the woman has yet to wake."

Captain Hollingswood glanced at Bray. "Normally Bray billets survivors at the White Eagle Inn until arrangements can be made. Why is that not the case now?"

"The inn?" Liam thought back to the dark, cramped, noisy inn. "That's hardly suitable for a woman and child. Nay. They'll stay here at Wyndcliff."

"If that is what you wish. Has the child told you any information? Names? Destination? Anything of that sort?"

Liam crossed his arms over his chest. "The child is named Mary Williams, and her mother is Elizabeth Williams. Other than that, she doesn't know or hasn't shared their destination or the name of their ship."

The officer pulled a bit of paper from his pocket, made a note, and returned it. "Every bit of information is useful, I suppose. If she shares anything else, let me know, but she is, after all, a child. I expect we'll have to wait until the woman wakes. We've placed officers at the beach for the time being, at least until the cargo is completely secured. The tinners from the north can be an unruly lot, and I want to avoid any lawlessness that might arise."

"Of course."

"We've checked with the office in Plymouth. There's no record of a ship failing to dock, but that's not saying a great deal. They could've been going anywhere. Normally there's at least one survivor to tell us of their point of origin or destination, but this is unusual indeed. It could be years before a foreign entity claims ownership of the cargo." Captain Hollingswood looked back at the two other uniform-clad officers who accompanied him and returned his attention to Liam. "Before we depart, might I have a word alone?"

Bray's shoulders straightened.

Liam had sensed that the relationship between the two men was a tense one. He was growing more comfortable with Bray's ways, especially after their interactions since the wreck, but it was not fair to judge a relationship after hearing only one side.

Liam nodded and the other soldiers and Bray excused themselves. Neither he nor Captain Hollingswood moved until the door to the great hall closed and the men could be seen in the courtyard.

Hollingswood stepped forward. He stared up at the plaster ceiling for several moments. His broad shoulders relaxed slightly. "It's been a long time since I've been in here."

The words surprised Liam. After hearing that Bray had been working with them, he assumed they would have been in here often. "Please, be seated if you would like."

The stoic captain broke his stance and sat down. "I knew your great-uncle very well.

Shipwrecks have occurred off this stretch of shoreline much before any of us were born. I have served as an excise officer for most of my professional career. I can say I've seen about everything."

Liam remained silent.

Captain Hollingswood rubbed his chin, then crossed one long leg over the other. "It is my understanding you are not from the area."

"I'm from Cornwall, but not this immediate area, nay."

"I trust you've encountered more in your time here than you bargained for."

Liam chuckled. "I suppose there is truth in that."

"I've lived here twenty years. We had an understanding, your uncle and I. He behaved as the model citizen as it related to the laws of shipwrecks and salvage, and we offered him assistance in whatever way we could. But he's gone now. And circumstances have changed. So I'm here to offer a friendly word of caution."

Liam's focus narrowed. "Concerning?"

Captain Hollingswood straightened. "You are the owner of the cove, and with that comes a great deal of control and influence. A great many people can profit from these shipwrecks and even the cove itself. My job is to make sure that lawlessness does not prevail. As a gentleman and the owner of this property, you must assist with that. There is no denying that these people are hungry. Greedy. They see the misfortune as an opportunity and descend on wrecks like vultures, plundering and scavenging at will. But with your arrival we have a unique opportunity to change this behavioral tide. Aye, they seek finder's fees and do help recover goods. That is lawful. No one disputes that. But the lawlessness that accompanies it is deplorable."

The grotesque sight of the men grabbing and pawing at the cargo even before the survivors were rescued burned in Liam's mind.

Captain Hollingswood's stare remained firm. "The free traders have their hands in everything, and your cove is no exception. 'Twould be folly to think otherwise. We've an idea of who the principal players are, but proving it is another matter entirely. Bray has been a part of this landscape for as long as I can remember, but his circumstances have changed. Like I said, everyone has something to gain, even those who appear to be law-abiding and wish to promote the greater good. Keep that in mind when you decide who to align yourself with."

Bray always seemed to be in the company of the local men. Laughing. Talking. He seemed so intent on following the law. "Are you suggesting Bray is contributing to lawless activity?"

Captain Hollingswood drew a deep breath, as if considering his words. "I'll be blunt. My men and I are tasked with keeping the peace, preventing free trading, and ensuring that the king receives the duties he is due, but Bray has been modeling his own form of justice and law, and it is a matter of time before his disregard for the law catches up with him."

Liam raised his brow. *Disregard for the law?* He cleared his throat, as if by doing so he could clear away the mixed messages and murky circumstances. "What is it you would have me do?"

"Your role is very clear. To uphold the law. You are to see that my office is notified immediately of a wreck. Your uncle used to send a man by the name of Tom, and that arrangement worked well."

Liam thought of the quiet manservant he rarely saw.

"Furthermore, you will notify us of those who are taking advantage of the situation. If you suspect free trading on any level, you are duty bound to inform us."

"And does Bray not do that, acting as my wrecking agent?"

Captain Hollingswood huffed. "Your man Bray considers himself a benefactor of the people. He is much more concerned with the locals and seeing that they retrieve what they will instead of notifying us, as evidenced by the fact that we did not learn of this wreck for a full day."

A bout of laughter could be heard from the courtyard — feminine, playful laughter. Miss Bray. Eager to see her, he looked out the window.

But it was not Miss Bray. It seemed a party had converged on the manor house, for a stately, crested carriage had parked in the courtyard, and two women stood just outside it.

"It appears you have other visitors." Captain Hollingswood moved to the window. "And it appears they will be much more charming than I am. I will leave you to your guests, but consider what I have said. I'll be in touch."

CHAPTER 18

Liam stifled a groan as he turned away from the window in his study. This day had started before dawn, and the incessant and difficult activities had taken their toll. He was hungry. Tired. And according to everything he'd been told, he needed to be out in the cove. Aye, the soldiers said they would be patrolling the shoreline, but he needed to see it for himself to know what he was up against.

Now two women and a man approached his house, and Bray greeted them and showed them inside.

Liam straightened his damp neckcloth and rubbed his hand over his face. He'd not shaved and scruff covered his jaw. He bent down to wipe mud from his boot with his handkerchief. He was hardly in a state to meet guests, but this would have to do.

Bray appeared in the doorway. "Visitors to see you."

"Who is it?"

"Mr. and Mrs. Traver from Verntin House, just north of here. Their daughter is with them."

"Do you know why they are here now?"

Bray chuckled. "I told you. Shipwrecks bring out everyone, from those depending on the salvage to those looking for amusement at the expense of others."

"Amusement?" Liam huffed. "Sounds like terrible entertainment."

Bray shrugged and raised a brow. "Or they could be here to see you. It's not every day a new master of the estate arrives."

Liam ignored Bray's sarcasm. "Where are they?"

"Just in the great hall. None of the other rooms are open yet. I can show them in here if you like."

Liam glanced at the untidy stacks of papers and sloppy piles of books and ledgers. "Nay, nay. I'll meet them there. Thank you, Bray."

The steward turned to leave, and Liam stopped him. "Are you returning to the cove?"

"Presently."

"Wait for me. I should like to accompany you."

"As you wish." Bray nodded. "The soldiers

are there now, so our presence is not as necessary."

"Where is Tom? I've met him once. Is he around?"

"I'm sure he's about. Why?"

"I'd like to talk with him at some point."

Bray gave a slow bob of his head. "Very well."

After Bray's departure, Liam forced his worries to the back of his mind and headed to the corridor outside the great hall to surreptitiously observe his guests. The man's back was to him, but it was clear his intention was not to assist on the moors, with his stark-white stockings and black leather shoes. Next to him presumably was his wife. A crimson pelisse hugged her ample figure, and an equally bright plume extended from her bonnet, which swayed and bowed with each movement. The young woman faced him. She was pretty, wearing a pelisse cut very much like her mother's but in a soft, pale-peach color. Her auburn hair was tidy and curled on either side of her face. Not a lock was out of place, and her cheeks flushed a becoming pink.

Liam ran his fingers through his hair, aware of how he must look. The last thing he felt like doing was entertaining, but there was no avoiding the visitors. He approached, and they all turned toward him.

Liam forced a smile. "Welcome to Wyndcliff Hall."

Mr. Traver stepped forward first. "There now, I say, it's about time a proper master was here at Wyndcliff, and I'm happy to welcome you to the area."

Liam bowed and shook his outstretched hand. "Thank you. My apologies for welcoming you here in the hall. I fear the sitting rooms have not been opened yet."

"Pay it no mind. We'll not stay and intrude on your evening, as we've heard your hands are quite full with business at the cove, but we have been dining with the Parsons, your neighbors to the east, and thought we'd be remiss if we did not stop by and introduce ourselves. I'm Roger Traver. May I present my wife, Mrs. Catherine Traver, and my daughter, Miss Lydia Traver."

Both women curtsied and Liam bowed. "Welcome to Wyndcliff, ladies."

Mrs. Traver stepped closer. "Oh, my only sadness is that your welcome has been marred by such activity. And so soon after your arrival! Why, the thought!"

Her husband stepped to her side. "Alas, the sea had her own agenda, did she not? How long have you been here?"

"A few days."

The man clicked his tongue. "Dodgy business, these wrecks. I count myself fortunate that my land does not extend that far."

"And where is your land?" Liam inquired.

"Just to the north of yours. And we're glad you are here. This old house has been empty for far too long. And we do hope you plan on entertaining in the same fashion as your late uncle. We have heard word that a woman and a child washed ashore. Could this be true?"

Liam's heart wrenched at the thought of the frightened child and the injured woman. "It is."

"Oh, such a sad tale!" The appearance of sympathy drew the older woman's brows together. "Do you think they will recover?"

He recalled the gash on Mrs. Williams's forehead. "I certainly hope so."

Mr. Traver cleared his throat. "I'd imagine you're grateful for a wrecking agent like Bray. He is well versed in handling such matters. But I trust you know his history." Mr. Traver leaned forward as if to share a great secret. "Such a fall from grace."

Liam nodded again. Aye, he was interested in learning more about Bray's past, but he was not interested in engaging in gossip.

Mr. Traver persisted. "In polite circles, of course, 'twas well known that Mr. Bray was unable to walk away from a wager. Then there was another rumor that he'd lost his money to blackmail. Regardless, it is a shame. A true shame."

Liam winced.

"Of course nothing can be proved," continued Traver. "Gambling. Free trading. Blackmail. It's all a sordid lot. And not at all appropriate conversation with ladies present."

Liam did not know how to take this. Was it a warning? Idle gossip? A play for power? He looked to Miss Lydia Traver, who up until this point had been silent, but she offered him a coy, flirtatious smile.

Liam stiffened. As if navigating the world of wrecks and smuggling was not enough, he would be forced to navigate the world of polite society as well.

And he did not know which was the most frightening.

CHAPTER 19

Had it really been two full days since the shipwreck? The hours, moments, sounds, and colors from the day's events blurred together, creating a lasting nightmare from which Liam could not wake. Thoughts of smugglers, dead sailors, and the unconscious woman under his roof robbed him of any peaceful rest, and another day in the wind and weather at the cove had been exhausting.

Aye, he'd not been at Wyndcliff even a full week, but he needed to think on something else, even if for a few moments. Now that he'd signed the papers authorizing Porter to move forward with their plans for the Aulder Hill pits, he could put thoughts of shipwrecks behind him and proceed with his plans for the estate.

As he made his way across the great hall to his study, soft voices and hushed laughter spilling from the parlor caught his attention. As he approached the room, warm yellow light spilled from its doorway. He'd not stepped foot in this chamber since his arrival. A cheery fire danced in the grate, and candles flickered on the tables and in the wall sconces. Two large paintings depicting fox hunts on the opposite wall drew his attention, and for the first time since his arrival, a part of the house seemed like a home — welcoming and warm.

He liked the feeling.

Miss Bray, clad in a gown of pale green, sat on the sofa before the fire. Her legs were tucked underneath her, and her arm was draped over the sofa's back. Her other arm circled around Mary. Their heads were inclined toward each other, and they were perusing a book. Miss Bray pointed at something, and Mary scrunched her face in a giggle.

It was good to hear laughter after such a difficulty. And to see such a pretty lady did no harm either. Did Miss Bray have any notion of how alluring she was, he wondered, sitting on the sofa, her blonde hair tumbling over her shoulders? How her hair caught the light, glimmering and lovely? How the slight dimple in her cheek begged to be touched?

He needed to stop this line of thinking. It

was not appropriate in this moment, after what had been endured, and her grandfather's warning rushed him. And yet he could not deny that his curiosity about her was growing, and he found himself thinking of her much more frequently than he should.

He cleared his throat, and they both looked up at him.

Startled, Miss Bray straightened, swung her stockinged feet down, and slipped them into the slippers on the floor in one fluid motion.

The domiciliary picture she'd conjured vanished.

"I did not mean to startle you." He entered the room.

"You need not apologize." Miss Bray smiled. "This is, after all, your parlor."

His gaze lifted to the ornate plaster flowers and vines adorning the painted ceiling. "I've not been in here. The last time I passed this room the furniture was still draped and it was dark."

"We've been busy, haven't we, Mary?" She hugged the child. "The weather kept us indoors today, so we thought we'd help Kitty open up this chamber."

"Ah, well done." He knelt before Mary. "And how are you today, Miss Mary?"

She stretched out her arm to show him her sleeve. "I have a new gown." She jumped up and shook out the folds of the pale-gray gown and pointed her toe in front of her. "Slippers too."

"So you do." He made a dramatic bow on his knees. "Quite lovely, my lady."

Miss Bray smoothed the blue ribbon on the back of Mary's gown. "One of the women in town sent it for her to wear."

"But look," Mary cried, scurrying back to the sofa and retrieving a bundle of yellow fabric from the sewing basket at the sofa's end. She held up a yellow gown with soft fabric and beads on the bodice. "Look at this one!"

Liam did not know a great deal about women's garments, but his three sisters chattered enough about gowns and trimmings for him to know this was no ordinary gown. It shimmered, and intricate embroidery embellished the hem. "That's very pretty."

"It was Miss Bray's when she was little. Not as little as me, but littler than she is now. She said she will make it smaller for me."

"Well now." Liam smiled. "You'll be the prettiest girl in the village with such a gown."

"My mama likes things that are yellow." Mary's smile faded, and she tucked her hand in Miss Bray's, leaned against her, then peered up at him with wide, dark eyes. "When is Mama going to wake up?"

Liam exchanged glances with Miss Bray, and she offered a little shrug of solidarity.

Mary had asked him the same question every time he encountered her, and the simple, sincere inquiry tore at him. As far as he knew, Elizabeth Williams had not stirred at all this day. He wanted to encourage the little girl, to offer her hope, but it would not do to lie to her. Each hour, each day that passed with no sustenance did not bode well. "Ah, poppet. I don't know."

Mary's face fell, and she was silent for several minutes before she looked back up at him. "Am I going to live here now?"

The question was innocent enough. Wasn't that what every person wanted, regardless of age, to be settled in a place that belonged to them and to where they belonged in turn?

"You are welcome to stay here as long as you and your mother need to."

Miss Bray reached for the book they had been reading and handed it to Mary. "Here. You look at this. I need to speak with Mr. Twethewey."

Mary did as bid and jumped back on the

velvet-covered sofa, clutching the book tight.

Liam stood and lowered his voice as Miss Bray drew nearer. "You've been very good to her. It does you credit."

"I'm not looking for credit." Miss Bray smiled and tucked her hair behind her ear. "Have you by chance heard from the surgeon today? He was to call and check on Mrs. Williams earlier this afternoon, but he did not come by."

"Aye, I did. There was an accident at the cove that required his attention. One of the men fell on the cliffs while recovering cargo and broke a bone. I believe Dr. Smith has been with him."

Her fair brows drew together. "Who was injured?"

"I-I don't know the man's name." He felt foolish for not knowing. It was something he should have paid attention to — the name of a man injured on his property. "Your grandfather was with him too. The man seemed quite comfortable with him there."

"Oh, there's that, at least." The tension in her shoulders seemed to ease. "He has such a way of comforting."

"Really?" The question was out of Liam's mouth before he could reconsider it. "It's only that he seems quite gruff to me. I'd hardly think him the nurturing sort."

"That's because you aren't well acquainted with him. Aye, I can see how one might consider him gruff. He does have a temper. But he's extraordinarily kind and —"

Liam could not help the chuckle that escaped his lips and interrupted her words.

"Nay, I insist!" she responded with a laugh of her own. "Ask anyone. The orphanage trustees. The Ladies League. The miners who have been left without work. He has been most generous with them. And with me. If it weren't for Grandfather, I would be . . ."

Her words faded, and as they did, the earnestness in them became evident. A flush rushed her cheeks, and she looked down, as if suddenly shy.

Liam had seen but one side of Bray — a defensive, domineering side. But he could not deny that most people had more than one side to their character.

"Oh, it's a shame, isn't it? Such a difficult week for our little community." Her sadness wrote itself on her features.

Would he ever feel the same way about the people living around him? He hoped so. He hoped they'd accept him in turn, although not knowing the name of the man who was injured during the salvage was not a good start.

Miss Bray tightened her shawl around her shoulders. "I worry for Mrs. Williams. I fear the worst will happen. She's eaten nothing at all. How can one survive with no nourishment?" She glanced back at the child. "Poor Mary has already been through so much. What if —"

"You cannot think such things."

"I can't help it." She lifted her chin and paused, as if determined to shift the conversation. "I don't suppose your welcome to Wyndcliff Hall has been a very pleasant one."

Pleasant? Storms, rain, a shipwreck, a house that had fallen into a state of disrepair, excise men at his door — *pleasant* was hardly the word he would use to describe his experience thus far. But he'd not show frustration. He forced a smile. "But what's to be done? It cannot be easy for you either. This isn't the first wreck you've encountered, but I doubt any are to be taken lightly."

"Unfortunately, 'tis a way of life here. Wyndcliff Cottage is the closest inhabited house to the coast, with the exception of Wyndcliff Hall, of course, and since Grandfather is the wrecking agent, he's always the

210

first to be notified."

Liam saw his opportunity to learn more about this odd system. "Who notifies him?"

"Local men are hired to watch the sea, especially during storms. There's too much at stake — for everyone — to miss a wreck. For years my mother and grandfather would not permit me to come down to the coast during a wreck, so I watched them from my window. They always said it was too dangerous, but one night I snuck down to the shoreline. I thought Grandfather would be angry, but he just told me to help away from the waterline and never said a word about it. I've been helping at every wreck ever since."

"And your mother?"

She did not respond. She only looked back to Mary.

Based on her words, it did seem odd that it took so long for the excise men to be notified. He pushed the thought down and focused on her and changed the subject from her mother. "Are you ever frightened of them — the wrecks?"

"They are scary, to be sure, but it is easier to put your fear aside when you think that someone's life is in danger." She paused and stared down at her hands. "You know, my father died assisting in a rescue."

Liam's breath seemed to catch. "I-I had no idea. I'm sorry. That must make this even more difficult for you."

She met his gaze once more. "I was very young. I don't remember it. But from the little I'm told, it was a night very much like the one that threatened Mary's ship. I suppose that is why my grandfather is so determined for the wrecks to be handled properly."

He searched for some sort of words to offer comfort, but what could be said? It seemed every moment brought about a new layer to this entire situation.

As if sensing his discomfort, she smiled. "I saw that the soldiers were here last night. They always come. For the wrecks they know about, at least. What did you think of our Captain Hollingswood?"

"A determined fellow. They're concerned that plundering is occurring." He watched her for a reaction. "Maybe smuggling."

She shrugged. "They always assume the worst. I've no doubt they intend to help, but the people in the village are good people. I believe that. Life here is hard for them, but they are not heathens."

"I never meant to imply that they were heathens. But you cannot believe that everyone down on that beach has the purest intentions."

"There's a great deal of want and poverty, but no one wants to see loss of life." She looked up at him and tilted her head to the side. "Where is the home you came from? Cornwall, is it not?"

"Aye."

"Were you near the sea? Did you not encounter shipwrecks there?"

"We were near the sea, very near in fact, but I can recall only one ship emergency, and it was a local fisherman. But our coast was tucked out of the way."

"Do you miss your home?"

The question stung. It was easy not to think about how much he missed his family when he was busy, but when he was asked specifically about them — Aunt Delia, Uncle Jac, Julia, Hannah, Sophy, and John — the sense of loss rushed him. "I have a great deal of family there. I do miss them."

"You are fortunate to have a lot of family. Just my grandfather and I are here."

For the first time since he arrived, he was having a real conversation. Not just a practical one, but a conversation to get to know another person. And not just any person. A lovely young woman.

What harm could be found in a little conversation?

"Your grandfather told me your mother now lives in Plymouth."

"She does." She watched the child for several moments before she turned back to him. "I expect to join her very soon. If all goes well, by year's end."

He stiffened, his momentary relief slamming to a halt. He did not like the thought of her leaving. "The end of the year is not very far away."

Footsteps sounded outside of the parlor, and he turned to see Rupert Bray in the doorway.

Liam tensed, realizing how the situation must look with him standing so close to Miss Bray. He felt like a naughty schoolboy caught doing something he should not. He took a step back.

Miss Bray straightened, but instead of sharing in his feeling of awkwardness, she smiled and drew near to Bray. "Grandfather." She placed her hands on the older man's shoulders and kissed his withered cheek. "There you are."

Bray smiled with grandfatherly affection. "Ah, Evie, my dear." He then turned hard eyes toward Liam, and any softness present when he beheld his granddaughter had vanished. "Evie, best see the child to bed and get to the cottage yourself. The hour is late."

Miss Bray knit her fingers before her, and for a moment Liam thought she might defy him. But then she resigned herself and reached for Mary's hand.

Mary and Miss Bray bid the men good night, then quit the chamber.

Leaving Liam alone with Bray.

Bray narrowed his eyes. "The beach is cleared, but Captain Hollingswood is in the cellar requesting to see the ledgers. Do you want to allow him access?"

Liam shrugged. "Why would I not?"

"You don't have to, of course. Those are your private documents."

"But I've nothing to hide. They're just ledgers and documentation. Am I right?"

Bray lifted a thick shoulder in a shrug. "It's never wise to let them know more than they need to know. They'll use it against you in the end. Use it against the villagers. Mark my words. You'd best keep your eye on that one."

"Interesting." Liam folded his arms over his chest. "He said the same thing about you."

"Bah, I don't doubt it. That man is out to line his own pockets. He gets paid for every arrest he makes and for what he confiscates in the name of the crown."

Liam followed Bray from the chamber. The man's harshness had replaced the welcoming warmth he'd shared with Mary and Miss Bray, but it seemed an accurate description of Liam's new life here. Sharp contrasts and unsettling transitions. Now more than ever he was determined to get to the bottom of the strange customs and happenings here. He needed to if he was to transform this property into the successful operation he hoped it would be.

CHAPTER 20

Much to Evelyn's pleasure, the next day broke fair and bright over the brown moorland and glistening sea. After days of misty rain and harsh autumn gusts, a welcome touch of warmth laced the breeze, and the desire to be outdoors filled her. If nothing else, a change in weather provided relief, for inside Wyndcliff Hall darkness and melancholy reigned.

Elizabeth Williams was still unresponsive.

Evelyn had spent the morning attempting to keep Mary busy, asking about her favorite animals, exploring the library, and searching for the kitten in the kitchen. Eventually they'd exhausted the indoor activities, and since the constant coming and going of the physician was making Mary anxious, they decided that a walk down to the beach was just the diversion they needed.

They made their way down to the great hall and encountered Mr. Twethewey returning from a ride. His windblown dark hair curled waywardly about his ruddy face.

Their conversation in the parlor the previous evening had surprised her. Up until this point she'd viewed his presence here as a business arrangement — the fulfillment of the instructions laid out by Mr. Treton. She'd assumed the young heir would sweep in and take charge, lording his position above them all, but recent events had bound them together in an unexpected way, crossing the lines of station and situation.

His face seemed more relaxed than it had the previous night. He'd recently shaven, and a dimple formed whenever he smiled. Even when he spoke. If she was not careful, her mind — and her heart — could trot down an unproductive path.

Evelyn had decided that she liked him, in spite of her grandfather's grumblings. The manner in which he interacted with Mary, fun and friendly, impressed her. Not many men would take the time to ensure such a child was cared for, much less happy. Yet every time he returned to Wyndcliff Hall, he sought her out, checking on her and making her laugh.

Once Mary noticed him, she giggled and flew across the hall. Her face flushed a sweet pink, and she held up the necklace around her neck. "Look, Mr. Twethewey!"

He chuckled and knelt next to her. "What do you have there?"

"Sea glass. Isn't it pretty?"

"Sea glass." He took it from her and held it up to the light. "Look at that."

"Miss Bray said it's all over on the beach." Mary bounced excitedly from foot to foot. "We're going on a hunt, and I'm going to find a piece and make my mama a necklace. You should come!"

He chuckled and then looked to Evelyn.

A thrill shot through her as their eyes met.

An unmistakable, unexpected thrill.

Oh aye, he was handsome. And for a brief moment, she thought she saw something in his eyes — a glimmer that made her feel he had noticed her too.

"Me?" He stood back up to his full height. "I am sure Miss Bray knows all the places to find sea glass. You don't need me to go."

"But it will be great fun!" Mary cried. "Don't you want to find some pieces? You could make a necklace too."

He laughed, a genuine happy sound, then glanced toward the afternoon sun. "All right, but a quick walk. That is, if it's all right with Miss Bray that I accompany the both of you. And only if you promise to help me search. I've never hunted sea glass before."

Finding herself the sudden focus of his attention, she straightened, wishing she would have taken a little time to tend her hair. But what did it matter? It was foolish to think that he considered her beyond anything more than Mary's temporary caretaker.

Plymouth — she must remember. Wasn't that her goal?

Together the trio traversed the windswept courtyard and made their way through the copse of trees down to the stony cliffs overlooking the cove. The gray-and-white seabirds swooped low and called noisily to one another, as if they, too, were happy for a glimpse of sunshine and enjoyed the warmth on their spread wings. Gone was the harsh sound of the wind whistling through the crags and stones. Instead, the lazy crash of surf on sand was almost like a lullaby, urging one to forget the horror that had happened here just two days prior.

Mr. Twethewey assisted both Evelyn and Mary over the rocks to the sand. Mary took off running, wild and happy and free, as if not a single care pressed upon her tiny shoulders, and Evelyn fell into step beside Mr. Twethewey.

It felt a little improper, almost, to be here

with them. They weren't alone, not really, and yet she was aware of how it would appear. But another part of her, a much more curious part, spoke louder than the little voice warning her of appearances. The part of her that wanted to know more about this man who was so kind to children, who seemed to have such grand ideas and dreams.

"Isolated here, isn't it?" He stared out over the water as it shifted beneath the clouds and lapped the shoreline.

She gave a little laugh and lifted her hand to still her hair from whipping about her face. "It should be. This is Wyndcliff land. Your property. There shouldn't be people on it."

"It's easy to forget that." He squinted as the sun glinted off the sea. "It's been a handful of days and yet it seems like an eternity, doesn't it? I saw the villagers on Market Day, but otherwise was beginning to doubt the existence of other people here until I saw everyone out on the beach."

"A wreck will do that. Brings out all sorts."

"Captain Hollingswood made it sound like the area was crawling with free traders and would be for days to come."

"And do you believe him?" She kept her face forward.

He shrugged. "I've hardly had enough time here to form such an opinion."

They continued on in silence as Mary chased the seabirds walking on the sand, splashed in the waves that darted past the waterline, and climbed up on one of the crags. They joined her there, where they searched in between the rocks, finding shells and stones but no sea glass. Eventually Mary tired of her search and raced along the shore with all the boundless energy of youth.

"She relies on you." Mr. Twethewey stooped to pick up a piece of rock, then launched it out to sea.

Evelyn followed suit and bent to pick up a shell, but instead of throwing it she added it to Mary's basket. "Of course I wish nothing but the best for her and her mother, but I will be sad when the time comes for her to leave. It is nice to be needed."

"It appears your grandfather is quite dependent on you. Does he not need you?"

"My grandfather?" She laughed. "My grandfather is a great man, but he is the sort who needs people to be dependent upon him, not the other way around."

"You said last night that he was very generous."

"And he is."

"You said he was generous with *you.* What did you mean?"

"Well, after my father died, he took my mother and me in and has seen to our every need. Even after my mother left, he has insisted that I remain here. He even saved my life."

"What?"

"It's true. Several years ago we attended a wedding in the village, and the celebration moved to Graer Beach, which is about half a mile west of here. It was dark, and I went too close to the water's edge. He always warned me about the sea, especially since it was how my father died. I was young, though, and not paying attention, and a wave crashed against me. My skirts became tangled and I fell, and the undertow was strong. I couldn't get my footing, and the waves kept rolling in. I would have died that night had it not been for him. He risked his own safety, jumped in the water, and brought me to shore."

She turned to see his reaction.

For several moments he said nothing — he only looked out to sea, the wind tousling his dark hair. She was not surprised that he thought Grandfather gruff. But she wanted him to see the softer, kinder side she knew existed, if for no other reason than to make the relationship between the two men less tense.

"The two of you seem to have an interesting dynamic."

She laughed. "Yes. Interesting. He wants nothing more than to keep things just the way they are and to keep me a child forever, tucked away in the cottage, away from all dangers, all possibility of change. I suppose that's why he is so terse with you. Oh aye, I've noticed the sharpness in his tone when he speaks with you. He does not handle change of any sort well, and your arrival is an adjustment for him."

"Does it not get lonely for you here, being so far from the village with naught but him for company?"

Evelyn bit her lower lip and looked down to the sand at her feet as they walked. If only he knew — if only anyone knew — the extent of her loneliness. But her pain was strongest where loneliness intersected with the rejection she felt from her mother. The fact that he recognized it affected her in a way she wasn't prepared for.

When she did not respond, he said, "I may have only been here a short time, but I don't know what I'd do without you."

The words stole her breath. They were unexpected. Warm. And far too personal.

She laughed to diminish the weight of the words. "Don't be silly. Marnie does everything around Wyndcliff."

"Nay, that's not what I mean."

He stopped walking and waited, as if expecting her to do the same.

After taking a moment to garner her courage, she turned toward him.

He stammered, "That is to say, I enjoy your company. With naught but your grandfather, Marnie, and Tom to speak with . . ."

His voice waned. They resumed walking and neither of them spoke again until they reached Mary, where they sat on the sand, sorting the bits of shell and rock she had collected, organizing them by size and color.

Then Mary's smile, which just moments ago had been bright, faded to a frown. The wind whipped her long, straight hair free of its plait. Her small, round face darkened as if a shadow had crossed over the sun.

"Is something the matter?" Evelyn asked, concerned at the sudden change in the child's demeanor.

Mary studied the pink-and-tan shell in her hands. "Is my mama going to get better?"

"I pray so," Evelyn said, then remained silent, giving the child space to choose words.

The girl's fist closed around the shell. "At

least the man is gone."

The vehemence behind her words startled Evelyn. She looked to Mr. Twethewey before she asked, "What man?"

"The mean man who yelled at my mama."

Alarm pricked Evelyn's spine. "Do you mean a man on the ship?"

Mary nodded, her gaze not straying from her hands. "I don't remember his name. He was mad at Mama, and she said that when we got to England, we would never have to see him again."

Evelyn chose her words with care. "Why were they arguing, do you know?"

"Mama was mad about the lights."

"What lights?" Mr. Twethewey interjected, his tone thin.

"The ones on the shore." Mary glanced up, squinting in the sunlight. "I thought they were stars, but Mama said they were too big to be stars. There."

She pointed to Brayden's Crag. "He said we had to get off, but then the ship hit something and it started to sink."

She spoke the troubling words calmly, and yet the words themselves were rooted in caution.

"He said you had to get off even before the ship started to sink?" Mr. Twethewey confirmed.

She nodded. "Aye. We were supposed to get in a smaller boat. But then the water started coming in."

Evelyn slid a glance toward Mr. Twethewey before she forced a smile and put her hand on Mary's shoulder. It would do no good to press the child for information now, not when she was so upset. "Well, you and your mama are safe at Wyndcliff Hall. I promise you that no one will argue with you, there will be no odd lights, and we'll make sure you get to where you were going in the first place. Won't we, Mr. Twethewey?"

Trouble brewed in his eyes, making them appear a shade or two darker, then a forced smile lifted the corner of his mouth. "Of course."

Once they had collected their shells and rocks, they walked back to the house in silence. Mr. Twethewey carried Mary, who was tired of walking. In the courtyard Mr. Twethewey put Mary down, and she ran to the kitchen to show Marnie her new collection.

Evelyn remained in the courtyard alone with Mr. Twethewey. Gone was the lighthearted nature of their conversation from when they first went down to the beach.

All was silent until he spoke at last. "Why

would there be lights on the cliff? Before dawn? Would it be the men watching the shore?"

Evelyn shook her head. "Nay. If there were lights on the shore it would signal a safe landing." Just the mention of lights made her think of the tales that had been whispered through the village for as long as she could remember. "There are stories, legends really, of dangerous men who'd use lights to lure ships to the perilous shores, and then once the vessel wrecked on the rocks, they'd rob the distressed ship of its cargo and, at times, kill the crew to cover their deeds. Like I said, they are legends. Of course, a much more likely reason would be that someone was trying to communicate with the ship."

"Do you think it's possible she was mistaken in what she saw?"

Evelyn shrugged. "I'm not sure, but lights in the predawn hours are fairly unmistakable. I'll tell my grandfather. He might know something of it."

Hoofbeats interrupted their conversation, and they both turned toward the main road.

A man in a black coat on a gray horse approached.

Mr. Twethewey's posture relaxed. "I know that horse." A smile spread across his face.

She lifted her hand to shield her eyes from the sun. As the rider drew closer, the resemblance to Mr. Twethewey was uncanny — hair so dark it was almost black. Vibrant blue eyes. Dimples in his cheeks when he smiled.

Mr. Twethewey jogged toward the horseman, the wind lifting his curly hair.

The visitor slid from his horse.

"Johnny, what are you doing here?" Mr. Twethewey clasped the newcomer's shoulder and shook it good-naturedly as he stepped closer.

"Uncle Jac got your letter. He said we couldn't let you face wrecks and excise men alone, now could we?"

Mr. Twethewey laughed and nudged the man with his elbow, and then, as if remembering her presence, he turned. "Miss Bray, may I present my brother, John Twethewey."

The man, a ganglier version of Mr. Twethewey, whom she guessed to be a few years younger, with ruddy cheeks and an easy smile, tipped his head in a quick bow.

"This is Miss Bray, the steward's granddaughter."

Laughter danced in his eyes. "Miss Bray."

Remembering her manners, she curtsied and brushed her hair from her face. Still stunned at the suddenness of his appearance — and the remarkable likeness — she smiled. "Welcome to Wyndcliff Hall."

230

CHAPTER 21

All eyes were on them.

Evelyn straightened in the pew and cast a glance to her right at Mary, who was seated next to her in her altered yellow gown and gray cloak. The child occupied herself by winding a length of blue ribbon around her small fingers.

Perhaps it had been a mistake to bring her to church, but the alternative had been too grim. To be in a home with a mother who had been unresponsive for three days — and an increasingly uncertain future — was worse.

On Evelyn's left sat Jenna, per their Sunday custom. Grandfather rarely accompanied her to church, but since her mother's departure, Jenna began sitting with Evelyn instead of her own family so she would not have to sit alone. Today was no different.

As the parishioners filtered in, Jenna

leaned close. "You've heard what they are saying, of course."

Her friend's tone suggested that she had some great secret to share, so Evelyn pivoted toward her. "Saying about what? I haven't stepped foot off Wyndcliff's property for days."

"That's just it." Jenna smoothed her hand over the tan wool of her pelisse sleeve. "Oh my dear, the villagers love nothing more than a good bit of gossip."

The sickening sensation that she was the center of conversation flooded her. "And what would that gossip be?"

Before Jenna could respond, the chatter around them stopped. Both women turned to identify the source of the interruption.

Mr. Twethewey entered alongside his brother.

"So that's the brother, then," Jenna whispered. "It's true. They appear nearly identical, don't they?"

"Word does travel fast." Evelyn faced forward once again, cognizant of the stares in her direction.

"Of course it does. He's the single most influential person in town now. Even more so than your grandfather or Jim Bowen."

Evelyn stiffened. She didn't like the reference to her grandfather and his influence.

Even though he was widely revered, the respect that people paid him did not translate to her. She looked around the small, ancient church filled with pews of people — people who knew her grandfather and people she knew by sight and reputation, but she was not exactly close to any of them.

"Your grandfather told my father that Mr. Twethewey is making a great deal of changes, including adding china clay pits to the moors between the village and Wyndcliff Hall. Father says Mr. Bray is none too pleased."

Evelyn was not surprised that everyone else, including Jenna, seemed to know more about her grandfather's opinions than she did. Marnie had been the one to inform her of the china clay pits, not her grandfather. He always said village business was far too indelicate for her.

Not wanting to appear uninformed, Evelyn whispered back, "Everyone has known that the clay pit would eventually come."

"Aye, but I've heard that Mr. Simms, who owns not one but two tin mines, is already campaigning against him, because he believes Mr. Twethewey will poach the mine workers. He says it is degrading to ask skilled mine workers to abandon their trade for naught but china clay. And then there is the matter with the shipwrecked woman."

Evelyn wrinkled her face. "Mrs. Williams? What could possibly be wrong with that? She's injured and requires assistance."

"It isn't proper!" Jenna's eyes popped wide. "You know that. She should be staying in the inn and not alone in his house."

Evelyn sighed. "Do you really think if anything improper was going on that I — or my grandfather, for that matter — would stand for it? What wouldn't be proper is if he left her and the child on the beach with no one to care for her."

"There's another thing." Jenna's voice lowered. Her brows drew together and she leaned closer. "As your friend, I'm concerned. Multiple people saw you walking alone with him on the beach. I only mention it to protect you and caution you."

Evelyn resisted the urge to roll her eyes. "Who saw us? Besides, we were not alone. Mary was with us."

"Oh, Evelyn." Jenna clicked her tongue. "I do hope you know what you're doing."

Evelyn gave a little laugh. "This is all nonsense. I care for the child and help the housekeeper with the injured mother. There is nothing improper about that, and I would challenge anyone who would dare say otherwise."

"Don't be angry at me, dearest." Jenna's eyes widened. "I'm not the one saying such things."

"I could never be angry with you, Jenna. It's just —"

Before Evelyn could finish her thought, Jenna's expression shifted and she stiffened as the two men walked up the aisle. Evelyn determined not to join everyone else in staring in their direction, but when the pair stopped to talk to Mary, it was impossible.

Mary's enthusiasm for Mr. Twethewey was evident, and she chattered with him happily.

Then he turned his attention toward her.

Suddenly every word Jenna had said seemed true. All eyes *were* on her, even more so than before he arrived.

She should have given more thought to appearances. Of course it looked suspicious for them to walk along the beach, even with Mary present. Of course people would question her coming and going so freely to Wyndcliff now that the master was here. And now he was focused on her.

Heat climbed her neck. Her cheeks. Her temples.

"Good morning, Miss Bray." His smile was easy, his manner casual.

She had no choice but to speak with him.

She swallowed her nervousness. "Good morning, Mr. Twethewey."

"Had I known you two were attending church today, we would have called the carriage. Did you walk all this way?"

She felt the weight of Jenna's attention on their conversation, not to mention the attentions of those in the pews behind them. She put her arm around the child. "Thank you, but we had a lovely walk, didn't we, Mary?"

She nodded eagerly in response and swung her legs beneath the pew.

Mr. Twethewey, seemingly unaware of the attention he was generating, leaned closer. "Could you point me in the direction of the Wyndcliff pew?"

She straightened. "It is the first one on the left."

He bowed, winked at Mary, and then the brothers continued down the aisle.

She did not need to look at Jenna to feel the criticism in her gaze.

Jenna's voice was now barely above a whisper. "They say he's working with the excise men, you know."

Evelyn cast a glance at a cluster of women across the aisle staring at her. "It's his land. He may work with whom he chooses."

"Oh my dear." Jenna shook her head.

"You'd best keep your senses about you. Keeping your good reputation is all about appearances, and you are in a dangerous position."

Evelyn gripped Mary's hand tighter as they made their way through the grassy moorland, careful to avoid the puddles that still remained from the rain earlier in the week.

The walk home from the village to Wyndcliff Hall took longer than normal, but Evelyn did not mind. She and Mary paused here and there to gather bits of heather and other moorland plants, and now Mary's arms were full of cotton grass and long grasses. Clearly, wherever Mary was from didn't have moorland. The new plants, although faded with autumn's dullness, fascinated the child.

After Jenna's warnings and the parishioners' questioning glances she'd borne all through the service, Evelyn was grateful for the solitude and freedom found here. The moors had always been a peaceful place for her, despite their tendency for strong winds. She found serenity in the bleak, barren landscape, and to see it all for the first time through the eyes of a child was just what she had needed.

But as they approached the iron gate surrounding the Wyndcliff grounds, Kitty ran out to meet them, her face pale, her eyes wide.

Alarmed at Kitty's expression, Evelyn slowed her steps. "What is it?"

Kitty stopped, glanced at Mary, then approached Evelyn, gripped her arm with tense fingers, and whispered in her ear, "She's awake!"

The simple words, hushed though they were, jarred Evelyn. "Stay with Mary." Not waiting for a response, she lifted her skirts and ran across the courtyard and through the kitchen entrance.

Panicked voices and a sharp cry met Evelyn's ears.

Legs shaking, heart racing, hands trembling, Evelyn raced up the narrow staircase, clipping the corner in her haste. Once on the landing she ran down the hall and swung into the chamber.

Elizabeth Williams sat upright against pillows, trying to push the blankets away. Marnie stood next to the bed, attempting to make the woman stay put.

Elizabeth's eyes were wide. "Where's my daughter? Where is she?"

Evelyn rushed forward. "Mary is here. She's fine. Elizabeth, she's fine."

"Who are you? How do you know my

name?" She attempted to get out of bed, but then grabbed her head as if suddenly accosted by pain. "Who are you? What has happened?"

Evelyn nudged Marnie aside and placed her hands on Elizabeth's shoulders to prevent her from getting up. "My name's Evelyn Bray, and you were in a shipwreck. But you are safe now, and so is Mary. Please, stay abed."

Elizabeth finally met her gaze. Her breathing slowed a bit and she stilled. As if just realizing she had a bandage on her head, she lifted her hand and touched it with her fingertips.

"You've had a blow to your head," Evelyn said.

"My other eye." Elizabeth's voice trembled. "I can't see well. Everything is . . . is . . ."

"Shh. You must stay calm. I'll explain everything." Evelyn looked toward Marnie. "Send Thomas for the apothecary right away. And Grandfather. And Mr. Twethewey."

Wildness flared in the woman's dark eyes. "Who *are* you?"

Evelyn stiffened. She had just answered the question. "I'm Evelyn Bray."

"And where are we?"

"You are at Wyndcliff Hall in South Cornwall," she repeated more slowly. "You were in a shipwreck. You and your daughter were rescued and brought here."

Fresh panic flared. "My daughter! My Mary, is she —"

They had just spoken of her daughter. Did she not remember? "Mary's safe. She's safe. She's here. You've been sleeping for a few days, but I'm glad you are awake."

"I didn't mean to do it. I didn't want to do it. He . . . He . . ." Her hysterical words stopped. She grimaced and put her hands to her head once more.

Evelyn tensed. What was taking everyone so long to arrive?

She'd never seen anything like this woman's erratic behavior. Not knowing what else to do, she crawled onto the bed and wrapped her arm around the woman's shoulders. Her entire body trembled, but eventually she relaxed and leaned against Evelyn's shoulder.

Mr. Twethewey rushed in, his face red, his hair windblown. He stared, as if not knowing what to say.

Elizabeth looked back to Evelyn. A tear escaped her eye. "But where's Simpson?"

Dread seized her. Had there been another child?

Evelyn swallowed hard. "There now, you've had quite an ordeal."

Footsteps pounded on the corridor outside the hall, and Mary, appearing very tiny and pale, peered into the room.

"Mama!" she cried, running to the bed.

Mr. Twethewey caught her and swept her up. "Let's not jump on the bed. Here, I'll help you." He lifted her and placed her next to her mother.

Mary sobbed against her mother, and Elizabeth embraced her child.

At the reunion, tears of happiness pooled in Evelyn's eyes. The emotion of the past few days, combined with her growing affection for Mary, welled within her. Not wishing to intrude, she stepped away from the bed and stood next to Mr. Twethewey in silence.

What relief Mary must feel to see her mother again, alive and awake.

Sudden and intense longing for her own mother tugged. How would Evelyn feel if she were able to suddenly see Mother? To embrace her and speak with her? Dorothea Drake had not been in an accident but instead chose a life away from her. This mother and daughter now clung to each other as if their very lives depended on the presence of the other.

It was as heartbreaking as it was beautiful, and try as she might, Evelyn could not quell the sadness — and loneliness — overwhelming her.

CHAPTER 22

The afternoon after Mrs. Williams's waking passed in bursts of sudden energy and slow periods of waiting. With the uncomfortable conversations at church all but forgotten, Evelyn threw herself into the tasks associated with helping Mary and Mrs. Williams, including bringing a tray of broth and tea up to the sickroom and keeping Mary busy while the surgeon assessed her mother.

And yet through all of these activities, uncertainty reigned.

After Mrs. Williams's initial awakening, she quickly fell back asleep, as if the events had been too much for her. Evelyn spent the long afternoon hours calming and soothing Mary, whose excitement at her mother's recovery had stirred her to a near frenzy.

Time would solve everything, or at least as much as it could. And yet impatience flared through her. Evelyn wanted all the answers. She wanted all of the pieces of the puzzle so she could arrange them into something that made sense.

And she was not the only one.

The excise men were notified and paid a call. Her grandfather had been pacing all day. Mr. Twethewey looked unnerved.

What was the name of the ship? What was their destination? Even one bit of information would be enough for them to set things into motion to help identify the owner of the cargo and get the Williamses to their rightful place.

But now patience was key.

The afternoon sun began its descent into evening, and after fetching a fresh tray of tea and broth from Marnie in the kitchen, Evelyn returned to the Blue Room to find Mary curled up at her mother's side, fast asleep. Elizabeth was awake, sitting upright and smoothing the child's long dark locks.

Evelyn tapped her knuckles softly on the door, and when Elizabeth noticed her, Evelyn stepped to the side of the bed.

"I'm glad to see you awake," Evelyn said softly, to avoid waking Mary. "How do you feel?"

She touched her bandage. "My head aches."

"I don't doubt it." Evelyn set the tray on

the table alongside the bed, next to the afternoon tray, the toasted bread from earlier appearing untouched. "Were you able to eat at all?"

Elizabeth stared down at her hands. "I ate one piece and drank some tea."

"You must try to eat. At least some bone broth. You've been asleep for three days. It will help you regain your strength."

Elizabeth leaned her head back against the wall and closed her eyes. "Three days. How is it possible I don't remember any of it? Everything is so foggy. I can't even recall your name."

"My name is Evelyn." She sat next to her on the bed and squeezed her hand. "Ask me as many times as you need. I don't mind. The surgeon said that this type of confusion is not unusual after a head injury. But you must stay calm and give yourself a little time to recover."

"At least my Mary is well. That's all that matters to me."

Footsteps sounded in the corridor, and Mr. Twethewey, her grandfather, and Captain Hollingswood appeared.

The captain spoke first. "We are sorry to disturb you, Mrs. Williams, but if you are able to answer a few questions for us, it would help us organize the details of what has happened."

Concern tightened Mrs. Williams's already taut features, but she nodded, smoothing a piece of hair from her face.

Evelyn stood next to the bed, hoping to offer support. It was an intimidating experience for Mrs. Williams, no doubt, to have three strange men in her bedchamber.

"Good." Forced lightness sharpened the captain's tone. "Do you know your destination?"

"London," she said quickly, but then her brows arched in confusion, and she nodded. "I think. London."

The captain rubbed his hands together, as if unearthing a great secret. "Do you recall the name of the vessel, by chance? Or perhaps the name of the captain?"

Mrs. Williams's trembling hand began to fuss with the blanket's edge. "I should be able to remember it, shouldn't I?" She looked to Evelyn, as if she knew the answer.

Mr. Twethewey stepped forward. "We've no wish to distress you, madam. Perhaps you can remember something different. Do you know where your husband or family are?"

Perspiration glistened on Mrs. Williams's brow, and the color seemed to drain from her cheeks. "I-I — My husband's dead," she began, almost as if asking a question rather than stating a fact. "Yes. He died in India. He was a sea captain. Mary and I are returning from India." She looked up, proud to have remembered the detail but also exhausted, as if the recollection of such a detail had drained every bit of her mental faculties.

"That's a good start." Evelyn smiled encouragingly.

"Indeed it is," Captain Hollingswood added. "If you were traveling from India, then it's likely the ship name will be on one of the trade logs, and it will give us a chance to learn a little more. Is there anything else you can recall? Anything at all?"

"I just can't remember."

Evelyn gripped her hand. "Earlier you mentioned someone named Simpson."

"Did I?" She frowned.

Evelyn nodded. "Does that name mean something to you?"

Mrs. Williams shook her head. Evelyn's shoulders relaxed. At least there was not another child unaccounted for.

"The surgeon said it is not uncommon to have a memory lapse after an injury of this nature." Mr. Twethewey's voice was kind. "Give yourself time."

"But what if I don't remember?" Her

question hung in the air.

"You will." Evelyn squeezed her hand again, hoping to calm her spirits.

Liam led the way down from the Blue Room, followed closely by Rupert Bray and the surgeon. After seeing Captain Hollingswood to the courtyard, the three remaining men crossed the great hall to his study, and Liam considered his current state.

It had been less than a week since he arrived at Wyndcliff.

A week.

In that time he'd been challenged in ways he never anticipated or even fathomed. Now the difficulty of assembling pieces of a puzzle lay before him, and he had no idea what the completed item was to be like.

"She can't remember anything." Annoyance colored Bray's voice. "Not a single thing."

"As I've said before, it's not uncommon." Dr. Smith adjusted his spectacles on his wide nose. "Sometimes an injured person will remember things that happened immediately prior to the accident. Sometimes they can only recall events from the very distant past. And then sometimes they cannot recall anything that happened before the accident. In all of my experiences, memory is usually restored. It just takes time. And patience."

"Time," Bray huffed. "That is good and well, but it does not help us in the least with the matter of this cargo."

Liam pushed open the study door and stepped inside, the room already growing dark with the setting sun outside the window. "We'll allow her a bit of time then, as you suggest. Surely everything will right itself soon."

Bray stepped to the dying fire and poked it back to life with growing fervor. "Maybe. Or until the excise men grow restless. Someone will have to account for the wreck and the cargo. This is all very suspect. Very suspect indeed."

"Suspect?" Liam uncorked the brandy on the small side table under the window, poured two glasses, and extended them to his guests. "I think it's best we permit the excise men to handle this."

"Bah." Bray snorted, smoothing his already-smooth cravat as he swirled the burgundy liquid in the short glass. "If you want this issue resolved, and resolved quickly, we'd best see to it ourselves. I suggest both mother and child be taken to Plymouth for recovery. The sooner the better."

"Plymouth?" Liam corked the brandy. "Why Plymouth?"

Bray ignored his question. "She'll be well enough to travel in a day or two, right, Dr. Smith? The excise office there can make connections. They are not your responsibility, Mr. Twethewey. Focus on your clay pits. That's what you want, isn't it? That will keep your hands full."

Heat rose beneath Liam's collar. Aye, the pits were important, but this was a woman and a child. He kept his voice low. "Of course Mrs. Williams is free to depart whenever she likes, but she's also welcome to remain here as long as she has need. I'll turn no one out of my house."

"Bah." Redness flushed Bray's face. "Such sentiment will march you straight down the path to problems. Mark my words, you're inviting all sorts of trouble for yourself."

Liam pressed his lips in a firm line and eyed the older man, with his bright crimson cravat and tidily combed white hair.

What made Bray fight him at every turn? Was it a battle for dominance? Was it the need for control?

It mattered not that their objective seemed to be the same — to protect the beach and those in the village — they always ended up on opposite ends of an issue.

Even now, as Bray's eyes locked firmly on Liam, his refusal to look away or even blink issued a challenge. "I know you want to be benevolent, but you've only just arrived. You know nothing of these people, this way of life. Whoever Elizabeth Williams is, she knows who has claim to that cargo — or at least she'll remember eventually. The locals want to keep it for themselves. If you get involved, you'll be the villain. You've made it clear that you intend to leave your mark on Pevlyn with the clay pits. That is all well and good, but if you want to be successful, you need to get the people on your side — who do you think will work in your pits? Don't create a situation you aren't prepared to deal with."

Bray grabbed his hat and was out the door before Liam could formulate a response.

Liam and Dr. Smith stood in silence for several moments until the echo of Bray's boots clipping the flagstone floor faded, and all that was left was the mantel clock's steady ticking.

At length the surgeon adjusted the satchel over his shoulder and tugged at the collar on his coat. "He's not entirely wrong."

Liam snapped his head up.

"There are more physicians in Plymouth," Smith continued, his voice soft and low in comparison to Bray's. "Physicians who have more varied experiences than I."

"But the child. Surely Plymouth is no place for her."

"She is not the first child to endure such a tragedy." Smith raised his sparse brows. "With proper sustenance, Mrs. Williams will be strong enough for a carriage ride to Plymouth within the week. I'd give a thought to Bray's words if I were you."

Liam stood at the window and watched Bray stomping across the courtyard. He suspected there was wisdom to what the men were saying, but something tugged within him.

To his knowledge, neither Bray nor Smith knew of Mary's account of the lights on Brayden's Crag. Perhaps it was an innocent mistake. Perhaps there was something more. But the tale still did not sit well with him.

The conversation turned from the feminine patient to the opening of the Aulder Hill pits, but even as the topic shifted, his uneasiness remained. Perhaps trouble was afoot at Wyndcliff. Perhaps not. But he needed to make sure he chose his allies carefully.

CHAPTER 23

Mixed emotions churned within Evelyn as she traversed the path from Wyndcliff Hall to the cottage. Elation. Sadness. Fear.

Challenges had met her at the day's every turn: Jenna's words had made her question her actions. Mrs. Williams had awoken, testing Evelyn's emotional strength. Mary was confused, and yet a spark Evelyn had not seen before brightened the child's dark eyes.

Evelyn recalled being young and looking at her mother in such a way, once upon a time, and harboring the deep-rooted belief that Mother could do no wrong.

She let her hair down and shook it out as she walked across the lane, running her fingers through her curls. She needed rest and quiet to sort her thoughts. A chill raced through her as gusts swept up from the sea, swirling the crunchy leaves at her feet, and the shifting clouds allowed only fleeting slivers of moonlight.

"Evelyn."

She jumped, her nerves on edge from the day's events. She jerked her head upward. "Oh, Jim. I did not see you there."

But he was not smiling — not in the way he normally was whenever he called on her grandfather. Instead, his head tilted to the side. His hair whipped about his unshaven face. "It's Sunday. I waited for you. There by the village."

Her hands flew to her mouth. "Oh, Jim, I am sorry. When we arrived home from church, Mary's mother had awoken, and I am afraid it's quite occupied my mind ever since. I completely forgot about our walk."

She expected the tension in his face to relax with her explanation. After all, it was important work and surely any person would accept her excuse.

Instead, his countenance darkened. "I suppose talking with William Twethewey has been occupying your mind as well."

Evelyn clutched her shawl tightly around her shoulders and narrowed her gaze to assess the evident flush on his face and the sloppy expression in his normally sharp eyes. "You've been drinking."

"I own a public house." He swung his arm out in a dramatic, sarcastic display. "Of course I've been drinking."

Anger began to bubble within her. She was tired. Worn. And in no humor for such behavior. Without another word she moved to walk past him.

But he reached out his gloved hand and blocked her path.

She drew a sharp breath, determined to keep control of her temper. "Please let me pass."

"You promised me a walk today."

His uncharacteristic insolence was almost frightening. This was not the Jim she knew. "I've changed my mind."

He threw his head back in laughter, loud and obnoxious.

By doing so was he trying to make her feel small? Foolish?

When his laughter subsided, the dark glint returned to his expression. "And why is that, may I ask? Is it because you've got your sights set on someone a bit higher and mightier?"

She refused to look away, although she might as well have been gazing into the eyes of a stranger. "I'll not have a conversation with you when you are in this state."

He laughed, the same deep baritone. Yet with every passing second the sinister tones hidden within his chuckle rang more sharply, pricking her nerves and raising her concerns. "Now, that's not very neighborly of you. Or maybe your idea of neighborly interactions has changed now that a rich man is at your doorstep."

"How dare you! 'Tis none of your business whom I speak with, and it's certainly not your place to comment on it."

His laughter faded, as did his smile, but his condescension thickened. "You poor, trusting child. You know what they say about him, don't you?"

Her stomach clenched. She didn't like being treated or thought of as anything less than a woman who knew her own mind, yet as much as she tried to force confidence to her voice, it came out light and thin. "I don't really care what is being said about him, or about anyone, for that matter."

"Well, do you know?"

She sniffed, crossing her arms over her chest.

"He's met with the excise men."

"Of course I know that. I saw them here myself."

"But do you know that he's turning his back on the people who serve his hand? Oh aye, that is true, my pet. As true as the blind adoration you have for him. He will single-handedly bring ruin to those who you at one time cared about. One. By. One. He will dissolve the income so many depend upon, even that of your precious grandfather."

She could not resist the bait in his words. "Income? What do you mean?"

He did not respond.

"You don't know what you're speaking of." She attempted to pass again.

He stepped closer. "Don't I? It concerns me that you think *you* know what you're talking about. Just wait, this will all come to fruition and you will see that old Jim is right, and you'll be begging to make an apology and be back. You'll be changing your mind about wanting to be by my side, but maybe I won't want to be seen with a woman who can so easily turn her back on her own people."

Shock at his bold statement momentarily robbed her of speech, and then at the sound of footsteps behind her, she turned to see her grandfather lumbering up the path.

Relief rushed through her.

Grandfather would not stand for this treatment, and he certainly would not allow Jim to block her path.

"And what are you two young people speaking of?" Grandfather approached, boasting his customary smile that had been all too infrequent of late.

"I was just going inside," Evelyn said flatly, glaring at Jim.

But Jim's words cut her off. "Your granddaughter promised to meet me for a walk today, but she did not come. I was asking her why."

"Oh, surely she had a reason." Grandfather's white hair fluttered in the night's breeze, his expression lighter than she'd seen it in days. "It's been a busy day at Wyndcliff, to the chagrin of us all. But then, you wouldn't just ignore Jim, would you, lamb? But now the day is done, and there's no time like the present for a chat. Come on in, Jim. Visit for a while."

She looked disbelievingly at her grandfather. Surely he could see what state Jim was in or, at the very least, smell it. "Thank you, nay." She pinned a hard gaze on Jim. "My head aches."

Without waiting for a response from either of them and with her face flaming with frustration, she entered the cottage kitchen. It was dark. Unusual for this time of night, and Bertie was nowhere to be seen. Evelyn's interaction with Jim had robbed her of every bit of patience, and she snatched the flint to light her own candle.

Oh, was it only a week ago that life had made sense?

It had been simple. Quiet. Perhaps dull. Her only focus was waiting for the day when her mother would send for her.

But now everything was different. Everyone was behaving abnormally.

Something was not right in the fabric of their little village — something that went beyond Mr. Twethewey's arrival, but she could not place her finger on it.

How she wanted to be free of it. Perhaps she should just pack her things and travel to Plymouth on her own, uninvited. Regardless of what her mother's current situation was, she would not turn her away.

Would she?

But Evelyn was not even certain her mother was in Plymouth at the moment, and then there was the matter of Mary and Elizabeth. They needed her.

She turned to climb the kitchen stairs to her attic chamber when the voices outside caught her attention. She stood still to listen.

"That granddaughter of yours. If I didn't know better, I'd say she was getting too involved in the happenings inside that house."

Her grandfather's voice was low. Rough. "I don't like that Twethewey man either, nor that brother of his, but it's harmless. She's just caring for the child and the mother."

"He's an opportunist. I'd wager my last penny on it."

"He'll tire of it all very soon, especially when he realizes how little control he'll have. Besides, he'll become distracted by his little clay pit project soon enough, and he'll have his hands too full with the angry mine owners to worry about anything else."

"And if he doesn't?"

"He will. I'll take care of that. And sober up. Don't get careless. We need our senses about us."

"We?" Jim's voice held a challenge. "Don't make this about us. It's about me, and what I control. I told you once before what was at stake, and I expect you to hold up your end of the bargain. Need I remind you of the terms?"

Evelyn's chest squeezed at the threat in Jim's tone. She waited for her grandfather's response.

At last it came. "Nay. No need."

"You might think you can control all of this, but we both know the truth. And I will not hesitate to —"

"Listen, I understand what you're saying," Grandfather interrupted. "I do."

"If you want things to continue as they are, you'd best make sure Evelyn sees things our way."

She lowered her candle. What an odd conversation. She'd always thought of her grandfather as the man in charge of the relationships with the villagers — the Bowens included. But now it seemed that Jim was dictating the terms. And what was it he was expecting of her?

She thought she heard footsteps coming her way so she quickly turned to leave the kitchen. As she did, she noticed that the door to the small pantry was open. She froze for a moment, then, as the men's footsteps retreated, she moved to close the door. But her candle's light reflected off something just inside the door.

Curious, she pushed it open farther. Inside were several casks — tall wooden containers, like the ones she had seen in the White Eagle Inn. Ropes were tied around them, and the entire lot was wet.

She'd seen enough wrecks to know what the casks contained. Ale. Or wine. Or something of the sort.

She lifted her candle to assess them more carefully. Writing of some sort was printed on them, but none that she could read. It appeared to be in a foreign language.

She shook her head. It was not unusual for casks to be retrieved at shipwrecks. But what were they doing here and not in the storage cellar?

Her grandfather often stored items from a wreck on Wyndcliff property. But in the pantry?

Tall tales were always racing up and down the coast about the art of free trading. The rights of the free traders. But Grandfather had been vehemently opposed to all such activity. He was known for his law-abiding ways. Even though he was often at odds with the excise men, he'd never go behind the law.

Would he?

CHAPTER 24

"What news from Penwythe?" Liam asked Johnny over breakfast the next morning. "Tell me of anything other than wrecks and excise men."

John laughed and rested his elbow on the table. "Oh, you know. Nothing much changes. Apple orchards for miles. Uncle Jac has his hands full with the fall harvest, and from what the women say, they expect Aunt Delia to give birth sometime next month. Julia's happily married to the Blake fellow, and it's all that Hannah and Sophy can speak of."

"Well, I'm glad you're here. It almost seems like we're at home again."

"Home? I'm surprised to be the one to point it out, but this is your home now."

Liam wiped his mouth and nodded.

"Are you not happy about it?" John prodded, taking a bite of ham.

"Of course I'm pleased with it. It's been

my plan my entire life. It's just not exactly what I expected."

"And what of life goes as it is expected?" John smirked. "Think of the people we know. For who among them has life gone as they had planned? And yet for most of them, it all worked out well enough in the end."

Liam considered his brother's words as he took a sip of his coffee. "I suppose you're right."

"Of course I am. I may be but eighteen years of age, but I received more than my fair share of the brains in the family."

It was Liam's turn to smirk. "Don't get ahead of yourself, little brother."

"But in all earnestness, all change takes time to get used to. So it's not exactly like you'd hoped it would be. You must make it like you want it to be. This shipwreck business is dastardly, but it will pass. I think it will, anyway. Focus on china clay. I'll help you."

"It's hard to think of that when we have a mother and child here, and we're no closer to finding out who they are or where they come from. But I did receive a letter from Mr. Porter. He will be coming back in a few days with men to start the hiring process."

"Well, that's a step. I'm sure you'll figure

it out. In the meantime, there are a lot of other things to think on."

"Such as?"

John laughed. "If I have to tell you, brother, then . . ." His voice faded away. "Miss Bray, of course."

Liam ran his fingers through his hair. He had hoped he'd been doing a decent job at hiding his interest in the young woman, but he should have known that John, who was not only his brother but his best friend, would pick up on it. "What about her?"

John threw back his head. "The two of you can barely look away from each other when you are in the same room."

"Nay."

"Aye. Like I said, I'm more perceptive than you give me credit for."

Liam shook his head to dismiss the thought.

But John had said that Miss Bray couldn't look away from him.

Was it true?

Even if it were, it would come to no end. She'd leave for Plymouth. He'd soon be busy with mining for china clay and the sort. But to think that a woman as lovely as Miss Bray would not be able to look away from him was . . . flattering.

A commotion erupted on the drive.

He groaned again. Never would he have guessed he would have so many visitors. Who could it be this time? The excise men? The surgeon?

Liam stood and left the table to intercept whoever it was. "I'll be right back."

He made his way through the corridor, and he could not have been more shocked to see Miss Lydia Traver and her mother just inside the great hall. "Mrs. Traver, Miss Traver." He plastered a smile on his face and bowed in greeting. "This is a pleasure."

"I do hope we've not called too early." Mrs. Traver bustled farther into the hall, not waiting for an invitation.

"No, no." He stepped back to allow her room to pass. "My brother and I were at breakfast."

"Indeed, I had heard your brother had arrived." She looked up, assessing the adornments on the wall. "News travels so fast in this area, does it not?"

He nodded. "That it does."

"But one can never tell rumors from facts, especially in these circles. It's always best to see to matters firsthand. Surely you agree."

He nodded, uncomfortable under the women's intense attention. He cleared his throat and remembered his manners. "Can

I offer you some refreshment? Or coffee at least?"

"No, I thank you. We don't wish to intrude on your morning activities, but we also heard that the woman you rescued has awoken. We needed to come and speak to you ourselves to help put our minds at ease. Poor woman."

"You heard correctly."

"And how does she fare?"

"She grows stronger by the hour."

"Oh, I am so glad," Miss Traver chimed in, speaking at last. "Mother and I were talking, and we have no doubt that you are the most accommodating host, but we wanted to show our support for the poor woman. If she washed ashore, she likely has none of the things a lady would require. So we have assembled a parcel." She extended a bundle wrapped in cloth. "A gown and other necessities."

"That is very kind." He took the outstretched bundle from her.

Miss Traver's eyes widened and she shook her head, sending the carefully curled locks on either side of her face bouncing wildly. "Oh, it is the very least we could do. My heart aches for both her and the child. Is it true they will be staying with you?"

"My home, such as it is, is open to anyone

who has need of it. Right now there are many unanswered questions, and they are welcome here as long as they require assistance."

"Oh, that is very noble indeed." Mrs. Traver touched her hand to her heart. "Such an undertaking for a bachelor. But then, I hear you are from a large family."

"Word does travel." He chuckled to hide his growing discomfort. "My younger brother, John, has joined me here to help with the china clay pits, and he is waiting for me in the breakfast room." Hoping to send a message that he was ready to return to his breakfast, he shifted the conversation. "But I do thank you for bringing these items. I'll see that they get to Miss Bray."

Mrs. Traver gripped her hands in front of her. "Uh, Miss Bray?"

Liam did not miss the hint of disapproval coloring Mrs. Traver's tone. "Yes. She's taken charge of our guests."

The women exchanged glances. Practiced glances — glances that begged for him to ask their opinion on the matter.

Liam raised his brow but said nothing.

Mrs. Traver tilted her head coyly. "The Brays are an interesting family, are they not? Oh, I remember the Brays from before Rupert's situation changed. Dorothea,

Evelyn's mother, used to be one of the favorites in our little society here. But after Mr. Bray's disgrace, everything changed. Gambling is such a bitter vice. In fact, I'm surprised Mrs. Bray sees fit to leave her daughter under his guardianship."

Liam was not comfortable discussing Miss Bray's private past with strangers. "I don't know. The Brays seem quite content to me."

"Oh, Mr. Twethewey. You are a man! Of course you think such things. There are subtleties that you probably miss, not to mention your tenure here has indeed been short. Mr. Bray is a volatile man. He was not always as such, of course. I recall passing afternoons with Dorothea Bray, and Lydia and Evelyn would play. But following her grandfather's misfortune and all that came with it . . ." Mrs. Traver's voice faded, and it was replaced by the sound of a door opening.

Miss Bray stepped into the corridor adjoining the great hall. She stopped abruptly when she noticed Mrs. and Miss Traver, and her brows jumped in recognition. "I am sorry. I did not mean to intrude."

He brightened, genuinely relieved at her presence. "Miss Bray. You are not interrupting. Please, join us. Mrs. and Miss Traver have brought a few things for Mrs. Williams."

Before Miss Bray could respond, Miss Traver spoke up, her voice sickly sweet. "Evelyn Bray. What a pleasure! It has been far too long since I have last seen you."

Her shoulders straightened. Her chin tipped up ever so slightly. Evelyn Bray was transforming right before him from a woman who flitted about the kitchen and the moorland to a lady. Her green eyes took on a sharpness. Despite the apron clinging to her and the looseness of her hair, every inch of her exuded ladylike mannerisms.

Miss Traver stepped toward her. "I am so glad to see you again."

Miss Bray returned a curtsy that rivaled Miss Traver's in its elegance. "Miss Traver. It has been a long time."

"Mother was just telling Mr. Twethewey how you and I used to play together when we were children, before your grandfather became steward here."

"I remember."

"But those days are long gone." Miss Traver lifted her chin. "Now I barely see you at all. It's a shame, really."

Miss Bray's smile seemed tight. "Thank you for sending the parcel. I am sure Mrs. Williams will be very grateful."

He thought the interaction was ending, but then Mrs. Traver inserted herself into the conversation between the two young women. "And how is your mother? La, I've not heard from her in ages."

"She's in Plymouth," Miss Bray responded.

"And pray, why are you not with her? I, for one, could not imagine being parted from my daughter for even a day. I fear the day when a young man makes an offer of marriage and takes her away from me."

Miss Bray's deep breath was tinged with annoyance. "My mother has recently married. I plan to join her in Plymouth very soon."

"Married! Ah, this is news indeed. But then again, we rarely hear from your mother anymore. Who might the fortunate man be, if I may ask?"

"His name is Archibald Drake."

"I am not familiar with the name, but la. Plymouth society is so far removed from us, is it not? I'm sure it is a wonderful match. I always adored your mother, and it saddens me that she no longer graces our small corner of the world."

Miss Bray swallowed. Hard. "I will pass along your well wishes. Please excuse me. I'm needed upstairs." She nodded toward the bundle in Liam's arms. "I can take that, if you like."

He extended it toward her, and she stepped close to take it from him. But she did not make eye contact with him. He'd gotten to know her well enough to read her — she was embarrassed. Ashamed. But why? Liam felt sick to his stomach, as if he had just witnessed a slight. He could not understand it, but something about it made him feel defensive of the steward's grand-daughter. A sadness flashed in her eyes. Sorrow.

Suddenly Miss Traver did not seem quite so lovely, the visit not so friendly.

The Travers, as if satisfied that they had accomplished what they set out to do, bid Liam farewell and left as suddenly as they had arrived.

Still confused at the odd interactions, Liam was eager to speak with Miss Bray alone, but as soon as she could politely excuse herself, she disappeared up the stair-case.

CHAPTER 25

Liam should retire. The hour was late. Dawn would come early. Even so, he paced his bedchamber. Tomorrow was the day — the Aulder Hill pits were to be officially opened. He'd confirmed all the details with Mr. Porter just that afternoon. The workers had been hired. Porter's men had arrived and were billeted at the inn.

A not-so-distant gunshot cracked, shattering the calm and slicing reality.

His heart lurched with the suddenness and then hammered wildly. Had he really just heard gunfire?

Then another shot rang out, followed by another.

Pulse thudding, he ran to the window and looked out to the blackness, searching for any sign of movement, but he saw nothing.

Determined to get to the bottom of the shots, he pulled on his trousers and tucked his nightshirt in as he stepped into the corridor.

Not a single rustling met his ears.

Had no one else heard it?

He bolted to his brother's chamber, flung open the door, crossed the space, and grabbed his sleeping brother's shoulders. "Wake up! Johnny, wake up!"

John groaned and rolled onto his side, his annoyance barely visible in the faint light slanting through his window. "What's the matter?"

"Gunshots. Did you not hear them?" Liam demanded. "How could you not hear them?"

"Slow down." Johnny sat up, shook his head, and pushed his unruly hair from his face. "Are you sure they were gunshots? I don't hear anything."

"Well, I heard them plain as day. I can't believe they —"

As if on cue, another shot echoed, cutting off Liam's words.

Johnny jumped from the bed.

The brothers stared at each other for several seconds. "Surely you heard that?"

Johnny's eyes were wide. "What are you going to do?"

"I'm going to go find the source." Liam's voice grew louder with determination. "And you're coming with me."

"You're mad." Johnny huffed. "I'm not going out there, and neither should you. Think about it! You could get yourself, nay, both of us killed!"

"Consider what Uncle Jac would do if he heard gunshots on his property. We both know he wouldn't rest, and we wouldn't respect him if he did. What if someone was hurt? Someone could be dying. Now, are you coming or not?"

John sighed, then reached for his boots at the foot of the bed.

Within minutes the brothers were dressed and downstairs. After retrieving pistols from the study, they made their way out into the night and onto the mist-shrouded court-yard. Tom, who'd also been roused from slumber by the shots, appeared in the doorway. At first Liam eyed the man skepti-cally. Since he'd arrived at Wyndcliff, Tom had been somewhat of a mystery. He seemed to materialize from thin air, but most of the time he was nowhere to be found.

Liam had no idea what he was up against, but at the moment he needed all the help he could get. And as much as Liam didn't want to admit it, he needed Bray's as-sistance. The man knew everything about the property. He motioned for John and Tom to follow him, and together they crossed the courtyard and the main road to the cottage.

He pounded on the dark cottage door.

No response.

He pounded with his fist again. And waited.

He expected Bray or at least Bertie to answer the door. But nay. After several minutes, a wide-eyed Miss Bray opened it, wrapped in a shawl. "What is it? What is the matter?"

Liam cleared his throat. "I need to speak with your grandfather."

She glanced to Johnny, Tom, then back to Liam, her brows drawn. "He's not here. I checked when I heard your knock. What's happened?"

Dread sliced through Liam. Where was Bray? Perhaps the steward had heard the gunshots and was already investigating. He ignored her questions. "If he returns, will you tell him I am looking for him?"

As she nodded her agreement, she grabbed his arm. "What is it? Is it Mary? Elizabeth?"

Before he could answer, a horse's wild whinny came from the direction of the beach, causing them all to whirl around.

His words rushed out. "Close this door and stay here, all right? Don't leave." He did not wait for her response and turned to Tom. "Captain Hollingswood said my uncle Treton used to send you to fetch them when he suspected trouble."

Tom gave a curt nod. "That's right."

"Do you know how to reach them now?"

" 'Course I do. There's an office over in Blight."

"Go get them. Now. Tell them we need their assistance."

He and Johnny left a confused Miss Bray, and once they were through the trees, he saw it: a single lantern light on the edge of Brayden's Crag — just as Mary had described. He looked eastward and saw lights at periodic intervals. But what did they mean?

He climbed the rock and looked down to the beach from the high vantage point. The moon flitted out from behind the clouds, illuminating a vessel not far from shore with its ghostly gray light. The ship was in distress. Its masts pointed sideward. No warning bell pierced the night air, and yet men crawled around like insects. Two shadowy figures ran across the beach. A whistle sang out.

"What is it?" Johnny's breath heaved from

the climb up the crag.

Liam filled his lungs with the frigid air. As much as he didn't want to admit it, he knew exactly what was happening. This was not the orderly wreck he'd encountered, when lifelines crossed the shores and good intentions trumped all others. Nay, this was quite different. Smuggling. Free trading. Contraband. Why else would this be occurring under the cover of darkness, and with no warning bell?

His options were few. He could pretend he didn't see it, or he could confront it.

If he was going to send a message to command respect, he had to do it now.

He lifted his pistol.

Johnny grabbed his arm. "Stop! What on earth are you doing?"

"I'll not tolerate this, not and be master." Liam wiped away the perspiration gathering on his brow. "Someone needs to take charge, and that's what I'm doing."

"But the excise men will be here soon," reasoned Johnny. "Let them handle it. And consider, we don't know where the gunshots came from."

Liam shook his head. "There's no one around us, and if the men on the beach know someone is here, they'll disperse. They don't want to risk getting caught."

"Are you sure?"

Liam nodded. Without hesitation, he shot his pistol in the air and then shouted loud and clear, "Every man found on this beach will be charged with trespass. Clear this beach now."

The shadowy figures' activity on the beach stopped, and as Liam suspected, they scurried away like rats, disappearing into the crags and around the cliffs. The lanterns went dark, and suddenly everything was eerily still.

"Come on." Liam descended the stony cliff.

"This isn't wise." Johnny followed him as he climbed down the precipice to the beach below. "Leave it for the morrow when there is light. Or at least until Tom returns with the soldiers."

But Liam ignored him. How could he pretend this wasn't happening, especially with the events of a few nights prior?

The ship, such as it was, was already nearly underwater. Bits of broken cargo and ropes and wood littered the beach, and as he drew closer to the scene, he stepped over a large, round pole and his eyes fixed on something before him.

He bent down and picked it up. It was wet, as if it had been immersed in water, and yet the hue of the item was familiar. He shook it out.

A crimson neckcloth.

Only one man wore such a piece.

Liam's blood ran cold.

Liam and Johnny waited for what seemed like hours. And it might have been. But no men returned to the beach. The waves were the only movement, the gulls their only companions. Only when the excise men arrived and had the beach under surveillance did Liam and Johnny climb up the cliffs and make their way back through the copse of trees.

With each step his mission became clearer. Liam would get to the bottom of this activity. He could never be successful with his china clay venture until he dealt with the lawlessness happening right under his nose. Wyndcliff Hall stretched before him. In the blue light of predawn, the scene looked peaceful, but it was a facade. Something dark, something sinister, was working right beneath him.

He was not sure whom to trust. The soldiers, the villagers, all had something to gain — some more than others.

And yet he could not ignore the signs.

Evelyn paced in the manor house kitchen

and clutched her shawl with renewed apprehension. She dare not step farther into Wyndcliff — not during the midnight hours with no one else present.

Mr. Twethewey had instructed her to stay inside the cottage. But how could she? Grandfather and Bertie were both absent in the predawn hours. Mr. Twethewey and his brother had both been clutching pistols. Tom had gone for the excise men. She'd heard hoofbeats. When she compiled those things with the other odd events of the previous days, such as the cask in her kitchen, it became blindingly clear that something was not right.

After what seemed like hours, the door flew open and both Mr. Twetheweys entered. The scent of the sea clung to them, but it did little to mask the irritation contorting their faces and flushing their cheeks.

"What are you doing here?" Liam Twethewey asked, not looking at her. He placed his pistol on the mantel and extended his palm for his younger brother's. "I thought I told you to stay at the cottage."

She jutted her chin out and straightened to gain as much height as she possibly could. "You don't really think I'd be able to remain inside after being woken in such a manner, do you?"

"You should go back home." He sniffed, smoothing his waistcoat.

"No, I won't." She stepped closer to him. "You must tell me. What's happened? I heard the hoofbeats. I saw the pistols."

Liam exchanged a glance with his brother. "Another wreck in the cove."

She shook her head in disbelief. "But I didn't hear the bell."

"That's because none was sounded," he snipped, his face drawn in irritation. "Apparently this particular wreck was more of a private gathering."

The meaning of his words sank in. "Do you mean —"

"Smuggling." He raked his fingers through his black hair, pinning her with his intense blue stare. "Or free trading. Or whatever you all wish to call it."

She stiffened at the harsh words. "How can you be sure?"

"There was a wreck, and no bell. Either someone found the wreck and decided to help themselves to the cargo, or someone caused the wreck and was gathering their plunder. Either way, something untoward happened right on my property."

"Was anyone hurt?"

Liam shrugged his coat from his shoulders. "Not that we know of. The excise officers are at the beach and will start their investigation when daylight breaks. We're on our way back there, but I'm looking for your grandfather. Have you seen him?" He hung up his coat.

The words shocked her. She'd just assumed her grandfather knew of it. He always knew about wrecks. "He wasn't there?"

Mr. Twethewey did not answer. Instead, he reached into the pocket of his hanging coat and retrieved a piece of cloth.

"What's that?"

He lifted it and shook it out.

Her blood froze within her. She recognized her grandfather's cravat immediately. She took it from him. "I don't understand."

He sighed, doing little to hide his annoyance. "This was at the site."

She narrowed her gaze, her own frustration mounting. "You are suggesting that Grandfather had something to do with this?"

"I'm not suggesting anything. I am only saying that this was there, in the midst of, well, whatever that was."

Alarm flared within her.

Surely not.

She shook her head. "That doesn't mean anything. Grandfather's always on the beach for one reason or another. He's the steward. He's your wrecking agent, for heaven's sake, and as such he knows every inch of this property."

Mr. Twethewey's shrug was offensively dismissive. "It seems a great many people have much to gain by these wrecks, and I am merely attempting to understand what is happening on my land."

"But you aren't suggesting. You're accusing." She stretched out the soaked neckcloth. His fingertips brushed hers as he took it back, wadded it up, and held it in his palm.

She looked up to John Twethewey leaning against the wall, studying the toes of his boots.

Fire flamed within her and her nostrils flared. "My grandfather has been a godsend to these people who had no leadership since Mr. Treton died. You are mistaken in your assumption of him."

"I sincerely hope that I am."

They stared at each other for several moments, and in that short span of time, she questioned what she ever could have found kind or good or attractive in the man before her.

He lifted his head. "And the men he associates with? Are you willing to vouch for their characters as well?"

"If you're referring to Jeremiah Shaw or Charlie Potts or Jim Bow —"

"Aye," he snapped when she mentioned Jim's name, silencing her.

She narrowed her gaze. "You assume that because Jim is an innkeeper and owns no land he must somehow be associated with this?"

She huffed.

Oh yes. She'd been sadly mistaken when she thought she saw kindness or fairness in Liam Twethewey. She must have been blinded by what she had hoped he would be, but now as he began to display his true colors, his real personality was becoming clear.

At length he sighed. His posture slackened. "Listen to me. Miss Bray, I —"

"You think you're better than Jim?" They stared at each other, and she recalled her last conversation with Jim. She had no idea why she was defending him, but she had to win the battle.

"I'm better than no one, but I do not trust people I don't know."

"Then I shudder to think what you must think of me." She turned to go.

"Evelyn, wait."

She stilled at the sound of her given name.

She'd almost forgotten John Twethewey was even there until he cleared his throat. "I think I will go back to the cottage, as I've been instructed."

CHAPTER 26

Strong, icy gusts blasted inland from the sea, which quite seemed to fit Liam's mood as they returned from Wyndcliff Hall to the beach. The hours had done little to soften his anger at finding smugglers on his beach, and the fact that he was no closer to identifying the perpetrators frustrated him further.

As they traversed the path through the copse of trees, Johnny matched Liam's quick pace step for step. "I don't mean to question you because, after all, you are the master of the estate."

Liam huffed at the sarcasm in his brother's tone, not breaking his stride.

"Do you really think it was wise to call out a warning to those men?" Johnny persisted. "One of them could have shot you as easily as they could have run you through with a sword."

"This is my land," Liam blurted out as

the wind tugged at his hair, his coat, his neckcloth. "I'll not stand by while vagabonds have their way with it. This is what I have been preparing for my entire life, Johnny. Either I take a stand now or risk losing it."

John scoffed. "Well, just make sure your life doesn't get cut short because you're trying to play a role you *think* you should play."

Liam chose not to respond.

John was right. It had been a foolish action. He had no idea why he'd acted so brashly. Perhaps the cover of darkness lent overconfidence. Or perhaps the knowledge that the soldiers would soon be on their way bolstered his resolve. Or perhaps he was simply growing weary of all of this — the shipwrecks, the uncertainty, the corruption, the mistrust.

Liam muttered as he stomped his way up the cliff that would lead to the shoreline. "Of all days for this to happen. Porter, along with the workers, are supposed to arrive in a few hours to open the china clay pits."

"You need to calm down, Liam. I understand you're frustrated, but that doesn't give you leave to take it out on everyone around you."

Liam stiffened. "You're referring to Miss Bray."

"You weren't fair to her. You all but accused her grandfather of being a smuggler."

Fair? John was talking about things being fair? What was not fair was that his land was overrun with illegal activity, and he had no idea how to stop it.

True, he'd seen the hurt flash in her green eyes. And it pained him to see it, but could he really trust that she knew nothing of this? After all, she lived under Bray's roof.

By the time they arrived back at the beach, dawn had fully broken, and vibrant pink and orange hues streaked across the silver-gray sky. White seabirds swooped and dove into the sea, now unusually calm, and a cool autumnal breeze wafted over the beach. All signs of the sinking ship were now gone.

But then Liam spotted the soldiers with their crimson uniforms on the beach. He and John made their way toward the soldiers to assess matters, and once they exchanged greetings, Liam explained the situation to Captain Hollingswood, spreading his hands out as if to paint a picture. "The vessel was over there, and lanterns lined this cliff. They dispersed immediately when I shouted a warning."

"And did your man witness this as well? Bray?" Captain Hollingswood inquired. "We'd be interested in hearing his side of the events."

Liam shook his head. The words were surprisingly difficult to say. "We did not see Bray last night."

The excise men exchanged glances, and Liam pressed his lips together. He knew what they were thinking. It was as obvious as if they had said the accusation aloud.

Captain Hollingswood turned toward him. "I believe you, Twethewey. Believe me, I do. But until we find something more concrete, there are no charges to bring, nothing to be done except to increase patrols on this cove. But even then . . ." His voice faded as he looked out to sea.

After several moments of silence, he continued. "I hope you understand the dire nature of this situation. It's an ugly business, and if you are right, there's no telling where the vessel came from nor what happened to her crew. I do commend you for sending Tom. 'Tis a good step to see we can count on you to handle situations in a similar manner as your uncle. All we can do at the moment is keep our eyes and ears open and hope for the best. Have you any idea who shot the pistol that woke you?"

Liam shook his head. "Nay. But men were swarming all over the beach. It could have been any one of them."

"Well, we'll probably never know who discharged the weapon, but it was lucky for us that they did. Otherwise we would never know about this event. It doesn't appear that anyone has been injured, at least not that we can tell. But we must be diligent. And we must put an end to this once and for all."

By the time the afternoon sun climbed to its highest point in the sky, Liam stood next to Mr. Porter at Aulder Hill.

What were the odds that the sun would shine so brilliantly, the breeze would blow so gently, and the clime would be so temperate on this significant day?

Word that they'd be hiring dozens of men to open and expand the forgotten china clay pits had spread quickly, in spite of the threats that the mining community would resist it. Now men lined up, from the very young to the very old, on the barren, rocky moorland, picks and axes in hand, signing in at the hiring station and gathering for the pit openings.

This was what should be occupying his early days at Wyndcliff Hall, not shipwrecks and gunshots in the night.

He'd met — or at least seen — many of the local men either on Market Day or on the day of the first shipwreck when the whole of Pevlyn descended upon his beach to save the ship. Clearly his handling of the situation had not bothered them too much, for they stood at the ready. There were faces, however, noticeably absent, including Rupert Bray and Jim Bowen. Charlie Potts was present. He'd only seen the man in passing, but he'd only ever seen him in the presence of Bowen or Bray.

Liam shook the thoughts away and was about to stand up on the speaking block when a flash of billowing blue fabric caught his eye. On the outskirts of the crowd stood a gathering of women. Miss Bray was there, off to the side, with her arms crossed before her.

He sucked in a deep breath at the sight of her there. Their argument had been a bitter one, and his thoughts on the matter still warred within him. He'd upset her, and yet she'd come out on this most important of days. Why, he was not sure, but something about her presence here infused him with fresh energy and resolve.

Porter approached the speech block first. He straightened his tall black beaver hat and pulled it tight to prevent the wind from disrupting it. He held his hand up in the air, signaling for the crowd's attention and waiting patiently for the chatter to die down.

"Men," he said, his voice deep and confident, "we are here today to begin digging for china clay. It's here at Aulder Hill. Beneath our feet. I've seen and touched the samples myself. This day is a significant one — for you, your families, and the village of Pevlyn. You've been selected for your strength. Your experience. Your enthusiasm. I have with me a dozen men from Staffordshire who have helped me establish several china clay pits and quarries all over Cornwall, and we'll teach you everything you need to know to be successful. After Mr. Twethewey addresses you, you will be divided into sets of six and given instructions, but for now, look here to our east. The grooves here will provide for your future. There is money in this land, and we'll find it."

A healthy, rowdy cheer erupted from the crowd, and Liam smoothed his damp palm over his breeches as he prepared to take Porter's place on the speech block.

Once the cheers died down, Liam stepped onto the block. The crowd watched him. Curiously. Expectantly. He drew a deep breath of the earthy moorland air. This was what he had come here for. To establish this new operation — to make something that could become important, productive, sustainable, and lasting.

He cleared his throat and spoke loudly. "Gentlemen, you stand here as a result of my late uncle's vision. Many of you knew him, and you knew of his enthusiasm for this project and his passion for providing for others. I'm told by Mr. Porter that many of you stood here in similar fashion well over a decade ago, with pick and ax in hand, ready to work, but my uncle's death and the will he left behind prevented further action. I am grateful for the legacy my great-uncle left me, and I intend to honor him to the best of my ability and make this goal of his a reality — one where we are all prosperous and endeavor to provide sustainable income for generations to come. You have put your faith in me. In Mr. Porter. Many of you have left employment elsewhere, and we do not take that for granted. If you have questions or concerns, my door at Wyndcliff Hall is open to you. We will face challenges, but let us face them together."

Mr. Porter handed him a shovel, and Liam stepped to the grooves in the rocky earth. He stabbed the ground with it, then pushed it farther into the earth with the heel of his riding boot.

The crowd cheered.

It was only after the celebration had died down that Liam saw Rupert Bray speaking with a cluster of men. He appeared as he always did, stoic and expressionless, cleanly shaven, with not a single white hair out of place. But one thing was different — his crimson neckcloth was noticeably absent.

Rupert left the men he was talking to and approached Liam.

Liam pivoted. "So you did decide to join us."

Bray drew his brows together. "Aye."

"I was looking for you this morning." Liam crossed his arms over his chest. "Perhaps your granddaughter told you."

His brows twitched at the reference to Evelyn. "I spent the night in town at the inn. I often do to see to estate business. But I'm here, as I told you I'd be."

Liam's brow raised at the mention of the inn. There was no need to drag this out. "There was a wreck last night, or perhaps you already know."

"A wreck?" Bray's head jerked up. "No bell was sounded. Are you sure?"

"John and I had the unfortunate opportunity to see it for ourselves. And to be awoken by accompanying gunshots."

Bray shook his head. "I've told you of the nature of that cove."

"And am I to understand you had no knowledge of it?"

Bray guffawed. His face reddened. "Of course I had no knowledge of it."

"The excise men were out here. They suspect smuggling. And so do I."

"I've made no attempt to deny that there's been a long history of trouble in that cove. A long history. Longer than you've been alive."

Liam narrowed his gaze. "Just so we are clear that my goal is to eradicate any smuggling on my property. And I intend to bring those responsible to justice."

The men locked eyes in a silent battle.

"We are clear," Bray said at last.

But as Bray stepped away, Liam's gaze returned to the blonde lady in the billowing blue dress, chatting with the woman he recognized from church and from Market Day. He'd not even been here two full weeks, but already what was happening was coming clear. Bray had been allowed too much power for far too long, and Liam would have to make that power crumble so he could build his own life. Bray would need to be held accountable for his actions, but where did that leave Miss Bray?

CHAPTER 27

In the week following the opening of the china clay pits at Aulder Hill, the atmosphere of the Wyndcliff estate settled into a quiet routine. Even so, Evelyn did her best to avoid Liam Twethewey.

It was impossible to bypass him completely, especially since she spent her days inside Wyndcliff Hall with Mary, Marnie, and Elizabeth, but she took care not to speak with him alone. Fortunately, business at the china clay pit occupied the landowner's daytime hours, and since Mr. Porter and John were both staying at Wyndcliff Hall for the time being, Mr. Twethewey was rarely alone. Every time she recalled how Mr. Twethewey suggested that her grandfather was involved in illegal activity, a fresh fire flared through her.

But angry as she was, each day brought a new measure of peace with the situation. As emotions cooled and the events quieted, she

297

came to think that perhaps things were not as dire and dramatic as she had first thought. The excise men had not been back to the estate since the overnight wreck, and life settled into a predictable pace.

Even now as she walked with Elizabeth, arm in arm along the sandy beach, she felt at ease and found comfort in the company and invigorating breeze. Mary ran ahead of them, clad in a heavy cloak, shell basket in hand, searching behind the crags and along the shore for treasures.

There was no denying that winter would soon be with them. The biting gusts that came from the sea and the gray clouds blocking out the sun seemed intent on their task, and if they continued, not a bit of the sun's warmth would filter through.

If one good thing had come out of this week, it was the evident improvement in Mrs. Williams. Each day she grew stronger, and her general health improved. Their walks along the beach were short, but Elizabeth claimed the sights and sounds soothed her, so Evelyn determined that they would walk there as often as she wished.

"How are you feeling now that you are out of the house?" Evelyn asked as they traversed the sandy path.

"My head still aches, but I am feeling better, I think." Elizabeth managed a smile.

"It was good to see you eating so well this morning. After not eating all those days, 'tis no wonder you feel weak. You must regain your strength."

"I'm very grateful for all that everyone has been doing to help Mary and me, but I feel terrible that we've had to rely on Mr. Twethewey for so long. I'm sure he is eager to be rid of us, what with his other house-guests and his endeavors."

Evelyn considered her words. She might be personally frustrated with Mr. Twethewey, but he had always been kind to the Williamses. "I've not spoken with Mr. Twethewey as of late, but I am confident in saying that he does not mind your presence here in the least. I understand he is from a rather large family, and I get the impression that he likes to have a lot of people around."

"Well, hopefully the officers will learn something soon. Mr. Twethewey has been naught but kind, though I fear your grandfather is not happy about my presence."

"My grandfather is stuck in his ways. In the past he always billeted any shipwreck survivors at the inn in the village, and he does not like to think of doing anything differently. But you mustn't take it personally. After all, Mr. Twethewey has the final say."

"I suppose you're right. And the last thing I want to do is bring any trouble. I know your grandfather is frustrated that I cannot remember more. I think he believes I am lying."

"Do not let him intimidate you. I promise, he is really a softhearted man under his gruff countenance."

The breeze swept low, disrupting their hair and skirts, and Evelyn smoothed her hair from her face. She glanced to Elizabeth, where she saw the healing wound and fading bruise. The surgeon said she no longer needed the bandage, but it was a frightful sight. The gash was not nearly as noticeable with her hair covering it, but with the wind lifting her hair, it was impossible not to see.

Evelyn cleared her throat. "Are you remembering any more? Grandfather said the excise men will probably be calling in a few days. It might be best to think about what you will be able to tell them."

"I think I might be, but it comes in snippets. I am almost fearful to say them out loud, for what if I am mistaken?"

"You must be gentle with yourself." Evelyn squeezed her new friend's arm. "Tell me what you think you know. Perhaps I can help."

Elizabeth drew a steadying breath. "I

know my husband died this past summer and Mary and I were returning to England. I have no family, so I cannot say with certainty where we were headed."

Evelyn looked again to the healing gash on Elizabeth's forehead. "Do you remember any events leading up to getting struck on the forehead?"

"I think I do, but I am hesitant . . ."

"Just try."

Elizabeth expelled the air from her lungs, her eyes scanning the horizon and watching Mary play in the sand. "The captain. I did not know him prior to departure, but he was an intimidating fellow. It was a cargo ship, that much I remember, not a passenger ship by any means.

"I think my husband must have been acquainted with him. Maybe we were traveling with him as a favor or something. I can't remember his name, but even now I can see his scarred face. Shaggy gray hair. Anyway, the voyage had been a long one, and we were so close to shore, but in the middle of the night, I heard a commotion and went above-deck. The captain was there with his crew, and he was yelling at me to get below the deck, and then I saw the lights."

"Mary told us of seeing lights."

"My husband used to tell me stories of

smugglers and how they would use lights to communicate, or even worse, use lights to lure a ship to perceived safety. Then the details are quite blurry, but I think he was going to try to land, I think to off-load goods. That frightened me, for I feared for myself and my daughter. I didn't know if they would let others board, or if we would be forced from the ship. If I remember correctly, the captain yelled at me to be quiet, then when I protested, he struck me. That is all I remember. Or that's all I think I remember."

"And you're certain you don't remember his name?"

"Simpson. Or Sampson. Or maybe that was his Christian name. Or maybe it's part of the ship's name. Oh, how ridiculous that I cannot remember!"

Evelyn kept her voice low. "You did ask after a Simpson on your first day here, so there may be something to it, but for now don't think on it anymore. I will tell my grandfather and Mr. Twethewey and they can share it with the excise men. Don't fret. With so many people intent upon learning the truth, it can truly be only a matter of time before everything is resolved."

"As for you . . ." Tears welled in Elizabeth's eyes. "You have been so kind through this process. I can't imagine what would have happened to my daughter and me if it weren't for your compassion."

"Please, do not mention it. I've grown quite fond of Mary over these weeks, and you too, of course. It has been lonely around here for so long."

They continued along the beach, playing with Mary and talking, until the increasing winds bid them to return home.

Evelyn had enjoyed her time with the Williamses, even though it had, at times, been frightening. But what would happen when they did leave? Who would she spend her time with? Would she go back to visiting Jenna on the weekends and spending the afternoons gardening alone? Mary and Elizabeth were a vivid reminder of how special a mother-daughter relationship could be, and as much as she enjoyed their company, it amplified her own feelings of homesickness for her mother.

Despite her own personal concerns, as she watched the Williams ladies play, she felt genuine excitement at their second chance at life.

How awful it would be to forget where you had come from and where you were going. But she could not help but compare their situation to hers. Whereas Mary and

Elizabeth had opportunity spreading before them, her own opportunities were dwindling, and Evelyn feared the worst.

CHAPTER 28

Evelyn paced outside Mr. Twethewey's study, slowly so her slippers made no noise on the stone floor. Marnie had told her that both Mr. Twethewey and her grandfather were inside. She needed to speak with them both.

Night had fallen well over an hour prior, and Mary and Elizabeth were now asleep. She could put this conversation off no longer. Elizabeth had shared more of what she remembered, and if her recollection of the events was accurate, the voyage must have been terrifying. Not only had she lost her husband, but to be treated so violently was more than one should be forced to bear. She owed it to her friend to swallow her pride and share what she knew with the man who could do something about it.

The paneled door to the study stood slightly ajar, and a gently flickering light spilled out. The rhythmic hum of voices and

305

the crackle of a fire echoed from within, and she stood outside the door, garnering her courage. At length she lifted her hand to knock on the door.

Mr. Twethewey's voice paused, then he said, "Enter."

She stepped inside. The men turned to face her. Grandfather's expression exuded concern. Mr. Twethewey's indicated surprise.

After several seconds, Mr. Twethewey jumped to his feet and extended his hand toward the empty chair next to her grandfather. "Miss Bray. Please, come in. Be seated."

She nodded and did as bid, nudging the door closed behind her before she moved next to her grandfather.

"I don't mean to interrupt." She wrung her hands before her as second thoughts about this conversation crept in.

"Of course you're not interrupting. We are only discussing the clay pits." Mr. Twethewey leaned forward behind his desk, his smile friendly. "What can we do for you?"

She sat down as she tried to remember exactly what she had wanted to say. She was not surprised at the odd little flutter in her stomach. She did not agree with what he'd said about her grandfather — she never would — but that did not change the fact that he was a handsome man, and despite all, he *was* kind. It was evident in the way he interacted with the Williams ladies and in the manner in which he dealt with his workers at the china clay pits.

She tucked her hands in her lap and licked her lips. "I'm here about Mrs. Williams."

"Mrs. Williams?" Mr. Twethewey's eyebrows rose. "What about her?"

"We took a stroll today on the beach, and she recalled more details of what happened the day of the shipwreck."

"That is wonderful!" A glimmer of genuine enthusiasm sparkled in Mr. Twethewey's eyes. "But why does she not tell us herself?"

"She's concerned that her memory is not yet steady enough to be trusted. Her recount of the events, if accurate, is quite telling, and I think she fears sharing false information."

Evelyn repeated Mrs. Williams's take — about the cruel captain, about the lights, and about the unscheduled stop at the cove. When she concluded, both men were silent for several seconds before Mr. Twethewey spoke. "So based on her words, the incident in the cove might not have been an accident."

Grandfather, at last, leaned forward.

307

"Before we give too much credit to what she says, we must remember she's had a significant injury. For all we know, her memory could be permanently altered."

"She seems quite lucid in our other conversations." Evelyn's frustration with her grandfather's constant negativity resurfaced. "She's told me that her husband was a sea captain and that he died of a fever in India."

Grandfather tilted his head to the side. "You are awfully eager to believe her, Evie, and I think it's because you want resolution. I want resolution too, but I'll not blindly believe everything until there is evidence to support it."

"We will let the excise men know," Mr. Twethewey declared decidedly, ending Grandfather's protest. "Thank you for sharing this information. If there is something illegal going on, as her story suggests, we want to make sure we're addressing it."

Grandfather huffed. "I'd be wary if I were you, Twethewey. I know you are fond of your guests, but I think it's time to send them on their way."

"Grandfather!" Evelyn interjected, shocked.

Grandfather ignored her and looked back to Mr. Twethewey. "How many times must I say it? The longer they remain, the more censure you draw." He surged to his feet and jerked his hat from Mr. Twethewey's desk, his face reddening. "I'm expected at the Polmann farm. The plow horse has taken ill, and I said I would stop by to offer assistance. Evelyn, dear, it's time for you to return to the cottage. It's dark outside. Make haste and be on your way."

Silence descended after he exited the study and his footsteps faded.

Evelyn's cheeks burned at the manner in which her grandfather had just spoken to her — as if she were a child. But she'd not show her hurt. Not in front of Mr. Twethewey. Even so, the awkward silence prevailed. She ignored her thudding heart and gave a nervous laugh, attempting to soothe the coarse nature of Grandfather's harsh words. "I don't know why he seems so angry. He's usually the first one to rush to someone's aid, regardless of their situation or circumstance."

Mr. Twethewey exuded calmness. His words were slow. Clear. "Perhaps he's helping someone else."

Evelyn's blood froze. She'd not really allowed herself to give any of Mr. Twethewey's words credit. But she'd just witnessed firsthand her grandfather's defensiveness. Could it be true? Could Grandfather be sacrificing the Williamses' comfort and security to protect someone?

Mr. Twethewey's blue eyes were direct. "We've had this discussion before, Miss Bray, and there is no need for us to rehash it. But I do want to thank you for telling me."

"I told Mrs. Williams I would mention it," she added hastily. "I know she would be grateful if you would notify the excise men."

Not sure what else to say or how to handle the discomfort within her, Evelyn moved to stand.

"Before you go — a word."

She stilled, waiting for him to speak.

"I think I owe you an apology."

She gripped her hands before her. So he *had* noticed it too — the discomfort, the distance that had been created between them.

"I was brash with you the other day." His tone softened further. "I shouldn't have questioned you about your grandfather. It was not my business. I was angry at the situation, not you. Please forgive me."

At his words, the weight of anger she'd been carrying all week began to dissolve. "Of-of course."

He stepped around the desk, bringing

with him the scent of sandalwood and leather.

As much as she didn't want it to, her heart lurched as he drew near.

He leaned back against the desk, not far from her, and crossed his arms over his chest. "The truth is, I'm concerned. That morning we last spoke there were lights on the beach, just like the ones Mary described to us. There was a ship, I saw it as plain as day, but within hours there was no sign of anything. It was as if it all evaporated."

Evelyn relaxed her shoulders as she considered his words. Conversation was flowing between them once more, and for that she was relieved. She also understood his concern. "I know the excise men patrol the beach and local men are hired to watch for wrecks at dawn, but have you thought of hiring other men? Men you chose yourself, and not ones my grandfather hired? Perhaps you'd have more peace of mind if you had more eyes watching the situation — the eyes of men you trust."

He lifted his brows and nodded. "That's not a bad idea. But like I told you the other night, trust is not something I bestow easily."

Evelyn let out a nervous laugh. "So I gather your trust in my grandfather has not increased."

"I have only known him just about three weeks."

She sniffed. "*I* trust my grandfather."

"That's fair." He nodded. "I would expect you to do so."

She looked up at him. "Do you trust me?"

It was a bold question, one that the grand-daughter of the steward should not be asking the master of the estate. But somehow, in the days since the first wreck, their recent argument aside, circumstances had forced them to a tighter bond than their relationship would regularly allow.

He drew a deep breath, one so serene and steady that she felt her own nerves relax.

"Since I arrived, Miss Bray, nothing has gone according to plan. The wreck. And you."

"Me?"

He stepped closer.

She tensed and her pulse increased.

"You asked me about trust. There are a handful of people who earn my trust immediately. They are rare, but you, I do trust. You, with your strong but genuine observation and your tender heart. I believe you want the best for those around you. I believe you want to see the good in those in your life."

Suddenly the air between them sparked. This was no longer a business discussion. Somehow, some way, it had morphed into something much deeper. Much more intimate. Even the way he looked at her had changed. Now his gaze was intentional, direct, as if searching her eyes for a reaction.

This was not proper. They were alone. Near each other.

Silently he reached forward and took her hand.

Her heart raced. His hand felt cool and strong around her much smaller one. Both peace and excitement flooded her in equal parts, heightening her every sense.

"Miss Bray. Evelyn, I —"

"What is going on?"

She whirled to see Grandfather in the corridor, hard eyes fixed on Liam. His face crimson, he stomped in.

Mr. Twethewey dropped her hand.

"Don't make me ask again," Grandfather thundered, stepping past her, nearly pushing her aside.

Mr. Twethewey stepped backward. "Bray, I —"

"I want none of your cheek and none of your excuses." Grandfather pointed a thick finger at the taller man's face. "I may be employed here, but did I not tell you? I'll not allow you to take liberties with my granddaughter."

"Did I not tell you?"

Evelyn straightened. What had Grandfather told him? "Grandfather, I —"

"Quiet, girl," he ordered, face shaking, without looking away from Mr. Twethewey. "How dare you touch my granddaughter's hand as if you had the right to."

"I have nothing but respect for Evelyn."

"Her name is *Miss* Bray, and if I see you touch her again, so help me, you'll regret the day you ever crossed paths with Rupert Bray." He whirled, hot wrath gleaming in his eyes. "Get out of here now, Evelyn. I'll not say it again."

There was no use in arguing. Still, with her hand warm from Mr. Twethewey's touch and her senses numb with embarrassment, Evelyn spun on her heel and hurried wordlessly from the study.

CHAPTER 29

What had just happened? Liam stood completely still in the deafening silence and solitude of his study.

He looked out the window but saw nothing but mist and blackness.

Just moments ago he'd been hand in hand with Miss Bray. It had been so natural to take her hand in his. And she seemed to return the regard. At least until they were interrupted.

He never should have taken such a liberty. What had he been thinking? And Bray — the man had a temper unlike anything he had ever seen.

Liam pressed his hands against his head and then rubbed them down his face, trying to determine the best course of action. As best he could figure, there were only two options that made any sense. He could dismiss Bray effective immediately. What master would accept such insolent behavior?

Or he could move past this and pretend it didn't happen.

In the end he was the one who had erred. He'd promised Bray he would stay away from Evelyn, and in spite of all the older man's faults, he'd been quite clear in his expectations. And Liam hadn't upheld his end of the agreement. Furthermore, he was beginning to have feelings for her.

"Did I hear shouting?"

His brother stood in the doorway, his blue eyes wide. Liam shrugged and motioned for John to enter.

John took a seat in the chair across from Liam's desk, bringing with him the solace that comes with someone familiar. "Well, are you going to tell me what happened?" John crossed one booted foot over his opposite knee, eagerness written on his face.

Liam filled his lungs and then blew out his air. "I'm not even sure where to start. Actually, yes, I do. Miss Bray just came by with news that Mrs. Williams recalled more about the wreck and believes the vessel was making a scheduled stop here."

"That's good then, right?" John shifted in his chair and leaned forward with interest. "Did she remember the name of the captain or the ship?"

Liam shook his head. "No, but it does

seem to corroborate what the excise men are concerned about — smuggling in my cove."

"Surely she'll remember in time. But that information did not incite shouting."

Liam sighed, loathing the thought of telling his brother what had happened. Yet what good would come from keeping it a secret? He needed help, advice of any kind. "Mr. Bray happened upon Miss Bray and me while we were talking, and he saw me holding his granddaughter's hand."

Laughter bubbled up in his brother. "What?"

Liam frowned at his brother's amusement. "This is serious."

Regaining composure, John straightened his waistcoat and pressed his lips together. "Of course it is."

"I've a mess on my hands that I've no idea how to handle."

Johnny sobered and leaned back in his chair. "My instinct is to tell you that I think Miss Bray a very lovely woman. You could do much worse, you know."

"I agree, and part of me thinks she shares the sentiment, but Bray warned me on my very first day here to stay away from her. I don't know what I was thinking to do such a thing. I saw only the moment."

"If you are drawn to her, then you're drawn to her. Sometimes attraction doesn't make sense. Unfortunately, the Twetheweys aren't exactly known for our conventional matches, although having that Bray fellow as a grandfather-in-law would put things in an entirely new light."

"I've made a mistake, I fear." Liam raked his fingers through his hair. "I should have exercised more restraint."

Johnny shook his head. "Even so, why would Bray be so against such a match? You are, after all, master here. If you aren't suitable enough for her, then who would be?"

Liam shrugged. There was a bit of truth to what his brother was saying. Either Bray already had plans for his granddaughter, or something was going on that Liam knew nothing of. Bray had told him she was practically spoken for.

"Don't be too upset about it. It was the mere hold of the hand, nothing more, right? It's not like you proposed marriage to the girl."

John was right. Liam took a lady's hand, nothing more. And yet he had a feeling it was not going to be that easily dismissed.

Humiliation flaming, Evelyn wanted nothing more than to escape to the solitude of her attic chamber to nurse her wounds and cool her embarrassment.

But it was not to be.

Grandfather raced after her in the black of late evening and overtook her in the cottage garden, just outside the kitchen. He grabbed her arm and forced her to the parlor.

Nervous shivers pulsed through every fiber of her being. She'd seen Grandfather angry plenty of times. But she'd never seen him mad at *her,* and now that she was on the receiving end of his wrath, its significance took on a whole new light. The parlor's candlelight cast hard, unbecoming lines on his wrinkled face, and his bushy brows framed hard eyes.

"Listen to me, girl, and listen well. I'll not have my granddaughter acting the tart, especially not with the likes of William Twethewey."

"You misunderstood." She shook her head emphatically. "We were only —"

"I may be old, but I know what I saw, and I'll not have it. Do you hear me? I've been lenient with you, and now I see I've been far too much so. Men like Twethewey are used to getting what they want. If that happened, then where would you be? Do you think he loves you? Do you think he would make you mistress of the house? He's not the innocent sort. He and every other man like him has but one intention. A touch of the hand? A caress of the cheek and then a kiss? Where do you think that leads? Nah. He is not for you, Granddaughter. You don't belong with a man like him."

"A man like him?" she challenged, her defenses rising. Did he really think her so incapable of reading another person's character? "What, an honest man who'd care for a child who had been fished out of the sea? A man who would strive to create employment for those on his land? A man who —"

"Bah!" Grandfather fired. "A man who swoops in to steal and change what rightfully belongs to those who live here, more like. A man who would seduce a young woman with no intentions of anything righteous. Aye. You sheltered child — you think everyone's intentions are good and pure."

"And who would you have me associate with?" She'd not back down. Not this time. "Jim Bowen?"

Her grandfather's eyes widened. His mouth snapped shut.

"I can't figure it out," she continued. "Jim has changed. He *is* changing, right before our eyes. His tone. His manners. His very countenance. And you are turning a blind eye to it! Why? To do so is unlike you in many ways."

Anger hardened his expression. "Best not to speak of things you don't know."

"Things I don't know? Then perhaps you had better tell me, because from where I stand, everything is looking odd, to say the least."

Instead of responding to her request, he stepped forward and lowered his voice. "That's the end of it. You'll not set foot inside the main house again."

Evelyn's mouth went dry. "But I am caring for Mrs. Williams."

"Yet one more reason that woman needs to go to Plymouth, her and her child. It isn't proper for her to be staying in the house with an unmarried man, especially one who is prone to take such liberties. Nay. Mrs. Williams is not your concern. Not anymore. You don't belong there."

"Then why don't you tell me where I belong, Grandfather? Because according to my mother, I don't belong here in this cottage, but I don't belong with her in Plymouth either. According to you, you would saddle me with an innkeeper who has a temper as broad as the sea and twice as fiery. And for what reason? Because he is influential? Among whom?"

"Enough!" he thundered.

She shrank back. She'd gone too far.

He stepped toward her, shaking his finger in front of her face. "I have tried to be patient with you. Tried to let you find your own way in the world, but enough is enough. It appears you have too much of your mother in you — the selfishness, the lack of discipline. You speak of Jim Bowen as if he were dirt beneath your delicate slipper, and such talk is a shame to me. You are the granddaughter of a steward. Do not believe your mother — you will never be anything more.

"You should be running to Bowen. Twethewey thinks he is the most influential man in the area? Bah! Bowen runs the entire area. Nay, Bowen *owns* the entire area. And he has taken a fancy to you. You'd be wise to welcome his advances, not those from some privileged, pompous boy who will run his estate into the ground. There now. You will think on what I've said. You *will* consider Bowen, because you don't belong here with me anymore. It is time for you to make your own way. I've enough with you now. Go upstairs."

She stared, disbelieving, at his glowering countenance. Had he just told her he didn't want her living here anymore? Had he just told her she needed to marry Bowen?

Confusion and questions stung, burning her heart and churning her mind. Without another word, she whirled and climbed the stairs.

At the moment she hated her mother for abandoning her as much as she wished she would come for her. At the top of the stairs, Evelyn paused at her mother's room. She had not cried until now, but here, in the magnified silence of the corridor, she wanted her mother. She wanted to be able to run to her, cry on her shoulder, find an ally. How she longed for that scent of rosewater that meant her mother was near. How she wished for the simplicity of the days when they would daydream of the future.

She put her hand on the door to her mother's bedchamber and turned it.

It held firm. She frowned. Was it locked?

She jiggled the knob again, but it refused to give way.

In all her years at the cottage, she'd never known the room to be locked.

Evelyn dropped her hand. Sadness overwhelmed her. She left the corridor and continued the climb to her attic chamber.

CHAPTER 30

The next afternoon, after Evelyn was certain her grandfather had departed for the china clay pits, she went down to the kitchen, where she found Bertie busy about the day's tasks.

Evelyn had been awake since dawn, but even so her head ached from the nearly sleepless night, and her eyes still felt puffy from crying. Part of her wanted to stay hidden away in her chamber's privacy, but another part of her wanted to escape the confines of the cottage.

Grandfather's harsh reprimands and words of Jim Bowen plagued her, and her grandfather's unwavering insistence on the innkeeper's merits was unnerving.

She didn't understand the change in his actions. She didn't understand it at all.

"What was all the yelling I heard last night?" Bertie prompted as Evelyn crossed the threshold into the kitchen.

Evelyn bit her lip. The cottage was small. If Bertie heard anything, there was no doubt she heard every word of the exchange.

When Evelyn did not respond, Bertie propped her hand on her hip. "From what I heard, your grandfather's keen on having you cozy up to Jim Bowen."

Evelyn gritted her teeth. She'd not fall prey to this discussion. In a village this small, any privacy at all was impossible.

"Isn't a bad idea," Bertie continued. "You know what everyone says about Jim, of course. Everyone's always looked to your grandfather to sort out the problems that befall us. But your grandfather's getting no younger. He's thinking of the future. Word is your grandfather has handpicked Jim to carry on his work."

"His work?" Evelyn raised an eyebrow.

"You know, the wrecking responsibilities. Seeing that the poorest of the poor have what they need to survive."

Evelyn had never really thought of her grandfather's village activities as an occupation. He had always been one to tend to the less fortunate, but even if that was the case, why was Jim so angry about Mr. Twethewey's arrival that first day? And why did he talk to her grandfather so meanly? There had to be more to it than what she knew.

A horse's whinny followed by the crunch of carriage wheels drew Evelyn away from her conversation with Bertie and to the drive separating the cottage from the main house.

She did not recognize the carriage, yet she watched it with interest. She arched her head to see through the windows and could tell several people were inside.

The sight of a large plume atop an auburn head drew her attention.

Evelyn's movements slowed. "It can't be."

The footman of the guest's coach opened the door and assisted a tall, slender woman in a striking red pelisse with gold braiding, a ruffled black bonnet boasting a crimson feather, and brilliant red kid gloves down to the ground.

The woman turned. Their eyes locked.

Evelyn's blood chilled within her.

My mother is here.

Not a letter.

Not a parcel.

But her mother, in the flesh, after well over two years, with her auburn hair elegantly curled and her green eyes flashing. Crystal ear bobs dangled from her ears. A fur muff covered her hands. Dorothea Bray — nay, Dorothea Drake — was at Wyndcliff Hall.

She appeared just as Evelyn remembered

her. And yet nothing like it. Was she dreaming? Had the events of the past days affected her to such a degree that she could not distinguish fantasy from reality?

As if drawn by some invisible force, Evelyn moved toward Wyndcliff's courtyard.

Her mother hurried toward her, arms outstretched. But instead of a smile on her face, her brows drew together. "Evelyn, dearest, just look at you! Your hair!" Eyes narrowed on the offending wisps, she brushed Evelyn's hair away from her cheek.

Questions bubbled within her, but before Evelyn could express a single one, two equally elegant women stepped from the carriage. They looked alike, both with chestnut hair and dark eyes. She found her voice and turned to her mother. "I-I can't believe you are here! But why?"

"Why am I here?" Mother smoothed the fabric of Evelyn's sleeve. "Is that any way to welcome your mother? Now, let me get a good look at you. Your gown is wrinkled, my dear! I hope you've not let yourself go over this time I have been away."

The criticism stung. Not that Evelyn cared about her hair. Or her gown. But did it matter? Her mother was *here*. Relief and happiness collided with buried anger and hurt. She wanted to demand to know why she had been gone so long at the same time she wanted to embrace her mother and not let go. It was simple, really, but simultaneously overwhelming. She turned her face into the breeze to let the cold air dry her tears.

"Darling," her mother said. "May I present my husband, Mr. Drake."

Evelyn had not noticed the man standing behind her until now. The tall man's awkwardly long limbs and long nose made him appear even taller than he actually was.

"Such a pleasure, Evelyn." The pitch of his voice seemed rather high for a man of his stature. "I am pleased to welcome you to our family."

Somehow Evelyn managed a curtsy to both the young women and her new stepfather, but with each passing moment she sensed disapproval washing over them. After all, she'd spent the night crying. She need not consult a looking glass to know she was puffy and pale. It has been hours since she ran a brush through her hair. This was not how she wanted her reunion with her mother to be.

Dorothea extended her hand. "Come and meet your stepsisters, Georgiana and Eleanor."

The two pretty young women stepped forward. They did not smile, but their gazes raked over Evelyn's simple gown.

Evelyn curtsied, summoning every memory of etiquette she'd been taught as a child. She was, after all, still a lady, despite what her grandfather said the previous night. She needed to remember.

"And where is your grandfather?" Mother asked. "If I recall, he was always roaming about this place, up to something or another."

"I'm not exactly sure." Evelyn was almost glad he was not here. Her grandfather and mother had never seen eye to eye, and she suspected it would be better for all concerned if she had time to warn him of Dorothea Drake's arrival.

The main entrance to Wyndcliff opened, and William Twethewey appeared.

Evelyn stifled an inner groan. No doubt the activity in the courtyard had drawn his attention. Her embarrassment at their last interaction flamed, and she was not ready to see him after their interlude the previous night. Not yet.

Her mother also noticed his appearance. Rupert Bray forgotten, she asked, "And who is this gentleman?"

"Did you not receive my letters?" Evelyn's frustration was mounting. She'd written several over the past weeks, and news about

Mr. Twethewey had been in every one. " 'Tis Mr. Twethewey. The new master at Wyndcliff."

Mother lifted her chin to assess the young master as he approached them, approval gleaming in her eyes.

How foolish Evelyn felt during this interaction. Small. Inadequate compared to the finely dressed women in the courtyard. She pivoted just enough to see Mr. Twethewey approaching them. The fleeting sun falling on his dark hair and strong shoulders only further emphasized his attractiveness — a fact that was not lost on her stepsisters, for gone were their sour expressions. Charming smiles and delicate curtsies appeared.

Mr. Twethewey was smiling, and his blue eyes fixed on her. He seemed calm and composed, as if nothing odd had transpired between them.

So different from her own present state.

"Miss Bray. I thought I heard a carriage but did not recognize it from the window. Have you visitors?"

Evelyn swiped her hair away from her face. She curtsied to greet him. "This is my mother, Mrs. Drake, her husband, Mr. Drake, and his daughters."

"Ah, well then." He bowed politely. "Welcome to Wyndcliff Hall."

"Mr. Twethewey," her mother exclaimed, eyes wide. "I am so happy to hear you are here at last. This manor home has been empty for far too long."

"That is right. I have been told you lived here once, if I am not mistaken."

"Yes, for a time." A flash of disgust crossed her mother's expression and she quickly changed the topic. "And the time has come for my daughter to leave as well. We've come to collect Evelyn home."

Evelyn jerked up her head. Had she heard correctly? "Collect me?"

"Oh, Evelyn, you goose. You speak as if you've not paid attention to my letters at all. We've come to take you to Plymouth. Has that not been the plan?"

Evelyn's breath caught in her throat, and she felt as if the air had been pushed from her.

This was it. This was what she wanted. And after the exchange between Mr. Twethewey and her the previous night and her argument with her grandfather, the timing couldn't be better. Could it?

Evelyn managed a glance toward Mr. Twethewey before she looked back to her mother. She wanted to say something of import. Something confident and witty. And yet all she could manage was, "Oh."

Her mother returned her attention to Mr. Twethewey. "We are headed to the west coast to visit the girls' cousins, and that should give you time to assemble your things, but then we will be back in a week or so to collect you. Why, Evelyn, I thought you would be more excited! You look positively dour."

Excited? After months — nay, years — of waiting, then such news was dropped so suddenly? "Have you mentioned this to Grandfather?" she squeaked.

"La, no. And why should I? In fact, I wish to not even see him if I can manage while I'm here."

Mr. Twethewey's eyebrows rose in unmasked curiosity. "The coast is still quite a drive from here. Surely you do not intend to finish your journey today."

"No, indeed not," Mother responded. "We will, of course, be stopping at a carriage inn. Detestable places, but what is to be done?"

A smile quirked Mr. Twethewey's mouth. "You are correct. They are the most detestable places. And that is why you must stay here, at Wyndcliff."

Evelyn's eyes widened and she bit her lip.

Her mother's hand flew to her chest. "Why, Mr. Twethewey, that is most kind."

"The Brays are an important part of life

332

here, and I could not, in good conscience, send you away to stay at a public inn. Please, you must join me as my guests."

Exclamations of delight circled the group, but Evelyn's breath caught.

This was all happening too fast.

But the charming host seemed warm, friendly, inviting. "I am sure Miss Bray has shared with you that we have a number of other guests under the roof at the moment, and the chambers are still being opened up after years of disuse, but if you can overlook that, we would be most happy to have you here."

A glance of Mr. Twethewey's eyes caught hers, almost as if to see her response.

And how did one respond?

He turned back to his new guests. "Welcome to Wyndcliff."

CHAPTER 31

Evelyn stood in the doorway of one of Wyndcliff Hall's guest chambers, feeling foolish as her mother shook out a gown for dinner and arranged her trunk and things for an overnight stay.

"Why did you not send word you were coming?" Evelyn repeated, after never receiving an answer in the courtyard. "I could have prepared the cottage for you."

"It was a sudden visit. The girls wanted to visit their cousins, and I have yet to meet them." Her mother scoffed. "But the cottage? Why, you must be in jest. You know I don't care for that place. And Georgiana and Eleanor would never be comfortable there."

But it is good enough for me?

Evelyn bit back the words that itched to be released. Instead, she stepped closer to the bed.

Her mother lifted her gaze to the heavy

wooden beams crossing the chamber's ceiling, oblivious to the emotions churning within her daughter. "I would expect this room to be much finer. Wyndcliff used to be so refined when Mr. Treton was alive."

"It has been vacant a long time, don't forget, and Mr. Twethewey has only arrived."

With a shake of her copper curls, Mother dropped the gown to the bed, moved to the looking glass atop the room's dressing table, and smoothed her hair. "You seem quite well versed in the happenings of Wyndcliff. Could it be that you've no reason to go to Plymouth after all?"

"What do you mean?" Evelyn knew full well the meaning behind the words.

"No need to be coy with me, my child. Mr. Twethewey! Devilishly handsome man. Do you not think so?"

Evelyn stretched her hand absently at the mention of his name, the memory of his touch so vibrant. She shook her head.

"Speak up, Evelyn. Do you remember none of the manners I so painstakingly bestowed upon you?"

"No, ma'am."

"That's better." Her mother stepped forward and smoothed her hand down Evelyn's hair once more and tsked. "Well then, perhaps it is for the best. Such a pretty girl, with that charming turn of your nose and those high cheekbones. La, child, with a little attention to your dressing, you will have no trouble finding suitors and a match that is advantageous for us all."

Was that all her mother cared about?

She'd been at Wyndcliff an hour and had not asked about anything — Evelyn's habits, her hobbies, how she spent her days. But then again, wasn't that how her mother had always been? This had been their dream — to find a suitable husband. And now it would come to pass.

"Why do you look so glum? I declare, you have barely even smiled since my arrival. It makes a mother feel as if you have been miserable all this time."

"Nay, Mother. I'm not miserable."

"Well then, I blame your grandfather. I often wonder if it was a lapse in judgment to leave you with him. But what can be done now?" She stroked Evelyn's cheek. "It really is good to see you."

Her mother turned back to her open trunk, signaling a change in topic. "It was most kind of Mr. Twethewey to invite us to dine with him, let alone stay the night. He said there were other guests?"

"Aye." Evelyn leaned against the bed's

massive post. "The house is quite full at the moment, actually. His brother, John Twethewey, is here, as is a gentleman by the name of Mr. Porter, who is one of Mr. Twethewey's business associates. And then, of course, Mrs. Williams and Mary Williams. Mary is a child and will not be dining with us, but she is here."

"Oh yes, the shipwrecked lady you mentioned in your letters." Mother lifted her gown to her chin and examined her reflection. "And this Mr. Porter, what is his situation?"

"Situation?"

Mother huffed and lowered the gown. "Is he an eligible bachelor? Of course, my goal for all three of you young ladies is to match you with gentlemen in Plymouth, but one must always be on the lookout, you know."

Evelyn stiffened. Her mother had lumped her in with her two stepdaughters. She thought back to the finery of the other girls, with their wool pelisses and ribboned bonnets. She was nothing like them.

"He's married, I believe. He's from Staffordshire."

"Well, what a waste then. And such a loss with Mr. Twethewey. Yes, as I said, he is handsome, but Wyndcliff holds such a detestable state in my heart that I could not imagine any one of my girls here forever."

Evelyn could not resist. "Then why have you not sent for me sooner?"

Shock crossed her mother's face, and she lowered the gown. But before she could answer, her two stepdaughters appeared in the doorway.

"Since my maid isn't with me, I thought you might dress my hair," the taller one said.

The smile returned to her mother's face. "Very well. Hurry in, Georgiana. And, Evelyn, you need to dress for dinner as well, won't you?"

Her mother turned back to the other ladies, and Evelyn felt very much like an outsider as Georgiana sat at the dressing table and her mother brushed her dark tresses. Evelyn quietly excused herself and took the servants' stairway to avoid being seen.

But there was no way to avoid seeing Marnie.

Evelyn wanted to run past her, to not allow anyone to think that her mother's arrival brought anything but happiness, but Marnie had borne witness to so much — she was present the day the Brays arrived at Wyndcliff twelve years ago. She'd been there for some of her mother and grandfather's greatest arguments. And most importantly, she had been here the day Mother left.

"There now." Marnie looked up from her task at the table as Evelyn came down the stairs. "This is a turn of events."

Evelyn's shoulders slumped. "I suppose."

"Aren't ye happy to see yer mother?" She paused in kneading her dough to swipe flour from her face.

"Of course I am." Evelyn even managed a little lighthearted laugh.

"An' are ye happy to meet her new husband and stepdaughters?"

Evelyn nodded. It would do no good to be negative.

But deep down she knew Marnie understood.

Marnie offered a small smile, wiped her hands on her apron, and stepped around the table to approach Evelyn. She patted Evelyn's cheek affectionately and then took Evelyn's hand in hers. "I may be nothin' more than a housekeeper, but I've watched ye grow all these years. For what it be worth, I am very proud of ye, an' I am here if ye need anything at all."

Evelyn smiled and embraced Marnie. "Thank you, dear friend."

A twinkle danced in Marnie's eye. "An' now we just wait until yer grandfather learns of her return."

■ ■ ■

Liam glanced around the table at the people assembled there. Somehow Marnie had managed to conjure a large meal in a very short period of time — the first real dinner Liam had hosted at Wyndcliff.

Everyone around the table was here for a different reason.

But it was Evelyn Bray he could not look away from.

He always thought she was beautiful, but tonight she was dressed for the occasion. Never had he seen her blonde hair so elegantly coiffed. Normally her hair hung loose and lovely around her shoulders and down to her waist, or bound loosely at the nape of her neck, but tonight it was twisted smoothly into a chignon at the back of her head. A gown of shimmering pale-green fabric accentuated her features, the shade of which made her unusually colored green eyes appear more emerald. The Cornish weather and winds demanded long sleeves and heavy capes, but tonight her arms were bare, and a coral necklace hung about her neck.

She was stunning. So much so that he felt more like a nervous schoolboy than the master of an estate.

He had to repeatedly remind himself that other guests required his attention.

Even so, everyone seemed quite comfortable — everyone with the exception of Rupert Bray.

He'd barely spoken since his arrival, and his brows were drawn in a straight line. His disapproval of the Drakes staying at Wyndcliff was obvious, but otherwise, everyone was chattering and enjoying the dinner Marnie had prepared.

To Liam's right sat Mrs. Drake, and on her other side sat her husband. On Mr. Drake's other side sat Miss Georgiana Drake, whom he'd learned was the older of the two daughters. To Liam's left sat Mr. Porter and the younger Eleanor Drake. On the opposite side of the table sat Miss Bray, Rupert Bray, Mrs. Williams, and John, who had the unenviable task of attempting to control any outbursts that might come from the old steward.

"China clay, eh, Twethewey?" exclaimed Mr. Drake, his high voice rising above the others. "Whatever made you get into such an enterprise?"

"Quite by accident initially," Liam responded quickly. "But then after a great deal of research and investigation, I saw the value in it. It came with the estate, really. My uncle laid the framework but died before he could see it come to fruition. With the help of Mr. Porter here, we are bringing it to life."

"I admire you men who are out in the elements to make your fortune. Ah yes, I admire it." Mr. Drake leaned back in his chair and gave his head a sharp shake. "A life behind the desk has its advantages, but nothing can compare to the wind in your hair and the sun on your face."

"I've always preferred life out of doors, Mr. Drake," Liam said. "My uncle Jac, who was my guardian, is in the business of apple orchards, and I always enjoyed it. And I am pleased that the clay pits are seeing early success."

Mrs. Drake leaned forward with interest. " 'Tis about time this area had someone at the helm. It is a lawless bit of land if you ask me."

"And just what do you mean by that?" Bray thundered, shattering the polite conversation.

Liam's jaw tightened at the outburst. He unfortunately recognized the look on the older man's face. It was the same expression that crossed Bray's countenance the previous night when Liam held his granddaughter's hand. Rupert Bray was looking for a fight, and he seemed to have set his sights on his former daughter-in-law.

"Why, Mr. Bray. What a thing to say!" Mrs. Drake shot back, reaching for her fan and fluttering it before her face.

"Ah, I see you, *Mrs. Drake,* putting on airs like you yourself were not from here, from mere miners. Aye, I don't forget how my son plucked you out of some mining village and made you his bride, a decision I still wonder over to this day. Oh aye, I doubt you'll not forget how a Bray rescued you from near poverty and brought you to the life of your betters."

Anger flared. Her chin shook as she fixed a narrow gaze on him. "Be that as it may, but I will also never forget how another Bray's reckless decisions and questionable ethics brought his entire family crashing to the ground."

Bray jumped from his chair and pointed toward a stunned Mr. Drake. "Your arrival into our family was a dark day, Dorothea, and I pity this man for the burden he is now saddled with."

Not a single person moved or spoke until the sound of Bray's hasty footsteps disappeared completely.

Liam looked to his brother, whose mouth

was hanging open at the display. Miss Bray's face paled.

But Mrs. Drake was not eager to let the conversation go. "The nerve of that man. What airs for a man who has fallen so far from grace. Mr. Drake, I am surprised you allowed him to speak to me in such a manner." Her face reddened, and the forced curls on either side of her face shook energetically. "That man will never change. La, I never met a more disagreeable person in my life."

Liam was about to offer an apology on behalf of Wyndcliff when a shaky voice from across the table spoke before he could.

As Miss Bray stood, the legs of her chair scratched over the stone floor. "And yet you thought him a suitable guardian for me these past two years?"

Liam jerked at the sharp words coming from Miss Bray. The argument between the man and woman had captured his attention, and he'd missed the change in her. Now her face flamed pink. Her chest heaved with what could only be anger, and her green eyes were pinned on her mother.

Mrs. Drake dropped her hand. "Why, Evelyn!"

Miss Bray dropped her napkin to the table with a trembling hand. "I fear my appetite is quite vanished. My apologies, Mr. Tweth-ewey." With a rustle of her skirt she turned. Her hasty footsteps echoed loudly on the stone floor as she withdrew.

Then all was silent.

"Well, that was unnecessary," Mrs. Drake muttered, fanning herself with her napkin.

Liam expected the mother to go after her child. But she did not.

Impatience surged through him. He wanted to jump up. To follow Evelyn. To make sure she was all right. But he could not do that to her, not without adding speculation to her name.

He was grateful when Mrs. Williams stood. "Please excuse me."

With much calmer movements than Miss Bray, she withdrew through the same door Miss Bray had.

CHAPTER 32

Blinded by tears, Evelyn fumbled with the parlor door on the far side of the dining hall. Why would it not open?

How quickly this mess came about. She was angry with her grandfather. Why had he chosen that moment to pick a fight with her mother?

Evelyn was also angry with her mother. She knew how to provoke her grandfather, and she displayed that knowledge brilliantly.

Most of all, she was angry with herself. She'd let her emotions and insecurities get the better of her, and she'd not been able to hold her tongue.

And she hated herself for it.

She shook the parlor door handle, trying to get it to swing free.

In truth, she detested everything about this situation. And the fact that Mr. Twethewey bore witness to it all — the messy, ugly truth — humiliated her beyond all else.

"Miss Bray."

She recognized the voice instantly, of course. Evelyn stopped jiggling the handle and turned, feeling more like a spoiled child at the conclusion of a tantrum than a grown woman.

The women looked at each other for several seconds before Evelyn released her breath in a huff.

Mrs. Williams did not say anything. She only reached for Evelyn's hand, looped it through her arm, calmly opened the parlor door that Evelyn had not been able to, then swung it open. It was cooler here, dark and comforting, a soothing balm to the anger that had raced through her.

"I don't know why I said that, *did* that," Evelyn lamented as they entered the darkened room. "I know I should be ashamed of myself. I should've held my tongue."

"You forget what all you have been through, what with your mother's sudden arrival. It would be a big surprise for anyone. And I don't know much about your story, other than the bits you've shared with me, but it's obvious some matters have been left unresolved."

Evelyn shook her head. "You're gracious, but I should be able to control my emotions better. After all, this is nothing like what

347

you have been through."

"Your journey is not mine, and mine is not yours." Mrs. Williams smiled in the dim light. "They are unique unto themselves, are they not?"

They stood in silence for several moments, allowing the peaceful stillness of the chamber to settle Evelyn's nerves. Her breathing slowed. Her pulse returned to its normal pace. "I feel like a fool. My mother no doubt hates me. I'm sure I embarrassed her in front of her new family."

"Your mother will understand in time."

Evelyn scoffed. "My mother does not know me." The words were barely whispered, but it was as if they had been shouted.

Mrs. Williams directed her to the sofa, where they both were seated. "There is so much I am struggling to remember right now. Details of life, while growing clearer every day, are still so confusing. But I do remember my mother. We argued. She did not want me to marry my husband. Oh, she forbade it. She screamed and cried, but I was such a headstrong thing. I ran away with him and did not see her for an entire year. I thought for certain we would never speak again. But then I received word that my father died. I went home, and we embraced and clung to each other as if there had never been a rift between us."

Evelyn looked over at Mrs. Williams. There was so much to this woman beyond what she knew.

"I hope I will remember more as time goes on. I scarcely even remember my wedding day. But I do remember the day Mary was born. There is an unmistakable bond between mother and daughter that must be nurtured if it is to survive and grow. I do not know details of course, but it seems like the one between you and your mother is broken."

Broken.

The word implied so much.

"But broken things, with care and attention, can often be mended, can they not?" Mrs. Williams paused, allowing her words to sink in. "You will go with her to Plymouth, then?"

Evelyn did not want to go. Not anymore. The dream they had shared together was now a nightmare. She wanted nothing of that life.

When Evelyn did not respond, Mrs. Williams continued. "You are a grown woman, though, with dreams and hopes of your own. Perhaps there is a reason you would want to remain here at Wyndcliff?"

Evelyn thought of the changes in her life here. She thought of the harshness in Jim. She thought of her humiliation in her last exchange with Mr. Twethewey. "Nay, there is nothing for me here."

"Are you certain?" Mrs. Williams prodded, her tone patient and soothing. "Mr. Twethewey is a very attentive man."

Evelyn flicked her eyes up.

Mrs. Williams shrugged. "I thought I noticed a connection between the two of you, but perhaps I was mistaken. I am, after all, not quite myself these days. You have not asked my advice, but I humble myself to think of us as friends. Give yourself and those around you a little time, and remember that feelings are only feelings. They are not facts. I am confident it will all work itself out." Mrs. Williams squeezed Evelyn's hand and smiled reassuringly. "What do you say? Shall we return to dinner?"

Evelyn groaned. The thought of returning to dinner after flouncing out did not appeal to her. Yet Mrs. Williams was right. She wiped her face, sighed, and straightened her shoulders.

Mrs. Williams led the way to the dining hall.

All eyes turned to them when they entered. The conversation fell silent.

"Please excuse me," Evelyn said, stepping to her seat. "I was out of line."

"Nonsense, we are glad you have returned." Mr. Twethewey's eyes were as kind — and painfully, as beautiful — as ever. "It's not the same without you."

She forced a smile, lifted her eyes, and for the briefest moment met his gaze. She was not sure what she had expected to find there, but the corner of his mouth lifted in the subtlest of smiles.

Perhaps he was embarrassed for her.

Perhaps he was amused.

Whatever it was, it would not do to give it too much thought.

Like Mrs. Williams said, she was overwhelmed with feelings. And feelings were just that — fancies and emotions, not actual facts.

Liam glanced at the clock before he returned his attention to Miss Georgiana Drake, who was entertaining them with a song at the pianoforte.

The lady was pretty enough, he supposed, with her dark hair and tall stature, but her musical talents left much to be desired. He glanced around the room. With the exception of Mr. and Mrs. Drake, it appeared the other guests shared his opinions.

But what was to be done? The day had been a long one. Sleep had been elusive the previous night after his argument with Bray, and spending the day on the moors with the china clay pits had taken much of his energy. Now, polite conversation and the smoothing of ruffled feathers had become tedious.

Indeed, if it weren't for Miss Bray's presence, he'd wish to leave the space instantly. He should be paying attention to the music, but his thoughts were drawn to her.

He'd seen her under many trying circumstances. He'd seen her physically carry a child to safety. Nurse a woman's head wound. Stoically stand by while her grandfather was accused of the worst. But this was a different side of her. Never would he have expected an outburst like the one she displayed at dinner. She was normally so controlled, but cracks were forming in her careful facade.

Whatever had happened between her and her mother must have cut her deeply.

To anyone who did not know her well, even her new family, she would appear quite calm at the moment. But he had been around her enough to notice the tight grip her fingers had on the edge of her shawl, not to mention the periodic clench of her jaw.

She was not herself.

After the parties bid one another a good night and retired to their individual chambers, Liam knew what he needed to do. Of all the guests, Miss Bray would be the only one to leave Wyndcliff as she made her way to the cottage, and he needed to talk with her. He had to. How could he not address what had happened the previous night when her grandfather interrupted? And now the thought of her leaving for Plymouth was driving him mad. He had no idea what he would say to her, no idea what he would do, but he exited the house and made his way to the cottage.

Once Evelyn was free of the confines of Wyndcliff Hall, she could not decide if the walk to the cottage was a welcome relief or justified punishment.

No one, including her mother, had asked where she was to stay that night. No doubt it was generally assumed she'd return to the cottage. Even if she'd been asked to remain in the main house with her mother, however, she would have refused, for emotions were running high within Wyndcliff Hall, and she didn't know how much more her heart could withstand. In truth, she preferred the cottage. At least in the tiny, humble abode there was a semblance of normalcy and continuity — and an odd sense of freedom.

She was grateful for Mrs. Williams, who had shown her such grace and kindness and had remained by her side the remainder of the evening, a constant encouragement when Evelyn felt she could bear no more.

But the dinner and entertainment were over, and Evelyn crossed the cobbled court-yard and traversed the path to the cottage. The wind mingled with the sounds of the distant sea, creating a symphony around her.

Would the sounds be the same in Plymouth? The scents? The breeze?

Now darkness was all around her.

But loneliness was all around her too.

Her mother didn't want her. She'd not even embraced her.

She hurried to her little cottage garden, barely able to see for the tears gathering, turning the shadowed greens and browns to a messy blur. Pain, sharper than anything she'd felt for ever so long, stabbed her chest and she gasped for air. As the darkness enveloped her further, a tear fell. And then another.

Oh, how had this happened? How had she gone from feeling content to wondering if she belonged nowhere and with no one?

Her mind raced with scenarios.

If only her mother had never left in the first place.

If only her grandfather had remained silent.

If only. If only. If only.

Swiping tears from her face, she stepped through the gate and stopped to sit on the bench there, mindless of how the wind tugged her skirt and pulled her carefully dressed hair from its pins. She did not want to go inside, not yet, when Bertie might be present — or even worse, her grandfather.

A figure in the shadows startled her.

At first she wanted to leap up and run, fearing it was Jim. Or perhaps her grandfather.

But Mr. Twethewey filled the garden space.

As if the day's humiliation was not enough, she was discovered crying like a child.

She immediately wiped her face with the back of her hand. He stepped closer.

She kept her gaze low. "You shouldn't be here."

"And you shouldn't be crying." In two paces more he was at her side.

She sniffed impatiently. "Please, can you

leave me be?"

But he did not move away. "Nay. Not when I know you are this upset."

She shook her head. "That is kind, truly, but I don't know why this — why any of this — should matter to you."

He drew a deep breath and stared out into the darkness before he turned his attention back to her. "Is it not obvious?"

At this she met his gaze. Did he really care? About her?

When she remained silent, he added quickly, "I take it you were not happy to see your mother."

"Happy to see the woman who has had nothing to do with me for two years? Happy to see the family I am clearly not a part of?" Realizing how bitter the words must sound, she sniffed and looked to the ground. "I am sorry. That was uncalled for."

"There is no need to apologize to me. For anything." He moved closer. "I only don't want to see you crying."

"I'm not thinking clearly, surely. This has been a difficult day, and I don't think I'm handling it well at all."

He sat next to her. Warmth radiated from him in the cold night, and she resisted the urge to lean closer to it.

They sat in silence for several seconds

before he rested his elbows on his knees and looked over at her. "I don't know how you could have handled this week any better. It's been a trying one, to be sure."

She shrugged. "I suppose the one good thing to come from this is that I will finally be able to leave for Plymouth after all this time." Her words sounded pathetically thin and unconvincing.

"And do you want to go?"

"I have been planning for it for so long. We all have."

"But I ask again, is that what you want?"

She did not respond.

He drew a deep breath and straightened once more. His shoulder brushed against hers, and she did not pull away. "I know you have not asked my opinion, but allow me to say this on the matter. Do not underestimate the satisfaction that can be found in making your own decisions and forging your own path."

"My path was planned many years ago," she said flatly. "And yours was too, if I'm not mistaken. You've said before that you have known your entire life that you were to come here and be master."

"Aye, you're right. My path was planned for me. But I think the difference is that I welcomed this one. And I am embracing it

— along with its challenges. And I am optimistic about what the future might hold. But your outlook seems different. You seem almost sorry to take yours."

She looked at him fully. "I hardly know what to think or feel anymore. I suppose I ought to figure it out quickly."

"Oh, I think you know. Deep down. It isn't something that changes. When you go to Plymouth, you might dress differently or keep a different schedule, but that person will still be in you."

A sound came from the cottage, and she looked back to it. Her nerves felt tight.

"You shouldn't be here," she blurted as the fear of discovery pinched. Then she shrugged. "Although I don't know why it matters. Everyone already has such low opinions of me. Of my mother. Of my grandfather."

"But you're not them. It will be easier for you to get past this if you recognize that distinction."

"I'm afraid there is nothing easy about this."

"It's not easy for me either, Evelyn." He leaned slightly closer to her. His scent of sandalwood and outdoors encircled her. "I would miss you if you went to Plymouth. I would miss you very much."

She flicked her eyes up at him.

"Without you, I fear things will be completely different at Wyndcliff Hall." Once again, he took her hand in his. Only this time there was no one to interrupt them — nothing but the song of the breeze and the rustle of the fading leaves overhead.

Her instinct was to pull away from him. But she remained still and allowed her hand to stay there in the warmth of his. If things were different — if he were not the master of the estate and she were not the granddaughter of the steward — the situation might have some other outcome. A future might glimmer, exciting and bright.

But she *was* the steward's granddaughter.

"Things are not simple, Liam. They never have been."

"Things are only as complicated as you let them be. As for me, I see something very simple. A man who is enamored and a woman who, if she were to let the wall around her down a bit, might warm to him. Eventually."

His eyes were so beautiful, so intent, that it pained her to see them.

"You say that now" — she diverted her gaze to her hands — "but . . ."

"I do not say such things lightly, Evelyn."

He was staring at her with eyes so full of

questions. She knew his expression would haunt her in the weeks to come, in the midnight hours when sleep would elude her.

She glanced back to the cottage. The night birds swooped down; the breeze blew. She'd been happy in that cottage, but something had been missing. Something she had never found. The distant crash of the waves on the shore — the sound that had always been so charming and soothing to her — now grated on her nerves and whispered a constant reminder of her confusion.

His words were sweet now, but what would they seem like when the emotions of the day wound down? Eventually Mother would leave, as would Evelyn, and Liam's life would resume. He had a future here, with his china clay endeavor. Would he really risk his position in society by marrying a steward's granddaughter instead of someone like Lydia Traver? For marriage was the only possible solution to their situation, and she doubted that either of them would be ready to think of such a union. After all, they really had not known each other all that long. A month, perhaps? Aye, emotions were ruling his actions now.

She had to put a stop to this line of thought, not only for her own sake but for his as well. It was chasing folly, and pretending otherwise would only lead to hurt.

Evelyn pulled her hand from his, straightened her posture, and forced steadiness to her voice. "What did you hope to achieve by coming here tonight, to say such things to me?"

He winced, as if shocked by the question. He hesitated, and that slight pause — the slight uncertainty that balanced in that silent moment — was enough to shatter the hope of something further.

In that moment she knew there was nothing more to be done. "Good night, Mr. Twethewey."

He grabbed her arm. "Evelyn, I —"

She did not turn around. "This is all for the best. You need to be here to run Wyndcliff. I need to go to Plymouth. It is as simple as that."

Evelyn did not give him the chance to respond. She gathered her skirts, pulled her arm from his hand, stepped into the dark kitchen, and closed the door behind her.

She could not bring herself to look back through the window.

She could not bring herself to step forward into the empty house.

So she sat on the floor and leaned with her back against the wall.

Life as she knew it was changing. She'd

begin anew.

She sniffed. She would not cry. Not any-more. After all, she'd started over before. But then she'd been a child and her heart's experiences were limited.

Time and experience had both educated her and taken a toll.

She liked Mr. Twethewey. In fact, he was the sort of man she believed she could love. An unmistakable thread bound them to each other. One of mutual understanding and respect. Never had her knees felt weak under another's gaze. Never had a simple touch of the hand ignited such longing.

But she was broken now. And she needed to heal.

CHAPTER 33

Evelyn tried to forget the interaction with Mr. Twethewey.

In the days following their conversation, she repeatedly pushed the memory of it to the back of her mind, only to have it resurface moments later. Nearly every time she closed her eyes, she could see the look of disbelief on his face when she discouraged his attentions.

Logically she knew she'd made the right decision, but the ache in her heart and the gaping emptiness in her chest suggested otherwise.

Nay, with the circumstances being what they were, it was best for her to leave and start afresh with her mother in Plymouth, regardless of how she felt about her mother's new family.

When evening fell, Evelyn found herself in her bedchamber, alone. Normally she did not mind solitude, but tonight was different. Her mother, stepfather, and stepsisters had departed for the coast the previous day, and Grandfather had been staying at the White Eagle Inn, claiming the need to be in the village to assist the pit workers. Evelyn would even be satisfied with Bertie's presence, but the maid also had seemed to vanish.

Now the wind howling against the outer wall was her only company. It rustled the dry ivy on the house and rattled the glass in the pane, proving its presence. The rag she had plugged the hole with had fallen again, and the breeze curled in at will. This time she didn't bother to plug it. She sat and stared at the sliver of moonlight sliding through the glass.

This room used to be a solace, a retreat from a world in which she did not feel at ease. It had hidden her safely away, and she had been comfortable with that. But now she felt its restrictions. Like a cage, it kept her in place, kept her from realizing what might lie beyond.

With a sigh she stood and stooped to finally pick up the rag that had been blocking the cool air from entering. It would not do to catch a chill, regardless of the circumstances. As she was about to stuff the rag into place, she stopped.

The sound of footsteps echoed beneath her window, followed by the sharp hiss of a whisper.

She arched her head to see out into the darkness. Tall figures cast long shadows across the stone courtyard. She quickly doused her candle and leaned forward. No fewer than three figures stood below, along the cottage's small stone wall.

Heart leaping and pulse racing, she tucked her hair behind her ear and leaned close to the hole in the glass, struggling to hear if she recognized a voice.

"We have to act tonight!" the first voice, low and gritty, whispered. It was Jenna's father, Jeremiah Shaw.

"Nah, too dangerous." Evelyn recognized her grandfather's voice in an instant. "I've told you before, you must be patient."

"Why? It's the perfect opportunity. It could take weeks for another vessel like this, and that will be far too late."

"You're daft," her grandfather jeered. "Twethewey's in tight with the excise men. Told you as much several times. No doubt the beach will be crawling."

"I don't know about that." Jim Bowen's lilt was unmistakable. "Besides, that woman's memory is returning more and more every day. You said so yourself. And Twethewey's in no hurry to send her away. Do you want her to be here if and when she suddenly recalls the details of that night? Besides, Simpson is nervous, and the last thing we need is more trouble with him."

Evelyn frowned at the name.

Simpson? Surely it was not the same Simpson Mrs. Williams had mentioned. Was it?

"Fine." Her grandfather's forced tone of composure recaptured her attention. "So what do you suggest?"

"We must get her away from here, one way or another. We'll get her on that ship tonight, and she'll be out of our hair by dawn," Jim hissed. "It *will* happen tonight. I'm tired of waiting. And you'll help me. Otherwise . . ."

The implied threat ended in silence.

"And the child?" Jeremiah Shaw blurted.

"She'll have to go too," Jim snapped. "Otherwise the mother will be bent on returning. The ship is bound for the East Indies. After such a voyage they'll not be back in England, mark my words."

Jeremiah cleared his throat. "And you're sure the ship is stopping in the cove?"

"Yep. She's carrying a shipment from Spain," Jim said. "The local men have already been notified."

"I don't like this," her grandfather grumbled.

"I don't like it either, but Simpson said we must. Do you want to make *him* angry?"

Evelyn had heard too much already. Talks of ships and danger, but what alarmed her the most was the talk of the Williamses.

She was still making sense of it when she heard the most frightening of it all.

"And what of Evelyn?"

Evelyn jerked at the sound of her name on Jim's lips.

"Are you sure she doesn't suspect anything? She's awfully thick with that woman."

Her stomach clenched. She thought she might be sick.

"Nah," her grandfather answered at length. "I took care of it. She'll not be leaving her chamber this night. She'll be none the wiser."

She whirled away from the window as all the bits of information slammed together.

So Liam's suspicions were accurate those weeks ago when he had found her grandfather's crimson neckcloth. Grandfather did have something to do with the comings and goings of these ships. The conversation she'd just overhead confirmed it, and the truth stabbed like a knife.

She had two options. She could forget she

heard anything — forget that she suspected her grandfather was involved in something dangerous.

Or she could tell someone.

She'd grown to care too much about Mary and Mrs. Williams, and she would not see them brought to harm. She would deal with the consequences of her actions later, but now she needed to get help from the only person she knew would not be involved with the local men.

She needed to seek Liam.

Evelyn tiptoed over to her door and jiggled the knob. Locked! So that was why Grandfather had been so confident that she'd not be leaving her chamber.

Irritation flared.

She whirled around. There were two other options for her to exit: the window and the access door in the floor that led to her mother's old chamber. Suddenly the fact that her mother's chamber door was locked the last time she attempted to open it made sense. Perhaps he'd been trying to contain her then too. But she knew how to unlock it from the inside. A key was always kept in the vase on the mantel. And surely Grandfather had completely forgotten about the trapdoor in the ceiling. He had not been in either chamber for years.

Hands trembling, she crossed her chamber, swept the rug out of the way, gripped the iron handle, and pulled on it. There was no ladder or stairs, so she knelt, lowered her legs through the dark opening, and then, using every bit of strength in her arms, lowered herself through the hole.

When she could lower herself no more, she dropped to the floor, holding her crouched position while listening to hear if anyone had noticed the thud. Satisfied her descent went unnoticed, she straightened and took a few steps toward the door to the corridor.

In a rush, strong arms grabbed her from behind. A large, calloused hand clamped over her mouth, and then a thick, wool-clad arm wrapped around her arm, pressing it against her body and immobilizing it.

Panic raced through her. She thrashed and writhed. Her assailant loosened his hold ever so slightly to tighten his grip on her, and she bit his hand. Hard. He jerked, giving her enough space to free her arm.

She ducked and whirled. In those split seconds her mind mapped the room. The fireplace. The candleholders on it. Nothing had changed in years. Trusting her memory, she lunged for the candleholders, grabbed a thick pewter candlestick with both hands, and swung it toward the staggering beast with all her might.

She landed her shot against something strong and sturdy. She did it again, aiming higher.

The man groaned and let loose a slew of swear words. She could hear him fall against the bed behind him.

He recovered quickly, jumped toward her, and knocked the candlestick from her hand.

She grabbed the second candlestick on the other end of the mantel. She swung again. Higher and harder. This time the man stumbled and fell.

And then all was silent.

Had she injured him? Killed him?

None of this was real. It couldn't be. It had to be a dream.

And yet every bit of energy coursing through her body forced her to flee.

Dropping the candlestick, she quickly located the extra key, unlocked the door with trembling hands, relocked it once she was in the corridor to prevent the man from leaving, should he waken, and stumbled down the stairs and into the night toward the sleeping Wyndcliff Hall.

Fear gripped Evelyn as she ran as fast as her trembling legs would carry her. She did not care who saw her. She just had to get to Wyndcliff Hall.

She swallowed a sob as she rounded the corner to the courtyard and a gust of icy night air struck her. She had to keep her senses about her. For Mary. For Mrs. Williams. For herself.

The moonlight cast fleeting shadows on the path leading to the kitchen entrance, and she gripped the door handle and flung it open. Not pausing to catch her breath, she fled up the back staircase to the Blue Room to make sure Mrs. Williams was still there.

Relief was sweet as Evelyn saw Mrs. Williams slumbering peacefully, with Mary by her side, both blissfully unaware of the developing plot against them.

She closed the door and stepped back to the corridor.

Just down the hall and around the corner was the master's chamber, where Mr. Twethewey was, no doubt, sleeping this very moment.

Dare she go to his chamber and wake him, especially given the events that passed between them?

She bit her lip in hasty contemplation. Did she have a choice?

There was no doubt the Williamses were

in danger. After the attack in Mother's chamber, Evelyn was very much in danger as well. She owed it to them, Mr. Twethewey, and even herself to sound an alarm.

She took several determined steps and then stopped abruptly. If she proceeded on this course, she'd be betraying her grandfather — the man who had single-handedly raised her these last years.

Could she do that?

But the man who'd locked her in her room was not the grandfather she knew. The man who would even speak of kidnapping a woman might as well be a stranger. The man who had yelled at Liam Twethewey was another version of the man she loved and had, at one time, revered.

And the innocent had to be protected.

Ahead of her to her right was a series of tall, narrow windows that overlooked the cove. It was dark, but far in the distance a swinging lantern gleamed through the night's mist.

And that was enough. Her decision was made.

Fresh urgency seized her, and she sped down the hall to Mr. Twethewey's chamber. She knocked, softly at first, and then with more intensity.

Rustling sounded from inside. Then footsteps toward the door.

She shifted her weight nervously and gripped her hands in front of her.

The door opened. He appeared, clad in his shirt and trousers. He raked his fingers through unruly dark hair. Surprise widened his blue eyes. "Evelyn."

She could not worry about what he thought of seeing her there, at his chambers, in the midnight hours. She blurted, "I think there's a ship coming into the cove tonight, and I think Mrs. Williams and Mary are in danger."

He jerked. "What?"

"I heard men outside the cottage saying it was getting too dangerous with Mrs. Williams remembering so much. They are planning to put her and Mary on a ship bound for the East Indies. And then a man attacked me in the cottage, and I —"

"Attacked you?" He gripped her arms. "Are you all right?"

"Aye, but I fear if we do not act fast, something dreadful might happen."

"Stay here." He disappeared inside his room and returned moments later more fully dressed and buttoning his waistcoat. "Are you sure you're all right?"

She nodded, but even as she did her eyes filled with tears. She was not all right. Fear, desperation, betrayal clawed through her.

He wrapped his arms around her and pulled her to him. She pressed her cheek against his chest, feeling his strength. His warmth. His comforting presence. For the first time since her grandfather had reprimanded her, she felt a calmness — albeit slight — return.

After several moments he straightened and lowered his head to look her in the eye. "I'll get John, and we'll check it out. Men are patrolling the beach."

"Are you sure?"

"They should be. Captain Hollingswood said —"

A crash, then a cry interrupted them.

They looked at each other for several moments.

"Mary!" Evelyn cried.

They ran down the hall to the Blue Room and flung open the door. A sharp breeze met them. The window was wide open and the bed was empty.

Mr. Twethewey raced to the window and looked down, and Evelyn followed quickly. In the courtyard lay a pile of rope that no doubt had been used to get down.

"Wake everyone. Have Marnie and Kitty place candles in every window. Let it be clear that Wyndcliff Hall is awake and watching. Then stay here, all right? I will not have you getting caught up in this. Do you understand me?"

She nodded.

"How many men did you see?"

"I heard three talking. I recognized Jim Bowen, Jeremiah Shaw, and Grandfather." Saying Grandfather's name aloud gutted her, but Mary and Mrs. Williams were at stake.

"And the man who attacked you?"

"I never saw his face. He was hiding in my mother's old chamber, but I don't know why."

"Whatever you do, don't go outside."

She nodded again, then reached for his sleeve. "Be careful."

CHAPTER 34

Liam stood in the study and devised a plan of battle based on what Evelyn had told him. Ignoring the slight tremor in his hand, he handed his brother a pistol yet again as uncertainty swirled.

The situation was unreal. Had they not just had a shipwreck, and now this?

How differently he felt holding the pistol now. The last time he took up arms, it was an almost naive display, as if he could sway the behavior of a band of smugglers by firing a pistol into the air and shouting a warning. His actions might have affected events for that one night, but clearly he'd deterred nothing in the long run, and the stakes were much, much higher.

"I sent Porter to get some of the men in the pit village to come and assist us."

"What of the excise men?" John suggested.

"I don't think they'll get here in time."

"Do you think the pit workers will come?" John checked that the pistol was loaded.

"I told Porter to pay whatever it took to buy their assistance. If what Miss Bray says is accurate, you and I alone would be no match for the men who did this. We need help and a great deal of it. Come on."

"I'm not sure Wyndcliff Hall is worth all this trouble." John donned his hat over his black hair. "Pistols. Shipwrecks. Angry grandfathers. Remind me again why you don't just sell this place and be done with it?"

Liam ignored his brother's sarcasm.

"I guess it's a good thing I came along after all." John huffed. "Not sure what you would do without me here. But I must say, if you're going to all this trouble for the sake of a pretty girl's attentions, then I think you're daft."

Liam wasn't doing this just for Evelyn, but he did have her in mind. She'd already been attacked. He needed to prevent something worse from happening. He needed to fight for the woman and child who had already been through so much.

"And Porter," John continued as they fell into step across the great hall. "You're sure you can trust him? He's a pit man, not a soldier or magistrate."

"I'm not certain of anything, John. But what other option have we? Whoever those men are, they've taken Mary and Mrs. Williams."

At the end of the great hall, John stopped, turned, and added in a more somber tone, "And are you sure you can trust Miss Bray?"

Liam's movements slowed as the meaning of his brother's words sank in.

It was true that he felt he'd developed a connection with Evelyn Bray over the past months, yet they did not have the advantage of time and the security that comes with a lengthy acquaintance.

Still, he had to trust his instincts. What other option did he have?

"I do trust her."

John shrugged. "Then let's go."

They stepped out into the night and crept along the edge of the house and under the shadows of the trees toward the forest bordering the cliff. No lights or voices could be heard, yet a strange energy charged the air.

They inched closer to the beach and watched the shore for what seemed like an eternity, until another group of shadowy figures appeared.

Liam licked his lips, then leaned to his brother. "Our goal is to rescue Mary and

Mrs. Williams and get them to safety. Then we deal with these men. Agreed?"

Johnny nodded.

They crept farther down Brayden's Crag to the beach, keeping close to the cliff. Liam feared they might be too late, but then voices, hushed and harried, carried on the whistling wind.

John tapped him on the shoulder and pointed toward the sea.

And Liam saw it.

A ship, large and black, waited off the coast, and upon further inspection, three smaller vessels were coming ashore.

"Liam!" John shouted.

Liam whirled in time to glimpse a large man with a handkerchief tied around the lower half of his face lunging toward him. Liam ducked the blow, and instead of backing away, he lowered his head and, using his shoulder, rammed the man. Johnny joined him, and together they pinned the man against the cliff. "Where are Elizabeth and Mary Williams?"

The man laughed from behind the kerchief, and even in the dark the man's eyes were harsh. "Look. There she is."

Liam looked over his shoulder. Someone was leading a woman in a white gown from the cliff to the boat. She was fighting. Flailing. And a wriggling bundle was hoisted on another man's shoulder. Mary.

Movement atop the cliff caught his attention. Black figures of men, too many to count, crested the cliff. At once they charged down Brayden's Crag, shouting and running. Porter had clearly come through, and the men stormed the beach.

The assailant took advantage of Liam's break in concentration and whirled from his grip, then threw a punch, wild and unwieldy.

A brawl ensued. Fists flew. Shouts rang out.

The pit men were charging the approaching sailors from the ship. In turn, the ship's remaining sailors ran in from the sea.

Liam had to get to the shore to make sure Mary and Mrs. Williams did not reach the ship. Leaving John to deal with the villain by the cliff, Liam ran toward the beach and straight for the Williamses.

The sea sprayed his face and bits of sand cut like glass as he ran, and yet Liam fixed his eyes on his target — the man holding Mrs. Williams — and he lunged toward the man, catching him by surprise and throwing him off balance. The man stumbled. Elizabeth broke free.

A gunshot rang out from somewhere. Then another. And another. On top of the cliff stood a row of horses and horsemen, their red coats vibrant even in the faint light. The excise men had arrived.

Liam didn't have time to consider how they found out about this. All he knew was he was glad to see them.

Liam grabbed Elizabeth's arm, pulling her away. "Run!"

"Not without Mary!"

He ducked the fist of the man and returned a punch of his own. His breath came in jagged gasps and his pulse hammered. He glanced at the man holding Mary. He was closer to the ship, standing in a couple feet of water, preparing to board.

Liam propelled himself toward the man. As he did, the sand devoured his booted feet, holding them firm like a vise. With every ounce of energy he freed his feet and grabbed the man from behind and whirled him around.

A kerchief covered his face and his hat was pulled low, but there was no mistaking Rupert Bray's eyes.

It did not matter whose grandfather this was or how many years he'd served the estate. At the moment, he was the enemy who was threatening a child. Liam punched Bray, and the older man crumpled in the waves and dropped the child, and Liam lifted her. She hugged him tight. With his other hand he grabbed an unconscious Bray and dragged him back to shore.

The excise men were down the cliff now. They added fresh power and energy to the altercation, and along with the pit men they quickly overcame the sailors.

Liam was not sure how much time had passed, but by the time dawn broke, the sailors and a handful of other men had been restrained, bound, and lined along the cliff.

The men were no longer hiding behind their kerchiefs.

Liam recognized some of the faces as he walked down the line, many of whom he'd seen his very first day at the inn. Jim Bowen. Jeremiah Shaw. Rupert Bray. He wanted to look each man in the eyes — each man who had violated his trust and used his property for ill gains.

Liam had almost reached the end of the line when he encountered a man he'd not seen before — a man with a full beard. Liam stepped toward Captain Hollingswood. "Who's that?"

"This is interesting." Captain Hollingswood lowered his voice. "That's Captain Leonard Simpson. From what I've gathered this morning, he was the captain of the ship originally transporting Elizabeth and Mary

Williams. Apparently he has been a special guest of Bray and has made several visits to this very cove over the years. Seems our friend Bray had a great interest in keeping his identity and location hidden after the Williamses were rescued."

The pieces of the puzzle slammed into place. "So the crew was not lost during that shipwreck as we thought."

"Not at all. My understanding is that they were rescued by Bray and his friends and swept to safety so we wouldn't be able to identify them — or their cargo. Essentially Captain Simpson here has been hiding right under our noses all this time. It seems that Captain Simpson has been part of a long thread connecting smuggled goods from India to Cornwall, and our friend Bray and Jim Bowen have been assisting him this past decade. Fortunately you and your brother intervened when you did, for they were going to get him back on a ship this very night to avoid detection, along with the Williams ladies."

Liam buried the frustration brewing within him. He had to keep his emotions in check. "How did you know to come here? We did not send for you."

Captain Hollingswood raised a brow. "Ever hear of a man named Charlie Potts?"

383

Liam nodded.

"He rode out and called us during the midnight hours. Apparently he used to be part of this ring but grew nervous when he heard Mrs. Williams and the child would be kidnapped and taken to the ship. He was the person who rang the bell during the wreck that brought us the Williamses, and he was the one who fired the shots that woke you up during the last shipwreck, or at least that's what he told us. Looks like one of the blackguards grew a conscience when a woman and child became involved and decided to alert us."

Liam glanced around. "Where's Potts? I must speak with him."

Captain Hollingswood scoffed. "You'll not see him again. He'll have too many enemies in Pevlyn now. These smuggling rings run deep. He'll likely never show his face in the village again."

Liam drew a sharp breath. He'd had an ally this entire time and didn't even know it.

"We'll bring our charges against these men," the captain said. "Free trading. Kidnapping. But you have charges to bring as well. Trespassing and so forth."

Liam nodded. He had no choice. He should be happy. He'd been here less than a month, and these men were going to be brought to justice.

And yet his property had been used for criminal purposes for all these years. It would take time to recover, to rebuild trust, and to establish new expectations.

But as he watched Bray stand there on the edge of the cliff, his chest ached. Not for Bray, but for his granddaughter who, no doubt, was waiting for him this very moment.

CHAPTER 35

Evelyn sat alone at the writing desk in her mother's chamber at Wyndcliff Cottage. Near her feet the candlesticks still lay on the ground — just where she had dropped them after crashing them against the man she now knew was Captain Simpson. Otherwise this chamber was completely empty and silent, with only the memories whispering from the walls and ceiling.

Betrayal stung.

Tears blurred her vision afresh. Everyone in this home had deceived her. Even Bertie had played a hand in this entire operation, tending to the captain and helping her grandfather send messages to the other men. On top of that, she'd kept several secrets from Evelyn, including the fact that a stranger had been secretly billeted one floor below her bedchamber.

What a fool everyone must have thought her. What a pathetic, insipid fool.

And now, on top of an already heart-shattering morning, more tasks needed to be accomplished. She looked to the paper in front of her and then to the quill in her hand.

Mother needed to know what had transpired. No doubt Mr. Twethewey would have her grandfather's position replaced by the week's end, and Evelyn would surely be required to vacate the cottage.

She folded the letter carefully and sealed it. She'd not ask Tom to post the letter, as she usually would. Instead, she'd take Ada to Pevlyn and do it herself, though she wasn't sure if the pony belonged to her anymore. At the moment, Ada was the one living, breathing thing that did not judge her. She'd be happy to see Evelyn, as long as she brought an apple from the barrel, so she did just that.

Evelyn rode Ada through the moors, completed letter in hand, and the silent, still morning air provided a bit of an escape. The bright autumn sun glinted on the golden-tinged flora. In the rare moments when the wind subsided, the sun's rays felt warm on her face, hair, and shoulders.

But her pastoral escape quickly vanished when she arrived at the village. She'd not really considered how fast the news of what had transpired would spread, but as she rode in, the stares started.

And they did not stop.

She concluded her business at the post office as quickly as possible, and as she stepped back to High Street, Jenna stood in the side alley by her father's shop. She motioned for Evelyn to join her. "You've heard what happened to my father, haven't you?"

Evelyn winced at the sadness in her friend's eyes. "Aye. I've heard."

"Oh dear, news of this is all over the village. As your friend I must tell you that everyone is saying you are behind this entire thing. Jim Bowen told some of the other men that you attacked Captain Simpson and informed Mr. Twethewey of their plans, but I know it can't possibly be true."

Evelyn froze. She wanted to deny it, if for no other reason than to ease her friend's mind. But she could not. How could she tell her friend that she did play a role in her father's arrest?

When Evelyn did not respond, Jenna tilted her head to the side and fixed her red-rimmed eyes on Evelyn. "You didn't have anything to do with it, did you?"

Weariness bubbled within Evelyn. She hated the thought that her actions had such far-reaching consequences. But had there been another choice? "Jim was wrong. I-I was attacked in my cottage, and I overhead some people planning to kidnap Mrs. Williams and Mary. I did notify Mr. Twethewey, but only to —"

"So it is true then." Jenna's tone hardened. "You did report the men. You betrayed your own grandfather. Jim Bowen. My father."

Evelyn stared at Jenna. "If you think I intended for my grandfather to be arrested, of course I did not!"

"But you did tell Mr. Twethewey."

"My concern was for the woman and child." Evelyn's voice rose in defense. "How on earth could I have guessed that half of the men in the village were somehow involved in illegal activities?"

Jenna's gaze narrowed. "Because of you, my father is arrested, not to mention your own grandfather. And you've heard about Charlie, haven't you? He's left with nary a word to anyone. Not even me."

Tears pricked Evelyn's eyes. She knew how much Jenna adored Charlie, and the pain in her friend's eyes was difficult to see. "I had no control over Charlie's actions. I knew nothing of him."

"Everything I love is now gone," Jenna hurled. "Evelyn, how could you?"

How could she make Jenna understand? Her defense sounded thin. Weak. "I was only trying to help Mary and Elizabeth Williams."

"All I know is that family is family. You chose practical strangers over your grandfather." Jenna narrowed her gaze. "I know the real reason you did this."

Stunned at the accusation, Evelyn shook her head. "What do you mean?"

"Mr. Twethewey, of course."

The words stabbed. "How can you say that?"

"He is handsome, wealthy, and poised to be the most successful man in the area. Many a woman has done much worse to secure the affections of such a man."

Her mouth felt dry as she tried to speak. "Is that really what you think of me?"

"I hardly know what to think. And I suppose you are off to Plymouth now, running away after you have hurt so many people. Good riddance, I say." Jenna spun on her heel and returned to her family's shop. And she did not turn back.

Evelyn drew a sharp breath, crossed her arms over her chest, and looked into the breeze, giving herself a few seconds to calm down.

She had anticipated, nay, expected a

measure of sympathy from her friend. But Jenna's hard countenance offered no comfort. Evelyn put one foot in front of the other toward Ada.

But Jenna did not call after her.

And Evelyn did not look back.

When Evelyn returned home from mailing her letter, she stepped across the courtyard to the cottage. How much longer would she call Wyndcliff Cottage her home?

She expected to find the cottage empty, but when she entered the kitchen, she saw Marnie tending the fire.

"What are you doing here?" Evelyn asked, surprised. Marnie rarely left Wyndcliff Hall on account of her bad leg. "Did you walk here alone?"

" 'Course I walked here alone. I may be old an' decrepit, but when my girl be hurtin', I can see beyond meself to come to her."

At the kind words Evelyn's shoulders sagged, and she allowed herself to fall into the embrace of the woman who had been more like a mother to her than her own had been. After feeling like she was the enemy of everyone in the village, she felt a strong sense of relief at being welcomed by someone who loved her.

"I'm glad to see ye." Marnie released her from the embrace and brushed a lock of hair away from Evelyn's forehead. "I was growin' quite worried."

"You know better than to worry about me." Evelyn offered a smile and removed her straw bonnet and hung it on the hook. "I went to the village to post a letter to my mother."

"An' what did ye tell her?" Marnie poked at the fire to encourage it to flame.

"Everything." Evelyn shrugged with a sniff. "I don't suppose there is a reason to hide any of it. I asked her if she could shorten her journey and come back as soon as possible."

Marnie looked up from her task. "Why did ye ask her that?"

"Well, I can't stay here. This is the steward's cottage."

"Mr. Twethewey is not goin' to throw ye out. Ye are a part of Wyndcliff Hall. *Ye,* no matter what yer grandfather has done."

Evelyn bowed her head as fresh tears trailed down her cheeks. "Am I? Because I feel very, very alone."

Marnie stepped closer and embraced her anew. After letting Evelyn cry for a few moments, Marnie smoothed Evelyn's hair once more. "He was askin' after ye, ye know. He was lookin' for ye."

Evelyn sniffed. She did not need to ask to whom Marnie referred.

"Young Mary an' Mrs. Williams were both lookin' for ye as well. Ye see? Ye do have friends, no matter what the people in the village might think. An' we'll not leave ye alone."

Liam fell into step with John and Mr. Porter as they walked along the china clay pits. The sun fought its way from behind the thick clouds, and seabirds swooped low over the faded cotton grasses. When he'd arrived at Wyndcliff, this stretch of land had been quiet and desolate. Now nearly three dozen men, axes or shovels in hand, worked the land.

It had been two days since the incident in the cove.

Two days since he'd last spoken to Miss Bray.

And two days since his entire standing in the community had changed.

He never would have anticipated that the event would have such an unexpected outcome. The men, who had up till this point barely noticed him, now greeted both John and him as they passed.

Porter nodded to a row of men on the far

side of the road. "I remember when we started this endeavor. You wondered if the men would be loyal, or if they would come and go between positions with the copper mines. Well, just look at them. They're grateful, you know, for the extra money in their pockets as a result of the raid."

Liam exchanged glances with John. He'd given Porter the approval to offer whatever funds necessary to recruit the men to stop the sailors, and it worked. Nearly a dozen of them had answered his call and helped until the excise men could arrive. "I am grateful for their assistance, but let's hope we don't need such aid again. John and I were no match for them. If you all had not come, the outcome would have been very different."

"An interesting tactic, to be sure, but it was creative, and most importantly, it worked. The amount you paid might not have been a huge sum to you, but to these men, it was monumental. It will change their outlook this winter. No doubt these men will be loyal to you for the rest of their lives."

Liam exchanged glances with John. "I don't want to buy their loyalty."

"They will always be grateful, but you also impressed them. It's not every day a man will spend money to see that a stranger and her child are safe."

Satisfaction spread through his chest at the words. Could it be that he was starting to accomplish one of his main goals — to be part of the community and make it better?

Porter's next words threatened that confidence. "There is one concern we have heard the men muttering about."

Liam swallowed. "And that is?"

"The Bray girl."

Every other sound faded into the background at the sound of her name. His spine stiffened. "What about her?"

"From what I can tell, the town is quite divided. The miners, the sort who were loyal to Bray, are obviously not on your side, but they are not your employees, so it doesn't really matter. They will tend to their business and we will tend to ours. But the china clay pit workers have taken up a cause of their own."

"And what has that to do with Miss Bray?" Liam asked as they paused to allow two men pushing a cart across the road to precede them.

"They don't trust her."

Liam huffed incredulously. "Do they realize she is the very person who discovered the plot and alerted us in the first place?"

"Aye, they know, but it does not matter. She carries the Bray name. After what has occurred, that is one of the worst possible offenses, and it will not soon be forgotten. There are, uh, rumors, that the two of you . . . well, that the two of you . . ."

"That I have affections for her?"

"Er, aye. It makes them nervous."

Liam laughed in spite of himself. "That's ridiculous. Besides, she is leaving for Plymouth any day. Surely that will quell any concerns."

"It's a shame. I always liked her, personally. But it is for the best. After all, things are moving in the right direction with these pits, and we are laying the foundation for a long and successful run. Loyalties are developing. You don't want to risk that. Is she still planning on going to Plymouth with Mrs. Drake?"

The words tasted bitter on his tongue. "As far as I know. I've not spoken with her on the matter."

Letting the topic drop, Porter stopped on the newly cut road and nodded toward a modest stone building with fresh white paint on the door. "There, the new count-inghouse. There can be no question now that this is a permanent establishment.

Congratulations, Mr. Twethewey."

Liam forced a smile as he assessed the building, but the smile could not mask the trepidation mounting within him. He had managed to find success in one area, but it was to the detriment of another, much more tender part — his heart. He tried to fight it, but with each day that passed, Evelyn seemed to slip further and further away from him. As it was, she would not even look in his direction. Her past words to him roared through his every thought.

"This is all for the best. You need to be here to run Wyndcliff. I need to go to Plymouth. It is as simple as that."

Perhaps it was time to admit she was right.

CHAPTER 36

The event on the beach had changed Evelyn's life, and now there was no going back. The few short yet significant days that followed felt like both an eternity and a blink of the eye.

She'd avoided Wyndcliff Hall and kept mostly to herself and the cottage. She'd received no response from her mother, and Evelyn's mind ran rampant. Once in Plymouth, she would be at the mercy of the Drakes and their hospitality. She had no other family, and she was no longer welcome in the village. She had no qualifications for employment and no money of her own. The more she thought about it, the tighter anxiety wound around her heart.

But for now she sat in her small kitchen garden, where the breeze rushed in, rustling the dead leaves and remaining flowers, and a little gray squirrel scurried up a leaning ash tree. Mary was with her, and together

398

they were clearing out one of the smaller flower beds to prepare it for winter.

They chatted about a variety of things, but safe, easy topics, like what happened to the garden in winter, when it would bloom again in the spring, and where exactly the cat liked to hide in the lavender. It was pleasant conversation, until Mary's countenance grew quite dark.

She sat still for several moments and then turned to Evelyn. "Why do scary things keep happening?"

Evelyn's heart squeezed. Aye, scary things were happening all around them. She had hoped the scary things were behind them, but in truth, the future, and the unknown lurking there, was the most frightening of all.

Mary fiddled with the stem of a flower and lowered it to her lap. "Mama says we are to go to London soon, when she remembers everything again. I've never been there. Have you?"

Evelyn shook her head, the realization that she had hardly been out of Pevlyn pressing her. "Nay, I haven't."

"Will you come with us?" Mary squinted against the bright sunlight.

Evelyn sighed and gathered her pruning supplies in her gardening basket. She had to admit the offer was tempting. Mrs. Williams, too, had extended it to her just the previous day. Evelyn was fond of Mrs. Williams and of Mary, but they had a life to return to that did not include her. Surely they would not want memories of their time at Wyndcliff Hall following them. "Nay, dearest. I am going to live with my own mother soon."

"Why isn't your mother here now? Doesn't she know you were scared?"

It was such a simple question — one with an impossibly difficult answer. Evelyn smiled to mask the uncertainty the question conjured. "Come now. Let's go down to the sea. Don't forget your basket now."

Satisfied that Mr. Twethewey would be at the Aulder Hill pits, Evelyn and Mary walked toward the courtyard, where Mrs. Williams was already present. Her eyes brightened as she saw them approach. "I was just looking for you!"

Evelyn could not deny how happy she was for Mrs. Williams. The young mother was healing — and a smile lit her round face. She exuded happiness. And why shouldn't she? The bruising on her forehead had all but disappeared, and the mark left from the gash on her forehead was shrinking. Beyond the physical improvements, a general sense of freedom suffused her.

How Evelyn envied it.

Her envy was quickly followed by crushing remorse. How could she think such a thing about a woman who had endured so much? For it was odd to envy the person she had been worried about and caring for all this time. Mrs. Williams's troubles seemed to be behind her, whereas the waves of Evelyn's troubles were crashing into her, fast and bold, and she had to weather the storm.

Mrs. Williams bustled toward her, hands outstretched. "Shall we all go for a walk while we still have the sunlight? Soon it will be too late."

Evelyn nodded, but a lump formed in her throat. For so long the paths and Wyndcliff walkways had been such a place of refuge and solitude. Would she ever possess such a place again?

They were about to head toward the path to Brayden's Crag, with its stony rocks and jutting forms, when Mr. Twethewey, his brother, and Mr. Porter walked through the gate.

She could blame the fluttery feeling in her stomach on the events of the past several days, but when her gaze landed on Mr. Twethewey, she knew the truth.

She wanted to be in his presence as much as she wanted to avoid him.

She wanted to talk with him as much as she wanted to hide every thought from him.

Oh, confusion reigned within her, and she had nothing like Mrs. Williams's excuse.

Mary, who was always enthusiastic to see the Twetheweys, ran up to Mr. Twethewey. "We are going on a walk down by the sea. I'm not scared at all to go there."

"I'm not surprised. You are very brave, aren't you? Well, there is nothing there that can hurt you." Mr. Twethewey swung her up in his arms. He glanced at Evelyn for a moment before he returned his attention to Mary. "I think you'll have a lovely walk. Are you going with your mama?"

She nodded, the blue ribbon in her hair fluttering wildly in the wind. "And Miss Bray. Will you come too? Mama said you would be busy, but you are here now, and you aren't busy at all."

He laughed, his blue eyes sparkling in the afternoon sunlight. "My dear, I would love nothing more than a stroll on the beach. John, Porter, will you join us?"

His brother shook his head. "I fear I have had too much excitement for one day already." Mr. Porter also declined.

They headed out to the beach — Mrs.

Williams, Mary, Mr. Twethewey, and Evelyn.

Mary bounded beside them, fueled by her childish energy. Once down at the beach, Mary ran ahead and Mrs. Williams chased after her.

Evelyn fell into step next to Mr. Twethewey like she had several times before, and yet everything felt different. The memory of their embrace and the touch of their hands hovered over them. It was impossible for her to pretend that the few moments they had shared did not happen. Did he think of their time together like she did?

At length he broke the silence and nodded toward mother and daughter. "They look happy."

Evelyn watched them run and then stop at the crag and bend to study something on the sand. "Hopefully from now on, their lives will be smoother than they have been."

They continued along the beach, their resumed silence broken by the crash of the waves and the call of the seabirds. At last he said, "You're much quieter than normal. I'm sure you have a host of thoughts on the current state of things."

She shrugged. "What is there to say?"

"In truth, it almost seems like you have been avoiding me."

"Avoiding you?" The very fact that he noticed rankled. "That's not the case at all. I just have a great deal to plan, 'tis all."

"And what are you planning for?"

Wasn't the answer obvious? "Plymouth, of course."

Initially he did not respond. But then his words were soft. "You do have friends here, you know. If you didn't want to go to Plymouth —"

"I don't think this needs to be discussed again, do you? It was never the plan for me to remain at Wyndcliff Cottage for as long as I did. And now Grandfather . . ."

"I have a question for you." His statement silenced her, and he squared his stance to face her fully. "If you would've known how everything would turn out with your grandfather, would you still have alerted me to what was happening the other night?"

Uncomfortable with the directness of his attention, she shook her head and started walking again. "I've asked myself that question so many times. I miss my grandfather and I hate that he's in jail, but then I see Mary and Mrs. Williams recovering and happy, and I could never live with myself if I'd not intervened."

"If it makes any difference at all, I believe you acted prudently." He fell into step next to her. "And I'm not just saying that because this is my property. It takes a great deal of integrity to behave as you have."

She sniffed. "Integrity, aye. But now I'm alone and dependent upon my mother and her new husband."

"Like I said, there are people here who care about you very much and would be sad to see you leave. Myself included."

They stopped and stared at each other. The wind whipped the length of her skirt against his legs and her long locks across her shoulders and face.

He lowered his head next to her ear to be heard over the wind whistling through the rocky cliffs. "Since my first day here, you have been the steadiest friend I have made. While so many others have seemed difficult to trust, you have been the one I have found as a true ally."

She did not know how to respond. The words were not romantic in nature, but they held intimacy. And what his words did not say, the intense expression in his eyes did.

"Please do not be in such a hurry to depart."

She looked down at his hands. Did he know what he was asking?

Did she?

She needed to change the topic. "I've been

thinking, and I've decided to go tomorrow and try to see my grandfather at the jail."

Mr. Twethewey winced and then shook his head. "Evelyn, no. I don't think that is wise. You have no idea what those places are like, and I —"

"He's my grandfather. Yes, I have heard about those places, and that is exactly why I need to go. He needs food. Clothing."

"I can arrange for him to have those things. You needn't take it on yourself."

"If I'm to have any peace at all about this, I need to let him know that it was not my intention to betray him. And I have so many questions I need answered. I can't leave Cornwall and not make sure he understands."

He propped his hands on his hips and stared out to sea for several seconds. "If you must go, I will accompany you. We can take the carriage."

"I could not ask that. I —"

"It would ease my mind. Don't forget, I'm equally responsible for what happened."

"We cannot go alone." She laughed in disbelief. "There is already enough —" She stopped.

"Enough what?"

"It's not proper, 'tis all."

"Marnie can go with us."

Evelyn could already hear the gossip. But what did it matter? She would be leaving this place. There was no way around it. Her family's reputation was already in tatters. What could be said now?

Mary ran up to her, halting their conversation.

They all walked back to Wyndcliff together, over the cliffs and through the copse of trees. Evelyn was glad to have had a chance to speak with Mr. Twethewey, but she felt only slightly more at ease at the thought of him accompanying her to visit her grandfather. One thing was certain: moving forward, she could not trust a single soul. Indeed, she could scarcely trust herself.

CHAPTER 37

Evelyn's stomach soured as the Wyndcliff estate carriage rumbled over the rocky moorland roads that connected their corner of Cornwall to the larger town of Bodmin.

She'd never ridden in the Wyndcliff carriage before. She never had cause to. Never did she go anywhere that was not accessible by a pony or a cart, and certainly she never dreamed that her path would take her to Bodmin Jail.

And yet that was exactly where she was headed.

Next to her sat Marnie, her head resting against the back of the seat, her eyes closed, her mouth open in noisy slumber. Across from her sat Mr. Twethewey. He was quiet, and his attention was focused on the moorland passing by. She could not ignore, in spite of the day's somber task, how handsome her travel companion was. His dark hair curled over his high collar, and the sunlight slanting through the window high-lighted the straightness of his nose and the brightness of his eyes.

Evelyn's anxious thoughts turned to her grandfather.

She wanted to see him as much as she wanted to avoid him. He'd had a hand in so many dishonest endeavors, and as more evidence of wrongdoing emerged, she felt increasingly deceived. Mary and Mrs. Williams could have died as a result of his actions. He had been careless. Reckless. Selfish.

She'd always thought of him as a benefactor — as one who would care for those around him. It was the image she had been led to believe, and she had done so eagerly. Now she wanted to hate him for the position he had put her in. And yet, despite all the deception and lies that had transpired, she could not. For in her heart, she loved the man who had cared for her and provided for her. And he loved her in return, there was no doubt in her mind.

As moorland gave way to the sights and smells of the town, her stomach twisted again. What would Grandfather think of her now that all was said and done? Did he believe, as so many villagers did, that she had betrayed him? Would he be pleased to see her?

She pulled her attention from the landscape to see Mr. Twethewey looking at her. He nodded toward the bundle of clothing and food in her arms. "You don't have to do this. I can take it in for you."

"Nay, I'm going." She gripped the bundle even tighter. "Besides, I can only imagine how angry he would be to see you there."

"I did nothing wrong. Neither did you." He paused, as if choosing his words. "I don't think you have any idea of what the conditions will be like in there. Trust me when I say that it's no place for a lady."

"He's my grandfather. And I'm the reason he is in there."

"Nay," he snapped back. "You're not the reason he is in there. He's in there as a result of his own actions, and nothing you have done or said could change that."

They sat in heavy silence again until buildings, smoke, dust, and people filled the view out the carriage windows.

Evelyn swallowed as they pulled to a stop in front of the foreboding stone outbuildings. She could feel the weight of Mr. Twethewey's gaze on her. She tucked her hand under the bundle so he could not see it trembling.

When the carriage stopped, he leaned forward and put his hand on the door. "Are you ready then?"

She nodded.

He exited the carriage and then extended his hand to help her down. She placed her gloved hand in his.

Marnie leaned her head out. "Be careful, dear. I'll be eager to hear how it goes."

Without removing her gloved hand from his, she nodded and turned back to the jail entrance in front of her. Bile threatened as scents of manure and rotten waste wafted from the surroundings, and now her imagination was coming to life as she tried to picture what was behind the guarded doors.

He leaned close. "You're trembling."

"What if he refuses to see me?" she whispered, her throat and mouth dry.

"I don't think he's in a position to refuse anything." Mr. Twethewey squeezed her hand instead of releasing it, then looped it around his arm. "Stay close."

She lifted her gaze to the tall iron gates and thick stone walls. Angry shouts echoed from somewhere in the distance. How she wanted to think she was brazen enough to do this on her own, but now as she saw the filthy men lurking in the shadows, she was grateful for his dogged insistence that she not come alone.

She inched closer to Mr. Twethewey as he led the way through the gates to the man guarding the large wooden door. "Mr. William Twethewey and Miss Evelyn Bray to see Rupert Bray."

The man eyed him. At first he did not move, then he nodded his greasy head toward the bundle. "What d'ye have there?"

Evelyn lifted the parcel.

"Give it to him," whispered Liam.

She obeyed immediately.

He dumped the contents out on the table next to the door. Her carefully packed parcel spilled forth. The bread and apples. The change of clothing. The dried meat and jug of ale. A piece of cheese fell to the dirty ground.

The man probed it with his dirty fingers and returned it to the parcel and then motioned for another man to come.

She swallowed, alarmed. What were they doing?

"We're too busy for visitors today."

Her eyes grew wide. It was not even noon. How could it be too late for visitors? Would they really not be able to see him after they'd come all this way?

"Nay," Mr. Twethewey countered firmly. "We intend to see him."

"Listen, unless you want to find yourself in the same predicament as your friend, you'll be a bit friendlier to those what run this place."

Mr. Twethewey did not blink. His gaze did not waver. He reached into his pocket, pulled out some coins, and dropped them on the table.

A smile slid over the man's face. "There now, that's a bit friendlier, isn't it?" He returned the parcel to Evelyn. "Come on then. There's a chamber inside where the lady can wait."

Evelyn cringed at the man's mock formality. She forced the tears of frustration and uncertainty to remain unshed. Mr. Twethewey tightened his grip on her elbow as he guided her into the waiting room.

"Are you sure you don't want me in here with you?" He shifted his gaze from the questionable jailer back to her.

She shook her head, drawing a deep breath of the foul air. "No. Thank you. This part I must do alone."

She watched as he left the room, and seeing his figure outside in the corridor gave her a measure of comfort.

He'd been right. About so many things. How she ever thought she could come to a place like this alone was beyond her.

After nearly half an hour, Grandfather huffed in, dirty and worn. She looked from the top of his unkempt hair to his dusty neckcloth to his torn coat. But as tired and as dirty as his clothing looked, a fire raged in his deep-set gray eyes.

He held his head high and smoothed his hair into place. "What are ye doing here?"

"I-I thought you might need this." She extended the bundle.

When he did not respond, she placed it on the only table in the room and slid a glance over to the jailer who was in there with them, watching their every move.

At length he grunted. "You shouldn't be here."

"I wanted to see you. I wanted to make sure you were all right."

"*All right,* is it?" He scoffed and shuffled farther in. "It's a little late for that now, isn't it?"

The accusation hit her with all the force of a slap. She swallowed and looked again to the jailer, whose dark eyes were fixed on her as if she were the last woman in the world.

"Did you come here alone?" Grandfather bellowed.

"No."

"Who came with you?"

414

"Mr. Twethewey is just outside the door, and Marnie is in the carriage."

"Ah yes. I see Twethewey wasted no time, swooping in to help the damsel in distress, eh?" He scoffed and then laughed. "My granddaughter and the master of the estate. Never thought you would have something like that in you."

The sarcasm in his words bit, but she straightened her shoulders. She had nothing for which to apologize. "I don't know what you think happened, but I —"

"I know exactly what happened. My granddaughter, who I raised, loved, and cared for, stuck her nose where it didn't belong and thought she knew best when she should've kept quiet. And now here we are. Not just me, but also many men from the village what raised you. Your friends. What you called home."

She pressed her lips together, her own frustration mounting. Any defense she offered would fall on deaf ears. She'd not acted wrongly, of that she was certain. How could she make him see? "Grandfather, I was attacked. In my home. I overheard a plan to kidnap the Williams ladies. What did you expect me to do? All of this was happening behind my back. I had no clue —"

"Of course you had no clue," he forced

out through gritted teeth. "I worked hard to make sure you had no clue — to keep you safe and out of such dealings. That was gentlemen's business. You were never to know. I did it all to protect you, and this is what you do!"

"Protect me? How?"

His shoulders slumped ever so slightly. "Things are changing in Pevlyn."

"Of course. Things are always changing."

"That's not what I mean. The balance of power is changing."

She narrowed her gaze and waited for his explanation. "You might as well tell me everything, Grandfather, or I will go on believing the worst."

"Every man is responsible for his own actions, and no, I didn't do everything in the best light. I used to be the most powerful man in our little world there at Pevlyn. Aye, it is clear. We did take part in smuggling and the sort, but it always was to help the less fortunate. That you must believe."

She eyed him skeptically. "But?"

"I was able to keep things under control for so long. Working with the ships and taking just enough to keep our community supplied. But I'm growing older, and the next generation is coming to light. Jim Bowen, child. About two years ago he surpassed me.

The next generation wanted him as their unofficial leader, not an old man like me. I did what I had to do to keep things running smoothly."

"I don't understand." Her brow furrowed, and she shook her head. "You always were trying to get me to consider Jim as a suitor. If he was as awful as you suggest, why would you do such a thing?"

"I just told you. Power, child. You are the granddaughter of the steward. What prospects have you really? Jim's methods might be questionable, but he is powerful and steady, and he set his eyes on you. Matching you with him would set you up for life in Pevlyn."

Disbelief surged through her. "I would have found out the truth about him eventually. Do you really think I would align myself with a man with such dubious values?"

"Are you really so naive?" He sighed as if disgusted. "Money, child! Do you really think I would have gone along with anything Jim said or wanted? I owe him money. A great deal of money. His father lent it to me way back when I lost my estate. I could not keep up with the interest. The amount grew yearly, and with it their power over me. And subsequently, you. Marriage, indeed. As if I would suggest that if I had any say in the matter. But they own me. And they owned every action I made as a wrecking agent. Once they teamed up with Captain Simpson and established regular routes, I was helpless to intervene. I was a puppet. A silly, foolish puppet doing as I was told. So you see, I shifted my tactics and behavior. For you. For me. For our future."

"For me?" She shook her head firmly. "Nay. Don't include me in your reasoning. I will not take blame for this. I would never, under any circumstances, have agreed —"

"One never knows what one will do when facing ruin. Don't be so arrogant to think you would be above such decisions. I did what I had to do in the moment." He turned away from her. " 'Tis time for you to go back to your Mr. Twethewey, who I am sure is making this entire experience quite cozy for you. You needn't leave your charity and you needn't return. As far as I am concerned, a woman who would act the way you did is no family of mine."

Fire blasted across her vision. "You don't mean that. You can't mean that."

"Don't come back here again, Evelyn. And when I'm free, you'll keep your distance then too."

Evelyn could only stare.

"Time to go," the jailer blurted, reaching for her arm.

She jerked away from his filthy hand. "Don't touch me."

She looked back at her grandfather, the past years racing before her. She wanted to say something — anything — that could mend the rift, but no thought presented itself.

So she stepped out. The vile air threatened to turn her stomach.

Mr. Twethewey reached for her arm as she crossed the threshold and guided her into the corridor. Feeling shaky and weak, she leaned into him, allowing him to guide her from this place.

She kept her gaze fixed on the wet, muddy ground before her. She didn't want to see any of the sights. She did not want to remember any of this, and yet it was burned into her brain.

CHAPTER 38

Liam snuck a glance at Evelyn. Her eyes were red. Dark circles had formed beneath them. Her cheeks, her lips were dry and pale. She jostled from side to side with the carriage's every movement without offering any resistance.

And he ached at the sight.

He had tried to warn her, tried to prevent her from experiencing what she did. But she'd been determined. It was that determination, that strength of character and conviction of spirit he admired so much about her. Aye, she should not have gone to Bodmin Jail, but he expected nothing less from her.

But that did not mean he liked seeing her in this current state.

She needn't say a word for him to know what she must be thinking. He'd been prepared for what he would see. He'd been to a jail before to visit his uncle's tenants,

420

and it had not been pleasant. But there was no way she could have known what had awaited her.

He glanced at Marnie. The older woman, who rarely sat still, had taken advantage of the carriage ride and was asleep across from them, head leaned back against the seat, mouth open.

He and Miss Bray were essentially alone as the carriage rumbled along. This time they were seated next to each other so Marnie could stretch out her sore leg, their bodies swaying with every divot in the road.

There were so many things he wanted to say to her. Words of encouragement and affirmation. Words of kindness and compliments. But he needed to be silent.

The carriage hit a rut, and she bumped against him.

The privilege of having her so close to him tightened his chest. He wanted to give her space, and yet they were so rarely alone, truly alone, and with Marnie asleep, now was the time.

"I'm sorry for the position this has put you in."

She stared blankly. "At least now I know the truth. There's power in that, isn't there?"

Silence prevailed, agonizing and long. He spoke. "Did you accomplish what you hoped to by speaking with him?"

"I should have listened to you from the beginning." Her tone was flat. "I never should have gone to that place."

He'd not heard the conversation between grandfather and granddaughter in that visiting chamber, but he could make assumptions. "Did he tell you anything about what happened?"

"Not really. If anything, I am leaving with more questions than I came with, but I do know that he believes his actions were justified. He told me Jim Bowen and Captain Simpson were behind everything."

"And do you believe him?"

"Aye, because it makes sense. Grandfather is a proud man. If he owes a man money, he would set it right. But I do think he sees the wrong in what he's done. Surely he must. Oh, Liam. I don't know why he chose this path. My mother was always very vocal about how she did not approve of the choices my grandfather made. I'd always thought her brash and judgmental, but I wonder if this is what she meant."

He stiffened. *Liam.*

She called him by his Christian name. Did she even realize it?

She was softening toward him. Otherwise why would she use his name?

He forced his attention back to the task at hand. "I'm sure such actions grew easier with time, especially after my great-uncle died and there was no one to answer to. As steward he had control over the property. He could use it as he would."

Her narrow shoulders drooped. "All this time, what a fool everyone must think I am. I had no idea."

"Your grandfather had a great deal of influence. He built a very effective shield around you, hiding you away in that cottage."

She huffed. "I thought people did not like me because of my mother or because of how I am or something I'd done. Now to learn that my grandfather was involved in such dubious activities — I feel like everything I've lived up to this point is a lie."

"Not everything is a lie."

She shrugged. "Like what?"

"Like me," he blurted. As he saw her there, injured and weary, he would not withhold anything that might offer comfort. She might not want to accept what he had to say about his personal feelings toward her, but it was true and honest. After so much hurt and betrayal, she needed to know she had a champion — someone who would support her and speak truth to her. "I admire you, Evelyn. I care for you. There's no lie in that. And I'm far from the only one. There's no lie in the kindness you've shown toward the Williams ladies or in how much Marnie cares for you."

A little sob caught in her throat. She looked down to her hands. "I suppose I must find an entire new set of truths to believe. I need to put this behind me. The sooner I can go to Plymouth, the better. It's time. I —"

"I do wish you'd reconsider that."

"And do what? It's been the plan my entire life. Go live with my mother and —"

"And what?"

"I-I don't know. Become a part of her life again. Be introduced into her society. I will figure it out. Maybe . . ."

As her words faded into forced resolve, Liam's stomach clenched.

She was rejecting him. She'd done it before, and she was doing it again.

The reality was sinking in, jagged and raw.

She'd said so many times that she would be leaving, but he hadn't wanted to believe her. After all, there was a connection between them — an unspoken understanding that bound them together — one that was fortified by their shared experiences. He'd made no effort to hide his regard. But now her words were even firmer than in the past. She intended to leave Pevlyn, leave *him,* and she was not going to change her mind.

The realization cut, and his words came out much more sarcastic than he intended. "Maybe find a husband?"

She jerked at the change of his tone, but her expression did not change. "Everything here is tainted for me. I don't belong. I never really have, but now more than ever. My only hope is a new life in a new place. I hope you can understand that."

Considering the conversation over, Liam turned and watched the landscape flash by. But he didn't really see it. His mind was consumed with her words. She had made her point abundantly clear, and this time he had no choice but to accept it.

Evelyn stood before the Drakes' carriage.

It was time. Her mother and her mother's new family were already settled inside.

They were waiting on her.

The breeze rustled through Wyndcliff's ash and oak trees, just as they had every day for as long as she could remember, singing their autumn song. Before her stood Wyndcliff Hall. Behind her stood the cottage, both structures poignant places in her life, and they would remain here long after she was gone.

She'd wondered for so long what this moment would feel like, leaving the only home she had ever known to chase the dream she and her mother had fashioned all those years ago. With Grandfather gone, she likely would never return to this place. And the thought sobered her.

She looked down the line of the people waiting to bid her farewell. Mary and Mrs. Williams were first. Tears moistened Mary's eyes, and Mrs. Williams offered her a small, reassuring smile.

"I will have you to visit in London once everything is settled." She gripped Evelyn's hand in her own. "I will never forget your kindness nor your friendship."

Evelyn embraced her and then lifted Mary into her arms. "Do you still have the sea glass and shells we collected?"

Mary nodded and swiped her hand under her nose.

"Good. Because I would like for you to make me another necklace with the green sea glass we found. Can you do that for me?"

Mary nodded.

Evelyn kissed her cheek and returned her to the ground.

Marnie and Tom stood next to her. Tom,

who was quietly in the background for as long as she could remember, and Marnie, who had stepped in as a mother figure once her own had left. She had known this moment would be a difficult one, but she had not anticipated just how difficult it would actually be. Before Evelyn could say another word, Marnie rushed forward and embraced her.

Evelyn hugged her tight.

"Now ye enjoy Plymouth," Marnie sniffed, "but ye always have a place with me should ye need to come home."

Evelyn nodded and smiled at Tom, who bowed.

Next to him was the farewell she dreaded perhaps the most. Liam and John Twethewey stood next to each other. Liam's smile was gentle but not the generous, unrestrained smile he usually offered her.

She had hurt him, she knew. And it pained her. She did believe he cared for her, and her feelings for him had intensified. After everything they'd endured together, attraction had grown to respect, and respect had blossomed to affection. But she had really only been in his acquaintance not even two months. He'd indicated numerous times that he wanted her to stay, but there had been no proposal. No reference to something more permanent. She could not remain here, hoping. Waiting. She had to think of her future, and for now she had to trust her mother and the plans they had made all those years ago.

At first neither of them spoke.

Half of her wished he'd repeat the sentiments of caring for her. Half of her wished he would propose then and there and secure her place here. But he only bowed slightly. "You will be greatly missed, Miss Bray."

Miss Bray.

Not *Evelyn.*

Their intimacy was already taking a step back.

As well it should, she supposed.

She'd considered what her parting words to him would be, but now her prepared sentiments fled her mind. A strange panic set in at the thought of leaving him. Because, yes, she was bound to him. She liked him. Maybe even loved him. And even more importantly, she revered him for his actions. She was happier in his presence than in the presence of anyone else she knew, and the thought of him moving on with his life without her in it stung.

But if he really wanted her to stay, as he had professed, he would have proposed marriage, or at least hinted at it.

And that he had not done.

She hesitated, waiting for some sign, something to show he'd had a change of heart, but none came.

Both Mr. Twetheweys bowed, and she curtsied.

At length Liam said, "Safe travels, Miss Bray. I hope you will find your way back to Wyndcliff one day."

She only nodded and looked back down at the line of people who had made up her world the last months and years, and then she stepped aboard the carriage. This chapter of her life was closing, and she was sad to see it go.

CHAPTER 39

"You stubborn fool." John clicked his tongue as the carriage rumbled away from Wyndcliff Hall and out to the open moorland. "I can't believe you are letting her go like this. Once she is settled in Plymouth, she'll never be back."

As they stood there in the sickening silence, the overwhelming weight and significance of his brother's words pressed upon him until he felt he could withstand it no more. "What am I to do? I can't change her decision. This has been her plan all along."

"Aye, but I doubt she meant for events to take this specific turn, what with her grandfather in jail and her mother marrying and all of the events that added up to make this very strange indeed."

John was right, of course. There could have been no way to predict that her grandfather would be involved in such underhanded dealings. Additionally, he'd seen the anguish that his betrayal had caused her. She'd shed real tears. Displayed real vulnerability.

He tightened his fists at his sides.

He'd told her he cared for her. Several times. And she had rejected him.

The thought of Wyndcliff without her seemed bleak and barren, even more than the moors stretching all around them.

The carriage cleared the iron gate, rounded the tree bend, and was gone.

"There is one practical way to get her to return, you know."

Aye, he knew to what John referred. The topic had come up on more than one occasion.

"I can't propose to a woman I've known for such a short period of time."

John sighed. "Spoken like a true romantic."

Liam's discomfort grew. "Too much change is transpiring. I've been here not even two months. Consider what has happened. The wrecks. The china clay pits. Bray. The Williamses. Do you really think it wise to make so many major decisions so quickly, and in the midst of such emotional situations?"

And yet, even as the words crossed his lips, he knew they were futile. He'd never experienced love, but Aunt Delia had always told him that when it came around, one needed to pay attention to it, for it might not come again. Hadn't Uncle Jac and Aunt Delia found love in a very short period of time?

Was this what she meant by it? This feeling of complete connectedness to another human being? This sense of being able to concentrate on nothing else?

It was all happening too fast.

But it was too late now.

And Evelyn was gone.

Evelyn pushed the tasseled velvet curtains aside and stared down to the busy street two stories below.

It really was a sight to behold. Vendors pushing carts rushed to and fro. Carriages and horses maneuvered their way through a sea of people. Activity — and excitement — surrounded her. So different from Pevlyn with its modest shops and sleepy atmosphere.

She stepped back from the leaded window, dropped the curtain, and returned to the padded, high-backed chair next to the roaring fire. With a sigh she picked up her needlework. She would need to improve her skills, for what else did ladies here do? There were no gardens to tend, no moorlands to explore, and not even any sea glass to search for. Nay, it was needlework, afternoon calls, and fussing over gowns.

Evelyn had been in Plymouth two weeks, and in that time her wardrobe had been completely replaced. New gloves, boots, slippers, pelisses, and cloaks lined her elegant chamber. She'd attended two balls, three dinners, and the theater. But even with all of these people around her, including her new stepsisters, loneliness plagued her.

She missed Marnie and her grandfather.

She even missed Jenna.

She missed the whispering wind over the moorland and the crash of the waves on the shore. She looked to the potted plant she was growing at the parlor's entrance. A sad replacement for her beloved heather and wild cotton grass, her lavender and chamomile.

But most of all it was Liam Twethewey who occupied her thoughts. He occupied her heart. Her dreams.

Had he engaged a new steward yet to replace her grandfather? The position would be an attractive one, and no doubt Liam would have no trouble selecting one from those who knew the area. Finding a man who was not involved in the smuggling ring might prove more difficult, but he'd be successful. Liam was the sort of man who commanded success, and that trait would serve him well. She also wondered after his china clay pits. He'd been so proud of them, and she wished him success.

But mostly she wondered if he thought of her. The sense that he was the one person who held the key to her happiness would not leave her. He'd told her he would miss her. That he wanted her to stay. Now she would never know if he actually felt that way or if his emotions were ruling his tongue.

Music sounded from the other room. The Drake sisters were about their music lessons. She'd never been taught. Now that she was here in their home, the differences in their upbringing were glaringly obvious.

Was this what her life had become? Feeling bored and useless, waiting for something — anything — to happen?

She decided to write to Jenna again. She hated the way things had been left after their dispute in the village, and if she could make things right via post, she would. But as she turned to the writing table in the parlor, her mother entered.

Evelyn straightened her posture and

smoothed her hair.

"How lovely it is to have you here, dearest. Everything feels complete now, does it not?"

Evelyn managed a smile, hoping it masked the emptiness she felt inside. "Yes, Mother. Quite complete."

"Tonight we will go to the dinner at the Petersons'. There is a young man of particular interest I want you to meet. Are you not excited at the prospect?"

Another young man to meet.

"Of course." She would lie, for her mother's sake. She'd smile and be a gracious guest. But her heart was very far away, and the longer she was away from Wyndcliff, the more certain she became — her heart was in the possession of Mr. Liam Twethewey.

CHAPTER 40

Liam should have been content. By all accounts, success was on his side. He'd opened the Aulder Hill clay pits, and already the effort was proving fruitful. He'd had a hand in banishing a smuggling ring from his property, and he'd reclaimed his beach. The villagers were starting to respect him, and he was even developing a rapport with the nearby landowners. Time and circumstances had changed everything, especially since the arrest of Rupert Bray and the other men three weeks prior.

Yes, he should have been content, but even with all of the advances he'd made, a pang of restlessness and vexation tremored beneath the surface.

And he knew why.

He tried not to think of Evelyn. He kept his mind busy and his schedule full. Even now Captain Hollingswood was a frequent and welcome guest, and as the tall man sat across the desk from him in the Wyndcliff study, Liam no longer regarded the man with suspicion.

"Things have been quiet in your cove, and I know I have you to thank for that." Hollingswood stretched out his booted foot and took the snifter of brandy Liam offered him. " 'Tis a nice change of pace around here. Of course, we will still have wrecks. 'Tis a part of Cornish life. But at least now perhaps the smuggling will lessen."

Liam should share in the man's relief, but he wondered if he would ever think of his cove happily now. Too much had transpired there. "At least it is all behind us."

And yet, even as Liam said the words, he wondered if the events would ever truly be behind him. Liam cleared his throat. "And have you any news of Bray or the other men?"

"Six men, including Bray, are being held in connection with the illegal activity in the cove, which in and of itself is a shame, for there were far more responsible, but it's a start. Those six men are to be brought to trial very soon. There is overwhelming evidence, not to mention witnesses. I've no doubt you'll be called as one of them. But truths are truths, and they always come to light in the end. I see you have taken on no new steward to replace Bray."

Liam shook his head and returned the bottle of brandy to the side table. "I'm doing well enough on my own. Besides, it is helping me learn my land."

"Wise man." Captain Hollingswood took a drink. "Never a good idea to trust another man too much."

Unable to let the previous topic pass, Liam asked, "What do you think will become of Bray and the others?"

"My instincts tell me deportation to Australia. They've committed a crime, but I don't think they'll hang for it. But if they're not deported, I'd be shocked."

Liam sobered. Deported. Miss Bray would never see her grandfather again.

As if reading his thoughts, Hollingswood inquired, "I haven't seen the Bray woman about. What's become of her?"

Liam sighed and leaned back in his desk chair. "She is living with her mother in Plymouth, as far as I know. They left about two weeks back. Our housekeeper has received a few letters from her, but I cannot speak about her other than that."

"Speaking of Plymouth, we've arranged transportation for Mrs. Williams and her daughter to London. One of my officers will escort them personally, but they will embark from Plymouth, where our main offices are. I'm sure you are eager to have your house to yourself. You've been kind to allow them to stay on so long."

"They've been model guests. I did not want Mrs. Williams to leave until she felt she was completely recovered. In fact, I will be sorry to see them go. Have you spoken to Mrs. Williams about it?"

"No."

"When do you intend for them to embark?"

"The end of the week. Will you pass along the message to them for me?"

"Of course. I am sure they will be grateful to see this ordeal come to an end."

The men talked for a while longer, but as they were talking, an idea formed. The talk of Miss Bray had prodded an already sore wound within him. But John had been right. It was not practical that he should ask a lady to stay without offering her something more permanent. And the more time that passed, the more certain he became.

He'd made a mistake that day when he watched Miss Bray get into the carriage. And now it was time to make it right.

CHAPTER 41

"Farewell, Mr. Twethewey." Mary wrapped her arms around his neck and gave his cheek an enthusiastic kiss. "Are you going to come see me in London?"

"Of course!" He bounced her in his arms. "One day I will come and see you in London. I promise. But you and your mother must promise to come and visit me at Wyndcliff again. You must come when it's summer and warm."

Mary nodded and then scurried down to the ground and back to her seat in the carriage.

Mrs. Williams stepped toward him next. "I cannot thank you enough for all you have done for my daughter and me."

He gave a slight bow. "You are most welcome. I wish you nothing but the best of luck on the second half of your journey."

A twinkle glimmered in her eye. "And now that we are in Plymouth, I wish you the very best of luck in your endeavor."

He raised his brow. It was no use trying to hide his intentions from Mrs. Williams. True, he had accompanied them from Wyndcliff Hall to Plymouth in preparation for their return trip to London, but he had another reason, a much more personal reason. And Mrs. Williams had been supportive.

Once he deposited the Williamses into the safe hands of the excise officer, Liam set about his much more personal business.

Captain Hollingswood, who often called Plymouth home, met him at the office. Liam had sent word of his intentions, and the captain had done some investigating. "At the moment the Drakes are attending a ball at the Andrews residence. It is a rather large gathering."

"Is it a private one?"

Hollingswood reached into his coat and retrieved a letter. "I've secured us invitations."

A grin spread across Liam's face as he took the papers from the captain. "You've thought of everything."

Hollingswood shrugged. "I'm happy to help. Think of it as gratitude for the assistance you've offered me with your cove, but now the rest of this is up to you, my friend."

After a short carriage ride to another street, they rumbled to a stop outside of a tall town house. Lights and music spilled from the windows and open doors. Activity and energy swirled in the air. By Hollingswood's account, Evelyn was here. After nearly a month, he was about to see her again, and he'd set things right once and for all. If she refused him this time, he was prepared to retreat back to Wyndcliff to nurse his wounds. But if she was agreeable, then the future spread broad and bright before him.

After gaining admittance, he smoothed his coat, slightly crumpled from travel. Strangers surrounded him. He wove his way through the ballroom. The cards room. The dining room. But he was searching for one person and one person only.

He thought he recognized one of her stepsisters talking with a gentleman in the corner, and his heart raced. Miss Bray had to be close.

And then he saw her.

She was standing alone, next to a window.

She did not appear necessarily happy, nor did she appear miserable. But she did appear beautiful, more beautiful than he thought it possible for a woman to be.

Her blonde hair was twisted and braided into an elegant chignon on top of her head. Soft wisps framed her face, emphasizing her high cheekbones and the soft slope of her nose. Her lovely green eyes took in the activity around her. Her gown of shimmery emerald emphasized the soft curves of her figure, and long white gloves extended to just above her elbows.

He swallowed his trepidation. 'Twas now or never.

The music started once again, and as the dancers shifted their attention back to their steps, he crossed the space.

And then she turned to look at him.

Recognition widened her eyes. A lovely pink flushed her cheeks. And most beautiful of all, she smiled. "Mr. Twethewey. What are you doing here?"

It took every ounce of reserve not to take her into his arms then and there. But standing at her side would have to suffice. He stepped as close as etiquette would allow. "I have just taken Mary and Mrs. Williams to the excise office. Tomorrow they are being escorted to London."

"They were here? In Plymouth?" She gave a little laugh. "Why, that is wonderful! Oh, I am so glad to hear they are so close to finally finding their home."

"Mrs. Williams and Mary both wanted to see you while they were here, but they needed to depart to reach their inn before the hour grew too late. I told Mrs. Williams I was coming to see you, and she asked me to convey her regard."

"How did you know where to find me?"

"Captain Hollingswood offered his assistance. He knew the Drakes would be in attendance tonight, and he secured us invitations."

Confusion wrinkled her brow. "So you came here to see me?"

"Yes. I've something I need to tell you. Something that has been in my mind since the moment you left." He moved even closer. "That day you left Wyndcliff, I made a mistake. A very grave mistake."

Her eyes searched his. "And what was that?"

"I let you go."

She straightened and drew a sharp breath.

He glanced around to make sure no one was watching, wrapped his hand around her gloved one, and guided her down a corridor. He opened the first door they came to. It swung open to a dark sitting room. He led her inside.

Once they were sheltered by the room's

shadows, he placed his hands on her shoulders, leaned close to her, and whispered, "What I should have done was beg you to stay. I should have done everything in my power to keep you with me. Because I love you, Evelyn Bray. What a fool I was. I love everything about you, and I never want to be parted from your side again."

A shaky smile replaced her more confident one. Her face was very close to his. Her scent of lavender teased him, and the memory of being with her flared fresh and compelling.

His thumb caressed the soft skin of her cheek. "So, if you will allow me, I am going to ask you the question I should have asked you before you boarded that carriage. Evelyn, dearest Evelyn, will you marry me? Will you come back to Wyndcliff and be my wife?"

Tears rushed to her eyes, making their green more vibrant. She drew a shuddering breath. "Oh, Liam. I have never wanted anything more."

He enfolded her in his arms, as he had wanted to do so many times, and lowered his lips to hers.

With the pain of the past behind them, they were free to start their new life together. And now that she was in his arms, their life could finally begin.

EPILOGUE

One year later

Evelyn watched as her husband took the platform at the Aulder Hill clay pits. Pride welled within as a cheer rose from the miners gathered, eager to hear from their leader.

Liam's words rose in the chilly late-morning air. "I am proud to share with you a successful venture. We have all profited, and I promise you that I will work to make sure we continue to profit for years to come."

After his speech and after shaking hands and talking with the men gathered at the foot of the platform, he turned toward Evelyn. Over the past year she'd watched him build his dream from mere grooves in the ground to one of the most profitable mines in the area — of any kind. He was doing just what he had set out to do — creating a legacy. Providing for the local population. And making a mark on the

447

Cornish countryside.

"I meant to tell you that I had a letter from your grandfather earlier today," Liam said as they fell into step with each other. "Tom brought it out to me just before the crowd gathered."

Evelyn raised her brow. She was pleased Grandfather was beginning to write to her husband more regularly, and despite the fact that they were separated by an ocean, they were still able to remain in contact. "Oh? And what did he have to say?"

Liam smirked good-naturedly. "He reminded me to check in on the Smiths and to make sure we make the yearly donation to the Ladies League."

Evelyn shook her head, combating the unavoidable sting of sadness that accompanied nearly every mention of Grandfather's name. "I would expect nothing less."

"He says he is well, of course."

"And yet, I wonder. He never was one to admit any sort of discomfort, was he?"

"I know you miss him," Liam said after several seconds.

"I do miss him." She nodded. "I regret that he won't be here to meet our child. I regret not being able to care for him as he ages. His absence leaves an emptiness that will not readily be filled."

Liam remained quiet, as he often did when this topic arose, to give her space. It was grief of a new kind, to know that one you love is alive but you can never see them, never speak to them. As a result of his actions, Grandfather, along with the rest of the men involved in the kidnapping and smuggling, had been transported to Australia and never again would set foot on English soil.

She heard her name called and turned to see Jenna Potts, formerly Jenna Shaw, and her husband, Charlie, crossing the ground toward them.

"Ah, and how is the new pit supervisor today?" Liam stretched out his hand and shook that of the ruddy-faced man.

Charlie chuckled. "Better now that the digging has begun on the north moor."

"As eager as I am to see progress." Liam smiled.

As the men talked of the future of the china clay pits, Evelyn extended her own hands toward Jenna. The road to repairing their relationship had been a long, difficult one, but as each accepted the fate of their family members, time had a way of smoothing out harsh edges and softening anger. Now both women were married. Both women were soon to be mothers. And both women had husbands involved in the china clay pits. Their long-standing friendship was being revived, and Evelyn was glad.

As the couples parted ways and Evelyn and Liam began the walk back toward Wyndcliff Hall, Liam paused to look out over the pits on the barren moor. Even though the ground was cloaked in grays, browns, and whites, a brilliant blue sky covered all.

"Just thinking, my darling." He clasped her hand in his and then looped it through his arm. "If your mother had had her way, you would be waking up somewhere much more refined. Plymouth. London. Do you regret your decision to return to this bit of moorland?"

Evelyn placed a hand over the swell of her belly. How could she regret it? She was content with her life. Fulfilled. And more at peace than she ever could have dreamed.

"All those years I thought I needed to escape to Plymouth. I thought my future resided there. I thought my happiness would look the same as my mother's happiness. But I feel so blessed that our life together has turned out the way it has. And you? Are you happy?"

Her husband shrugged, a boyish grin on his clean-shaven face. "I might be," he teased. "I'll be happier when we are alone, though."

She hoped the thrill that shot through her at his words would never diminish. And they walked together, hand in hand, back to Wyndcliff Hall.

ACKNOWLEDGMENTS

The Light at Wyndcliff is the third and final novel in the Cornwall Novels series. Each of the books in the series was a joy to write, but there was something special about this last book! I know I've said it before, but it is so true — it takes so many people to mold a book from the glimmer of an idea to the finished product that you find in the bookstore.

To my family: Your support and encouragement inspires me daily!

To my writing friends, and especially KC and KBR: Thanks for walking this road with me.

To my editor, Becky Monds, and to my line editor, Julee Schwartzburg: You guys challenge me in such a positive way. Thanks for coming alongside me to polish this story. And to the rest of the publishing team — from sales to design and everything in between — you guys are amazing!

To my agent, Rachelle Gardner: Thanks for taking this journey to Cornwall with me! It would not have been possible without your guidance and advice — not to mention friendship.

Last but not least, a very special thank you to my readers: You are such an inspiration! Thank you for your enthusiasm and for sharing the love of story with me.

DISCUSSION QUESTIONS

1. In this novel, Evelyn's father is dead, and she feels abandoned by her mother. Even so, she lives with the hope that her mother will call for her and invite her into her life. How do you think the absence of Evelyn's parents shapes her character and actions?
2. Who is your favorite character in the book? Why? Who is your least favorite character in the book? Why?
3. How do you think the arrival of Mary and Elizabeth Williams affects Liam's view of shipwrecks and potential illegal activity on his property?
4. Liam is only twenty-two years of age when he inherits Wyndcliff estate. Do you think his youth affects his approach to his new-found authority?
5. Do you think Evelyn's mother truly loved her? Why or why not? What about her grandfather? In your opinion, did he love her?

6. Evelyn and Liam form a strong attachment in a relatively short period of time. Do you believe in love at first sight? What about after a month or two? How long do you think it takes for two people to fall in love?

7. In the story, Evelyn is faced with either doing what is right or protecting someone she loved. Have you ever been in a similar situation? If so, how did you handle it?

8. If you were the writer of this story, what would come next for Evelyn and Liam?

ABOUT THE AUTHOR

Sarah E. Ladd received the 2011 Genesis Award in historical romance for *The Heiress of Winterwood*. She is a graduate of Ball State University and has more than ten years of marketing experience. Sarah lives in Indiana with her amazing family and spunky golden retriever.

Visit Sarah online at SarahLadd.com
Facebook: SarahLaddAuthor
Twitter: @SarahLaddAuthor
Pinterest: SarahLaddAuthor

The employees of Thorndike Press hope you have enjoyed this Large Print book. All our Thorndike, Wheeler, and Kennebec Large Print titles are designed for easy reading, and all our books are made to last. Other Thorndike Press Large Print books are available at your library, through selected bookstores, or directly from us.

For information about titles, please call:
(800) 223-1244

or visit our website at:
gale.com/thorndike

To share your comments, please write:
Publisher
Thorndike Press
10 Water St., Suite 310
Waterville, ME 04901